W9-ADE-106

SHIFTING TRUST

MADONA SKAFF-KOREN

Renaissance
Diverse Canadian Voices

This is a work of fiction. Any similarity to any events, institutions, or persons, living or dead, is purely coincidental and unintentional.

SHIFTING TRUST ©2021 by Madona Skaff-Koren. All rights reserved. No part of this book may be used or reproduced in any manner whatsoever without written permission except in the case of brief quotations in critical articles and reviews. For more information, contact Renaissance Press. First edition.

Cover art by Louise Koren. Design by Nathan Frechette. Interior design by Phillip Tran. Edited by Evan McKinley, Vicki Martin, Myryam Ladouceur, and Phillip Tran.

Legal deposit, Library and Archives Canada, October 2021.

Paperback ISBN: 978-1-990086-05-2

Ebook ISBN : 978-1-990086-14-4

Renaissance Press - pressesrenaissancepress.ca

Printed in Gatineau

We acknowledge the support of the Canada Council for the Arts.

Canada Council for the Arts   Conseil des arts du Canada

For my husband and daughter
Who patiently live with a writer and still love me

CHAPTER ONE

Matt peered at Hyde Park, barely visible through the rivulets of rain on the window pane. He could just make out the garbage trucks loading up recycler bins from Sunday's art festival. Then they silently lifted off and disappeared into the low dark clouds.

He'd arrived in London early so he'd be able to play tourist before the conference started. No rain was going to stop him. So, yesterday, umbrella in hand, he'd joined the countless people strolling through Hyde Park to check out the artists that had set up their plastic clad displays. Eventually, he'd abandoned the search for a souvenir and taken pity on his soaked and shivering bodyguard to return to the hotel empty handed. His bodyguard somehow forgot to pack a weather-sensitive suit—or maybe he didn't own one. But he'd also refused to carry an umbrella insisting he had to keep his hands free. He'd even refused to share Matt's umbrella because that would hinder his view. Seriously, the guy needed to relax.

A loud thud from the next room startled him. He reached the adjoining door just as a loud knocking threatened to rip it off its hinges. He opened the door to find a dishevelled, giant of a man eclipsing the doorway. A forty-year-old man with short white hair glared at him.

Cahill. His bodyguard. Rumpled blazer, partly unbuttoned shirt, and only one shoe suggested that he'd slept in his clothes. Matt felt a twinge of guilt at staying out so late touring London's nightclub scene.

Cahill shook a finger at him as though scolding a child. "You didn't wake me."

"I thought you could use the rest," Matt said. "We didn't get to sleep until after two this morning. It's barely seven..."

"You were planning to sneak out again, weren't you?"

"It's just breakfast here in the hotel."

"I can't protect you," Cahill paused to take a deep breath, "if you keep sneaking out."

"You're taking this bodyguard thing way too seriously," Matt said, with a laugh. Cahill's glare intensified. Wisely, Matt became serious. "Look, I already apologized about leaving my room without telling you…"

"Yesterday afternoon you said you were going to have a nap. Next thing I know, you're in the bar downstairs meeting with a man who is a security risk. A man, I might remind you, who insisted you meet him before the conference even started."

"It was just an informal get-together with some of the delegates staying at this hotel. Nothing sinister. Let's not get paranoid." Matt laughed as Cahill scowled. The guy had no sense of humour. "Look, this is a high-tech conference. You know, exchange of information and all that. I can't learn much if I stay in my room. Besides, I was careful. I stuck to the cover story."

"That doesn't matter. You're not going anywhere without protection." Cahill crossed his arms and moved to block the door to the hall.

Matt nodded at Cahill's clothes, saying, "That's not exactly what I'd call proper dress code."

"Shit!" Cahill said, looking down at his untidy clothes. He held up a warning finger. "Wait for me. I mean it!" He stomped back to his room, slamming the door behind him.

Matt felt a twinge of regret for giving him such a hard time. He never wanted a bodyguard, but the Canadian government had insisted. At one point, they'd suggested he have a private hover car fly him to the conference. At least he was able to put a stop to that. Fortunately, his hotel, the Plaza on Hyde Park was close to the Lancaster Gate underground station, and the government had agreed he could take it. Especially since the conference was only a few stops away.

Of course, had Drake come as he was supposed to, he'd probably have insisted a car take him everywhere. Even to the bathroom if he could have managed it. Stupid bastard. That reminded him to try the phone number once more. Using the hotel com system's 'incognito mode', he keyed in the number and listened to the endless hollow rings. How could someone not have voicemail these days? Maybe they objected to the subcutaneous implants, but there was an endless variety of skin contact phones available. Like the patch he wore on his right wrist. Easy to remove. He hit *end* with a grunt. He had to finish getting dressed.

He searched the dresser drawer for his favourite navy tie, which went best with his grey suit. He cursed when he pulled it out. He'd forgotten that his co-worker, Aidan Monette, had insisted on helping him pack. It would have been okay, but as soon as Matt's back was turned, Aidan had happily undone and ironed every single one of his ties. With a huff, he turned to the dresser mirror to tie it.

"Damn it! Damn, damn, damn," he muttered, as he fumbled with the knot. As much as he loved wearing suits, he still couldn't make a knot and never undid one after he succeeded. Maybe that was one secret he should have told Aidan.

The rest of his research team teased him for being so conservative because he wore his hair short and preferred suits to jeans. But he knew that suits made him look older, more distinguished. He had expected to be in his element at the conference. That smug feeling, however, shattered last night when someone called him "the kid from Canada." Kid? He was thirty-two years old for Christ's sake. He didn't think he looked that young, especially with the tuft of gray at the hairline, which was very obvious in his dark hair.

When the other delegates invited him to join them for dinner, the excitement of attending his first elite international high-tech conference overcame his jet lag and exhaustion. He'd enjoyed himself despite seeing Cahill at a nearby table, scowling as he sipped a coke.

Eventually, the idle chitchat turned to shoptalk, as Matt knew it would. Agonizingly, he'd managed to maintain his research's cover story. Despite few details coming from him, the other men and one woman were very open about their work. This morning using his own wrist phone, he'd fired off a quick message to his research director back in Ottawa. After two years, he knew Laura Jessup well enough to be sure that the snippets of information would intrigue her enough that she'd be on the next flight to England. He smiled.

His smile vanished when he examined the third failed attempt to tie a knot. He dropped his arms to his sides to study the mess, not sure how to fix it. He thought about asking Cahill for help, but considering how angry he was, the guy would probably just strangle him. A heavy sigh, a couple of yanks, and it was halfway decent. It would do for the rest of the week. No way in hell was he going through this again with another tie.

He heard a knock on the door and a muffled voice in the hall. Cahill letting him know he was waiting. "I'll be right out," he called.

Matt scooped up his wallet and room card from the night table and dumped them in the inside pocket of his jacket. Slinging the jacket over his arm, he opened the door expecting to see Cahill in his usual loitering stance. No one. Maybe the guy had to go to the bathroom. He knocked on the guard's door calling, "I'm late for breakfast so I'll just meet you downstairs." Silence. "Okay?" Cahill would be mad, but this time he had tried to co-operate.

At the elevator, he nodded 'morning' to a man dressed in a dark charcoal suit. The man just put his gloved hands in his trousers' pocket and turned away to face the elevator. Matt ignored the rudeness, refusing to let it ruin the day for him.

The elevator door opened and Matt hesitated when he saw a man dressed in dirty coveralls holding a key in the control panel.

"I guess this elevator's not working," Matt said, and turned towards the staircase.

He barely made it a step when the suited man shoved Matt into the elevator. Slammed him face-first into the wall. Pain. His eyes burned. Tears flowed. His nose felt broken. He dropped his jacket. Reached for his face. Someone yanked his arm behind his back. They pinned him against the wall. Jagged fingernails scraped the phone off his wrist. A sharp stab in his neck. Too late to pull away. Vertigo slapped him.

"Cahill, help..." He barely heard his own strangled whisper. No chance anyone else could.

He sucked in a deep breath to cry out again when a large hand clamped over his face, crushing his already throbbing nose. He gagged at the stench of mechanics grease mingling with anaesthetic.

The salty tears mingled with the taste of blood in his mouth. Numbness spread through his body. Anaesthetized legs failed him.

In Ontario, Tyler Demir had been enjoying the drive through the late spring snow squalls until the north-south navigation system crashed. Forced to switch to manual driving mode, the relaxing four-hour trip from North Bay to Ottawa transformed into six hours of white-knuckle steering.

March was doing its best to ward off spring's imminent arrival with a snowstorm that blanketed the entire province and eastern Canada. As he neared the city outskirts and was considering pulling off the road, which wouldn't have been too difficult since he was barely able to stay on it, the skies cleared.

Demir pulled into the nearly deserted parking lot at 5:15 in the morning. The sun hadn't risen yet to erase the night sky. The stars looked deceptively close, due to either the crisp air, or because he was tired as hell after driving all night.

He yawned widely as he pulled into a spot near the nondescript single storey building. As he reached for the ignition to shut off the Mazda, the engine shut off. A quick inspection of the power gauge and he shook his head at his good luck of making the last few kilometres literally on a couple of electrons. He hadn't had the chance to charge the car when he'd arrived in North Bay and driving through snow drifts had drained the battery charge more rapidly.

He pulled on the hand brake. Yawning again, he rested his head on the steering wheel. Thinking he was still driving, he jerked awake, heart pounding. He slammed on the brakes. Grabbed the steering wheel. Fully awake, he laughed at himself as he pulled the key out of the ignition and put it into his ski jacket pocket. At this hour, the only cars here belonged to Internal Security's night shift, including, he noted with a smile, the very old blue Volvo.

He checked himself in the rear-view mirror. Christ, he looked like crap, especially with his bloodshot, brown eyes underscored by dark circles. He finger-combed his dark, curly hair hoping to tame it, but eventually gave up. He got out of the car dragging his backpack behind him. He could pack a week's worth of clothes into a backpack—including a suit.

He slung the pack over one shoulder and then shut the door, not bothering to lock it; after all, in a high security installation, who'd try to break in?

After plugging the car in to charge, he trudged through the snow on the uncleared sidewalk towards the office building with the bold lettered sign CYBER INC. He stopped to peer into the woods behind the building, wondering why the shadows seemed so deep. It took a moment for him to realize that one of the floodlights was out. He continued. Inside, he greeted the elderly commissionaire at the front desk. Demir removed his ID card from his jacket pocket and clipped it to his shirt.

"Good morning, Mr. Demir," the old man said, as he barely glanced at the ID card.

"Morning, Frank. I just noticed one of the lights on the north-west corner is out. Also, the sidewalks haven't been cleared."

"Oh," the older man said, with groan. "The maintenance bots must be acting up again. I'll call it in immediately."

"Thanks," Demir said, and continued around the corner, greeting another man, this one in his thirties, seated behind a desk. He wore a plain dark suit and an ID tag identifying him as Internal Security.

"Morning sir," the man said. "Welcome back."

"Hi, Bryan. Anything exciting happen while I was gone?" Demir asked.

"Let me think," Bryan began, as though searching his memory. "You left about fourteen hours ago... Nope." He laughed and added, "Except that Mr. Abraham came in around 4:00 a.m."

"Hard to miss that ancient Volvo in the parking lot." Demir continued to the elevator behind the desk. He placed his hand on the palm reader and looked at the sign above it that read, ONLY LANDLINES IN USE BEYOND THIS POINT. He remembered how, on his first day at work, he'd laughed and thought, 'back to the 19th century.' It still made him smile. The elevator door slid open. Inside, he punched the button for

Sub 1, Internal Security's level. The door whooshed shut.

On Sub 1, Tyler Demir headed down the hall, passing the squad leaders' offices where he sheepishly tiptoed by. Not that he was avoiding Abraham, but he wasn't in the mood to be lectured on driving all night.

The narrow corridor soon widened into a circular reception area with the secretary's modular desk in the middle and offices to either side, his and the chief of security's. Between both rooms was his favourite low-tech device. The coffee machine. He selected large and strong, only remembering at the last second to shove a mug under the spout. Oh, he thought, that's what the faint beep was...

He took a cautious sip as he entered his office and stumbled over someone's legs. Abraham was sitting in the armchair near the door.

"What the hell!" Demir barely saved his coffee.

"Hey, you're back." Abraham stood up, took Demir's backpack, then gave him a not quite playful punch in the shoulder. "I knew you'd be stupid enough to turn around and drive back. And with auto-drive down... Glad you made it in one piece."

"Gee, *Dad*, I told you not to wait up." Demir laughed.

Abraham was about a half inch taller than Demir's own six feet and a couple of years older, with no evidence of grey in his short cropped brown hair. Friends for over twenty years, they'd left the RCMP together and joined Cyber's police force: Demir as second-in-command of Internal Security and Abraham as one of three shift leaders.

Demir sloughed off his jacket, tossed it on the coat rack as he sat at his desk and turned on his computer, all while trying to take another sip of coffee.

"Sorry if I worried you. The storm wasn't that bad when I left, but about an hour into the trip, driving was hell."

"I wish I hadn't called you last night. I just thought you should be aware that the chief was heading out of town," Abraham said. He tossed the backpack in the corner, then rolled the leather chair closer to the desk before settling comfortably into it.

"I'm glad I only had a couple of beers at the bar when you called. More and I don't think I'd have made it back. When the storm knocked out the nav-corridors, fuck what a nightmare." He shook his head. "Shit, I used to drink a hell of a lot more and stay up for days."

"Don't forget you'll be turning 40 next year. You gotta slow down."

"Hey, old man, look who's talking." Demir smirked playfully. Then turned his attention to the computer to check messages.

"Ty, I told you we could manage for a day."

"With a scientist out of the country? It's not a good idea for both me and Henderson to be away. Besides, I promised my friends that I'd go back next week. No big deal." Demir scrolled through the messages looking for any that were flagged 'urgent'. "You know, I'm pissed that Henderson didn't tell me he was going out of town to see some musical, or play, or whatever the fuck it was." Demir broke off. He took a sip of coffee to calm down.

"Guess he figured it was only Toronto and..."

"But he actually insisted I leave Sunday." He took a bigger gulp, scalding his throat. So much for calm. Too late to spit it out, he finished swallowing and added, his voice rough, "I could've postponed my trip."

"Go home. Sleep. I promise to call you if anything comes up."

"I'll sleep here."

"Where?" Abraham looked around. "There's barely space for your desk and a file cabinet in here."

"Right there," Demir pointed to the floor by his desk. He got up, grabbed his backpack, and said, "My pillow..." Dramatically pulling his jacket off the coat rack, added, "...my blanket. We've slept with less than that on long stakeouts."

"Well, at least you're getting rest," Abraham said. "I'll see you in a few hours."

"An hour should be enough."

"Yeah," Abraham said. He looked like he wanted to say more, but left without another word.

Once the door was closed, Demir tossed his jacket and backpack on the floor and sat down to finish going through the new messages. Communications had relayed Cahill's routine check-in yesterday. There would be another later today.

Next, he logged into the chief's computer to check for anything that required immediate attention. Regularly checking Henderson's messages seemed to be the only way to find out what was going on these days. Not telling Demir about the holiday in Toronto could have been a genuine oversight. But Demir wouldn't have known about the last-minute change in travel arrangements for Dr. Stoddard to go to the conference if Cahill hadn't mentioned it in passing.

He leaned his head on his hand, yawning widely. Maybe Abraham was right and he shouldn't have rushed back. He yawned again as he rested his head on his arms, staring sideways at the screen, hypnotized by the screen that started to dance before his eyes.

He couldn't move. He could barely breathe. What happened? An earthquake? Was he trapped in the elevator under rubble?

As a scientist, analyzing the unexpected was second nature. He concentrated on the facts.

No, he wasn't under rubble. He was sitting up. His hands limp on his lap. But his wrists hurt. His fingers felt numb. Something was keeping his hands together. He wiggled his fingers to try to get the circulation flowing. He started to call for help and panicked at the paralysis in his face. No. Calm down. Not paralysis, but something stiff on his face. His lips were partially open and he felt around with his tongue. A strange taste. Glue? Very rigid on his cheeks—duct tape maybe?

Gradually his head cleared enough for him to try to open his eyes, but a blindfold stopped him. The throbbing roar in his head gradually transformed into a car engine. Dizziness was in fact the movement of a car driving at high speed, along a winding, pothole ravaged road.

All the facts told him one thing. He was being kidnapped. That was ridiculous.

He tried to tell his captors that they were making a mistake. With leaden arms, he reached for the tape.

A hand seized his arm. Tore his sleeve. A sharp stab. An injection? He choked against the tape on his mouth. He gasped as searing lights flared in his mind's eye. He had to keep his brain awake. He fought to speak to them.

This has to be a mistake. The words danced around in his head mocking him with their silence. His captors had to hear him. The thoughts blurred but one floated to the surface.

Drake, you bastard...

CHAPTER TWO

Tyler Demir sat up with a grimace, rubbing his neck. He should never have closed his eyes. Checking his watch, he came fully awake. Shit! It was almost noon. He stood, carefully stretched his arms over his head, felt the muscles protest as he listened to the crunching snap of vertebrae. A hot shower and change of clothes would help. Working his mouth, he decided mouthwash would chase out whatever had died in there.

Halfway through a series of head to shoulder stretches, a light knock at the door interrupted him. The door opened slowly, and Abraham peeked in.

"Hey, you're awake!" He stepped all the way in holding the door open.

"No thanks to you! Why didn't you wake me sooner?" Demir asked.

"I tried, but you couldn't hear me over your snoring. How about breakfast?"

"Sounds great. Just give me a minute to shower." Demir picked up his backpack then followed Abraham out the door. "I'll meet you up top in twenty minutes." He paused at the secretary's desk. "I should leave Yasmin a note to say I'm back and..."

"It's taken care of," Abraham said.

Showered and teeth brushed, Demir felt human again. Dressed in black slacks, a t-shirt and grey pullover, he put on his ski jacket and met his friend outside the building, twenty minutes later. He was hungry enough that even cafeteria food sounded great.

In the cool air, Demir's headache vanished. They joined the many employees from other buildings who were out enjoying the sunshine during their lunch hour. The bots were still busy clearing the snow from the far side of the parking lot, but at least the sidewalks were clear.

As he and Abe came around a building, Demir saw movement out of the corner of his eye. He turned in time to see a white-tailed deer bounding into the woods. It always amazed him that nature could survive in a constantly shrinking island of green, surrounded by a six-lane highway on one side and industrial parks and warehouses on the other.

Minutes later, they arrived at the six-storey biology building, which housed the main cafeteria. Taking their tray to a table near the windows overlooking the woods, Abraham cleared his throat as they sat down. A sure sign he wanted to say something difficult.

"What is it?" Demir asked, on guard, as he unwrapped his tuna sandwich.

"Nothing, really," Abraham paused. "Well, after you left for North Bay, Henderson called to tell me that he was heading to Toronto for some play."

"I know. That's why I came back early. Remember?" Demir put his sandwich down.

"And he specifically told me not to bother you. I knew you'd be mad if you didn't know about his trip, so I called you anyway."

"You're reading too much into it. He's been bugging me for a while to take a holiday." Demir picked up his sandwich. "He just didn't want me to cancel my trip. Besides, it was only for a couple of days."

"Sure." Abraham started to unwrap his own chicken sandwich, then practically slammed it on the table and snapped, "He's been leaving the day-to-day operations of Internal Security to you for the last year."

"I know," Demir said, keeping his voice level, hoping Abraham would calm down. "Like I said, he probably just wanted me to take some time off. No big deal."

"You really gotta stop defending the guy. He's not doing his job,"

Abraham said, taking a big bite of his sandwich and chewing hard as though it was tough. Demir was amazed he didn't break a tooth or two. The guy never was any good at hiding his feelings.

Demir took a bite of his tuna sandwich and was startled by the taste of salmon. He hated salmon. A gulp of his coffee forced it down. Then he ate it quickly, in part to just get it over with and in part to avoid talking to Abraham. He'd never admit to his friend—he barely wanted to admit it to himself—that his friend was right. If Demir hadn't kept trying to justify Henderson's actions over the past year, the job would become completely unbearable instead of annoying. The chief only had a few years to go before retirement, so it was reasonable that he left more of the workload to him. Training him to take over. Right? Maybe.

"Hey, Ty," Abraham leaned forward to whisper.

Demir leaned forward as well, expecting something important.

"How about her?"

Demir checked where his friend was looking to see a pretty redhead at the cashier.

"I was wondering how long it would take you to try to set me up." Demir shook his head and chuckled.

"Not your type?" Abraham started to take a drink of his Coke, then stopped to add, "I guess you prefer brunettes with emerald-green eyes."

"Shut up," Demir snapped, feeling his cheeks burn. With less emotion he added, "Just cut it out, okay?"

Demir was grateful that they finished their lunch in silence. After driving all night and even with the few hours of sleep he'd managed, he was too tired to be patient with Abraham's matchmaker act and really didn't want to be teased about emerald-eyed brunettes. When finished, Abraham picked up both trays and they headed out of the cafeteria. He didn't fail to nudge Demir as they passed the redhead. Demir elbowed Abraham in the ribs with a smile. Tough to stay mad at the guy.

Outside, Demir inhaled deeply. "Hmm. Air smells fresh."

"Yeah," Abraham said, as they returned to their building. "Hard to go underground with all this outside."

As they stepped out of the elevator on Sub 1, Abraham asked, "Need anything? I should go do some work myself, since this is my actual shift."

"No thanks." Demir returned to his office. The petite blonde secretary looked up from her desk and gave him a big smile.

"It's true, you really are back. I never know when to believe Mr. Abraham."

"I just can't leave this place for long," he said, with a warm smile. "If you need me, I'll be in my office."

Closing the door behind him, he hung up his jacket on the coat rack, then sat down at his desk to check messages. It was just after 1:30 p.m. and still no message from Cahill. He sent a quick message to Operations, in case they hadn't passed on the routine check-in. His heart skipped a beat when he saw a message from Laura Jessup, Cyber's Director of Research. With a grin at this rarity, he opened the message with the subject line, "Welcome back."

Then sat back, mouth agape, staring at the message.

"Dr. Jessup," Demir said, "you can't fly to London on a whim."

Not what she wanted to hear, he noted, as she glared at him with those beautiful, unremitting emerald-green eyes. She brushed back loose strands of light brown hair worn in a French braid today. Though it was still pretty, he preferred it loose. He mentally shook himself out of that mindset, telling himself to concentrate. He avoided her gaze by looking at the holo-image behind her desk. A lighthouse overlooking a colourful ocean sunset. Her substitute for a window, she called it.

"That message from Matt makes it more than a whim," she said, finally. "He suggested I meet him at the conference and talk to the scientist myself."

Demir rubbed his left temple, looking at the message printout in his hands. When he'd first left the RCMP, he'd thought private security would have a much more relaxing pace. It wasn't long before he discovered that guarding the Prime Minister had been less stressful than dealing with Laura Jessup.

"Why don't you have a seat?" she said.

He turned and suppressed a grin at the sofa, which was covered with files and books, and was the main reason her desk stayed so neat. With an embarrassed laugh, she hurried to the coffee table to clear off two chairs by stacking their contents on the other two seats. He was impressed that the ever-growing tower didn't topple over.

"Sorry," she said, sheepishly as they sat down. "I just find working with hard copies much easier. Guess I'm a throwback."

"No, of course not, ma'am."

"This is more comfortable, don't you think?" she said, in a gentle tone that put him on guard. He knew there would be little chance of reasoning with her. "Once Aidan gets here, we can finalize things." Damn, but he knew her well.

As though on cue there was a knock on the door and Aidan Monette came in.

"Hey, Demir," Aidan greeted him, cheerfully.

"Mr. Monette." Demir smiled back. Complete with jeans bearing a hole in one knee to shoulder length unruly brown curls, the man looked more like a street kid than a genius in everything technical. Demir always enjoyed reading his daily t-shirt message but today's was hidden beneath a grey lab coat.

"I found a great deal for us on an overnight flight tonight!" Aidan said.

"What?" Demir jumped to his feet.

"I'm going to pay for my own flight," he added quickly.

A migraine was imminent. Time for a new approach. He looked at her and stated flatly, "I'm sorry but I don't have the authority to approve travel out of the country, so you'll have to wait until Mr. Henderson gets back. In a few days."

Demir prepared himself for the inevitable argument but was saved when the office door opened. Expecting Laura's secretary, he saw instead Paul Drake, the project's most senior, most talented, and most detested scientist. Drake slammed the door shut behind him.

Though barely in his mid forties, Drake bore the aura of an elderly man who believed the world owed him a debt. His pale face was framed by short, straight black hair that fell into uneven bangs across his forehead.

His eyes were so dark that pupil and iris were indistinguishable. He always seemed to look past you. His expression always said, 'I'm better than everyone and I have to keep reminding you because you are so stupid'.

"Drake," Laura said, her tone guarded.

"Jessup," Drake responded, with his usual haughty British accent. He approached Laura, openly ignoring Demir and only cast a superficial glance towards Aidan, who stood with arms crossed and feet apart, watching the older man with undisguised contempt.

"My supplies have been delayed at customs," Drake stated, pausing as though expecting her to take immediate action.

"I don't have time to look into it now. I'll be leaving for London tonight."

"You can't go," Drake snapped. Then he paused to take an uncharacteristic breath before he added more calmly, "Who'll run things here?"

"How about you?" she shot back.

"That is not amusing in the least!" Drake said.

"Yeah," Aidan added, his arms falling to his sides. "Don't even joke about something like that."

"Dr. Jessup," Demir cut in, "we haven't established the fact that you are going. When Mr. Henderson gets back…"

"Are you insinuating that we need your police force's permission to travel?" Drake demanded.

"No sir, of course not," Demir said, biting back a suggestion of where the bastard could travel to. "There are procedures…"

"I did *not* think so," Drake interrupted, and turned his back on him. To Laura, he said, "You must use your contacts to get my supplies released from customs. I have perishable standards in that shipment."

Aidan snapped, "Why the fuck don't you just go and get them yourself?"

"I am much too busy."

"Sure," Aidan continued. "You claimed to be too busy to go to the conference, so Matt had to replace you. Busy? Doing what? Anything that's come out of your section has been Matt's work. Everyone knows it."

Demir expected to hear a tirade, but Drake's only reaction was a slight tensing of his jaw muscles.

"Aidan…" Laura stood to come between the two scientists.

"I don't know how Matt put up with you for the past two years!" Aidan continued undaunted, glaring at Drake over her head. "No one else could stand to work with you for more than two minutes."

"Dr. Jessup," Demir began, hoping to diffuse the argument. This time, the phone interrupted him.

Laura leaned across her desk to answer.

"It's for you, Mr. Demir."

"Thank you." He took the phone. "Demir here."

"Abraham here."

"Yes?" Something in Abraham's voice made a knot form in Demir's gut.

"London called. Dr. Stoddard's missing."

"What? When?"

"Just before 7 a.m., London time. Stoddard was on his way to meet other conference delegates for breakfast. He never made it. Witnesses saw a man matching his description being dragged out of the side entrance by two men."

"Where the hell was Cahill?"

"They're still looking for him. Ty, Scotland Yard's sure it's a snatch."

"Shit!" Demir rubbed his eyes. "Why the hell didn't they tell us sooner? Never mind. Recall Henderson. I'm on my way up."

He hung up then saw the frozen tableau of blanched faces before him. A result of his non-professional reaction. Where the hell was his training? He filled them in on the conversation as Aidan moved closer to listen intently. Drake remained motionless near the coffee table, his eyes narrowing slightly as he listened. Other than increasing pallor, Laura showed no outward expression.

Without warning, Aidan dove at Drake and punched him in the face.

"You bastard!" Aidan's voice was hysterical with fury. "They'll kill him when they find out they got the wrong man!"

Demir managed to stop a second punch from landing on Drake's mid-section. He pinned Aidan's arms behind his back as the younger man continued to struggle.

Laura stood in front of Aidan, calling his name gently, trying to calm him.

"Ma'am, please," Demir spoke through clenched teeth as the younger man fought to get free. "I don't think I can hold him much longer. Move away."

Drake had recovered his footing and now stood motionless. His expression unreadable. Blood flowed from his nose unchecked.

"Come on." She pulled Drake out of the room by his arm. Just before the door closed, Demir thought he'd seen Drake mouth the words, "I'm sorry."

Impossible, Demir reasoned. Drake never cared for anyone but himself.

Once they were gone, all fight left the young scientist and he crumpled to the floor. Demir knelt beside him.

"It's his fault," Aidan gasped. "It should have been him." Trembling, he leaned his head against the chair.

Demir awkwardly patted Monette's shoulder trying to console him, praying Laura would hurry back and take over. He was never good at this paternal stuff. But he did excel at being territorial and now all Demir wanted to do was get to Operations and find out how a simple conference trip had got so fucked up.

CHAPTER THREE

After Laura watched Drake lock himself in his office, she sprinted back to her office. She had barely opened the door when Demir dashed out. Damn! She'd wanted to question him. Get more details about what happened in England.

Her mind a maelstrom of questions, she tried her best to console Aidan. Maybe he'd picked up on her anxiety, or reality was finally sinking in. His breathing became ragged, he began to cry in short gasping sobs. By the time the doctor arrived, she'd had to hold him still for the doctor to administer a light sedative.

Within minutes they were able to get Aidan to his feet and managed to walk Aidan, now a silent zombie, to medical. From there she phoned her bewildered secretary to have her call the other two scientists to her office. With bile rising in her throat, Laura broke the news of the kidnapping.

Their reaction—stunned silence. Then a barrage of questions. Laura's only answer was "I don't know," which frustrated her and the others so much that she soon put a stop to the discussion with a promise to call a staff meeting after she got more information. Everyone filed out of her office in silence, looking more like stoop-shouldered day labourers after a full shift than scientists. Only her secretary was left behind.

"Is there anything I can do?" Edna Esteban asked.

"No, thank you," Laura said. "Oh, maybe you could get Mr. Demir on the phone for me, please."

"Do you want me to find out about any developments?"

"Thank you, no. I'd rather talk to him," Laura said. When Edna hesitated to leave, she added, "That's all for now."

"I'll get him on the line right away," Edna said, as she stood and quickly left the office, closing the door silently behind her.

Like a mouse scurrying across the floor, Laura thought. But it wasn't a derogatory thought. Edna had been at her side from the first moment Laura had taken over as research director nine years ago.

Back then, low morale had darkened everyone's mood. After the government had moved Cyber into the underground facility, the previous research director had taken security measures too far. He'd insisted that all scientists work independently, going as far as to monitor offices and the lunchroom for any unauthorized technical discussions. Within a short time, he'd transformed a cutting-edge facility into a crumbling empire-building dungeon.

Given the option of early retirement and an added incentive of an overly generous severance payout, he'd accepted. He'd stayed on for a week to show her the ropes. Patiently, she'd smiled and listened to his paranoid rules for ultimate secrecy, turning those legendary ropes into a quagmire of knots. Rumour was that he suffered from early Alzheimer's. Her best guess was that he was simply an idiot.

Through the entire breaking in period, Edna had helped her transfer into the position seamlessly.

The phone on Laura's desk rang, startling her out of her musings. She grabbed it before the second ring. But before she could speak, Edna's voice, not Demir's, sounded through the receiver.

"I'm sorry, Dr. Jessup. I spoke with one of the Internal Security officers. They said Mr. Demir can't come to the phone now and that they'd call you the moment they have any news."

"Damn," Laura muttered, then spoke aloud, "didn't you tell them I wanted to speak to someone?"

"He hung up before I had a chance. Should I call back?"

"No, it's all right. They're right, I shouldn't be interrupting them. Thank you, Edna." She hung up, not meaning to slam the receiver. She had to be patient. There was nothing she could do except let everyone do their job.

She turned to lose herself in the holo behind her desk, imagining herself in the white lighthouse, overlooking a vast ocean and a serene sky painted with a myriad of reds, purples, and darkening blues. The sunset view usually helped her escape to a calming solitude when deadlines or high-level bureaucracy stressed her out. This time she didn't want to be calm. She needed to do something.

Laura left her office for the laboratory level.

The elevator doors opened on Sub 3 and Laura paused, listening. The hum of the air circulating system was surrounded by a surreal silence that reached deep inside her as a reminder that no one was here. No laughter. No jokes. No voices at all.

The underground facility had been constructed in the early 2000s. Built first, this level was better thought out and enjoyed higher ceilings and wide corridors. There were four spacious labs set to the right of the elevator, plus three smaller ones around the corner, a low temperature electron microscope room, and sterile clean room.

Breathing deeply, Laura finally forced her feet to take her to the first lab. It was the one that Drake and Matt shared. Or more correctly, that Drake allowed Matt to use. She shook her head wondering if Drake's self-centered nature stemmed from being an only child who was never taught to share by overindulgent parents.

She took another deep breath before entering the spacious lab. It was quiet, save for the humming of the incubator and the whispering whoosh of the laminar flow hood. She turned towards the two large, flat computer screens on the wall, and her heart thudded when she saw one active screen displaying schematics. For a second, she irrationally thought that Matt was here working.

No, he'd forgotten to shut down his computer in his rush to throw together a paper to be presented at the conference. Though it made more sense for Drake to simply hand over his own prepared talk, he'd refused, asserting that he planned to deliver the same paper at an upcoming conference and didn't want the 'junior scientist' to mangle his work. With everyone's help, including grudging assistance from Drake, Matt finished with barely enough time to go home, pack, and catch the flight to England.

Matt would present their progress in the field of neurotechnology. He'd had a hard time finding enough details—that he was allowed to include—that would satisfy the scientific audience, but not enough to compromise the top-secret classification of their research. Eventually he'd found the right balance. Laura smiled, remembering how he'd practically danced out of her office when she'd finally approved his presentation.

Their research was based on early attempts to grow brain organoids in vitro. The culture had matured and organized to form synapses and soon brainwaves could be detected. The initial driving force was to get a better understanding of brain development and disorders such as Alzheimer's. That work had stalled amid public controversy and ethical questions about growing sentient brains in vitro. But in reality, the work of those scientists were still years, if not decades, away from their goal.

Cyber built on that early work. They used the brain organoids to train nanites to find and repair injuries or heal neurological disease. And their work, thanks to the top-secret rating, continued unhindered by public opinion. They were close to human trials. A simple injection and the nanites would find and repair the damage.

She wandered about the lab and, despite herself, laughed at the printout of a news article from over a decade ago that was posted on the wall. In bold letters the headline read, *PETRI DISH FLIES SIMULATOR*. Scientists had grown an organoid in culture that could control the pitch and yaw of an FB-50 jet simulator.

Cyber's work was already light years beyond that modest ability, and someone had scrawled 'Bloody Amateurs' under the headline. Everyone had assumed Aidan, the usual practical joker, was responsible. However, Laura recognized the neat handwriting, disguised to look messy, as being Drake's.

Her good mood vanished as the emptiness of the lab surrounded her reminding her that Matt was missing.

She wandered aimlessly about until she eventually stood in front of the door to her own, much smaller, lab. She'd set up this lab to test some of the ideas she'd come across while doing literature surveys. As an administrator, she didn't need to do any hands-on research herself. But what sane person could survive by only reading other people's work and writing reports?

Working in the lab also helped her stay centered and calm. She knew that once the shock wore off, her staff would start knocking on her door with questions. And she'd reassure them that she was looking into things and information was coming in. Make them believe that she was in charge.

Even though she felt as lost as they did.

Demir left Laura to console Aidan and raced up one flight to Operations, taking the steps two at a time. Barely winded, he pushed open the door to Operations. Two men studied several computer monitors that displayed the security status within the complex itself as well as the building above. Abraham had his back to the door and was looking over the shoulder of one technician at the computer display.

Demir checked the holographic projection on one wall with the schematics of the underground facility. Each individual had ID implants or skin patches that showed on the schematic. Sub 2 housed the scientists' offices, a couple of briefing rooms, as well as the infirmary. The red dots of the scientists were there, including the green dot of Cyber's medical doctor. On the schematic, this level was a maze of corridors originally designed to be much larger, but soon after construction had begun, they were already grossly over budget. The designs were scaled back on the fly, leaving many corridors leading to dead ends.

By the time construction reached Sub 1, *cramped* was given a whole new meaning.

The blue dots of Internal Security showed them on this level. The two secretaries represented by yellow dots were outside their respective boss' doors. The cleaners, when they did come in, were represented by blinking white dots.

For now, the scientific staff would stay in the complex until he knew what threat, if any, existed. Bodyguards would very likely shadow them outside. It would be Henderson's call, but it was also standard procedure.

"Anything new?" Demir joined Abraham.

"Scotland Yard's tracking down leads," Abraham answered, as he returned his attention to the screen.

"And Cahill?" Demir asked.

"No word yet."

Demir chewed his lower lip. Cahill was a seasoned man who would have protected Matt Stoddard with his life.

"And Henderson?"

"Sir," the tech said, as she turned her head slightly to answer, "I haven't been able to reach the chief and I've left messages at the hotel. Mitchell's on his way to Toronto to get him."

"Why send the new guy?" Demir asked Abraham. "He's been here barely a year. Why didn't you send someone with more experience?"

"Lives five minutes from the airport, so was able to be on the flight the quickest," Abraham said. "In the meantime, we got the local cops at the hotel waiting for Henderson until our boy gets there." He checked his watch. "Which should be in less than an hour." Before Demir could ask, he added, "We managed to nab a military plane courtesy of Major Kirby."

"Good," Demir said. It wouldn't be long now and he could hand control back to Henderson where it belonged. To Abraham he said, "Did you get all the information from London?"

"Right here," Abraham said, as he handed him a red file folder.

Demir opened the folder to find a single sheet. He read aloud, "Dr. Matthew Stoddard seen leaving the Plaza on Hyde Park Hotel with two unidentified males at 6:55 a.m., GMT. Scotland Yard is investigating." Demir turned it over to check if there was any more on the other side. "This it?" He looked at Abraham who nodded. With a grunt, Demir added, "I'll make some calls."

"Mr. Demir," one of the other techs said, "surface just called. Major Kirby is on his way down."

"I'll meet him in my office," Demir said. He snapped the flimsy folder closed, creating a tiny puff of wind. To Abraham, he said, "Let me know when the other squad leaders get here."

Demir left Operations, half anticipating, half dreading Kirby's visit. When Cyber Inc. first became a joint venture with the government, it was agreed that security would be handled by a private security force with Kirby only acting as the liaison with the Department of National Defence. Somehow, he always seemed to be too closely involved for comfort. This time, his interference would be welcome if it helped get

Matt Stoddard back faster.

As Demir rounded the corner to his office, the secretary, Yasmin, pointed to his office and mouthed, "He's here." He nodded thanks, wondering how the hell Kirby had got down so fast.

Demir opened his office door and was startled to see Kirby seated at his desk, talking on the phone. Anytime Kirby visited, he'd sit behind the boss' desk, and Henderson would let the bastard stay there the entire meeting. Bristling, Demir closed the door quietly and waited. After all, the call could be about their missing man.

Kirby's face was a street map of deeply etched lines reflecting the military operations he'd lived through. Though in his late sixties, you could see that he'd once been quite muscular, but had allowed a beer belly to take hold. Instead of a uniform, he wore a simple dark suit.

"Thank you. Keep me updated," Kirby said, as he hung up. Demir deliberately came around the desk to stand near him. Kirby smiled and stiffly stood up. "Hope you don't mind my using your chair while I was on the phone. My back's been bothering me with all this dampness. Damn Mid East war, you know. That area just can't stay calm."

"No problem," Demir said, slightly ashamed of his own show of authority, though not enough to relinquish his seat. He sat down, motioning to the chair on the opposite side of his desk. "Please."

Kirby sat, with a heavy sigh. "I understand you've got the troops in Toronto tracking down the old man."

"The local police are at the hotel until my man gets there. By the way, thanks for the plane."

"No trouble," Kirby said.

"Any word on Cahill, yet?"

"They found him alive."

"Thank God! What happened to him?" Demir, though relieved, was also annoyed that Kirby hadn't led with that fact.

"They found him bound and gagged in a linen closet," Kirby said. "Pretty beat up, but he'll be okay. I don't have the full details of what happened, but looks like he was taken out of the way to get at the scientist."

"Was he able to identify who did it?"

"Unfortunately, no," Kirby said with a sigh. "They knocked on his door and thinking it was Stoddard, he opened it without any concern. They sucker punched him." He paused as though debating whether to continue. Nodding slightly, more to himself than to Demir, he added, "I do have some information and I don't see any reason to wait for your boss to get back. We've found Stoddard."

"Great!" Demir said. "Where is he?"

"I don't have an exact location, you understand. For security reasons. MI5 has tracked him to an old mansion in the countryside. About two hundred kilometres north of London."

"So, they're mounting a rescue," Demir said, hardly able to believe that it was almost over.

"Yes. Local authorities are preparing to move in." He checked his watch. "Oh, they've been getting ready since about 11:30 our time."

"That's three hours ago! Why didn't they tell us before?"

"They did. I just wanted to make sure everything was on track first."

"You mean *you* knew."

"DND is always informed first," Kirby said, matter-of-factly. "MI5's special unit should be in position by 1600, our time. Stoddard will be snug and warm in his own bed by tomorrow night. However," he leaned forward resting his elbows on the desk, as he looked past steepled fingers. His voice even and commanding. "You should keep this between you, me, and Henderson, until I tell you otherwise. There's no point getting everyone's hopes up. Just in case."

Demir stared back, unsure which kind of answer he should give. Tell him to go fuck himself because everyone was worried about Matt and deserved to know? Or tell him to go find the rock he climbed out from under? Finally, he realized there was only one answer.

"Yes, sir."

"Good," Kirby said, as he stood up and strode out of the office, all signs of stiffness miraculously gone.

Demir fumed. Other than asserting his control over Internal Security, it hadn't been necessary for the bastard to come here in person. Consciously forcing his shoulders to unclench and relax, Demir spent the next half hour calling old friends and contacts from his RCMP days, trying to get information that Kirby should have supplied.

About an hour later, armed with what little new information he'd managed to collect, he took his handwritten notes down the hall to Tech Support. An easy matter of entering the info, then copying on to four e-pads for the meeting with squad leaders. He finished quickly and deleted the information from the stand-alone computer, as was protocol. As he rolled his chair back, the deafening crunch stopped him. Slowly he looked down. One e-pad lay under the wheel, crushed.

"Damn it!"

"Sir," the IT tech said, as he got up from the other terminal. "I can take care of this for you."

Just then, the phone rang. The tech answered and after listening briefly, hung up and said, "Sir, the squad leaders are waiting in the briefing room for you."

Demir looked up from the floor at him. "I deleted the original info. And these are encrypted, so you can't copy from them." He stretched out his hand to give the tech his notes.

"Not a problem. I can get the info back."

"But I just deleted it."

"Everything gets put into the deleted directory," the tech said. But just as Demir was about to speak, he added quickly, "The directory contents are permanently deleted nightly, at midnight."

"So for several hours, sensitive material is hanging around for anyone to access?"

"Uh, no sir," he stammered. "Not anyone. Just me. Anyone else needs clearance from the chief." When Demir remained silent, the tech slowly sat down and silently, looking embarrassed, copied the information. He handed him a new e-pad.

Demir stared at him for a few seconds. More than anything, he wanted to grab him by the throat and shake some sense into him. He was a new hire, barely six months. Maybe that's how they did it out in the corporate world, but not here. Calmly he said instead, "You're going to change that. When someone hits delete, then it's to be gone. Immediately."

"But sir, some of the scientists..."

"Immediately deleted." Demir waited for him to nod, before leaving the room that felt even smaller than when he'd first entered.

A secret installation meant special measures were to be taken.

Satellite phones didn't work here. All internal phones were hard wired. The network was internal only, with no access to the open Internet, even for research. Outside electronic communication came in and went out through a separate, highly shielded route. Even these e-pads were so highly encrypted that only the appropriate DNA could unlock them. DNA that belonged to him and the three squad leaders.

And Henderson, of course.

Before he knew it, Demir stood outside the briefing room. He paused, his hand on the doorknob. He sucked in a deep breath, held it for a few seconds, then let it out slowly. He opened the door to find three grim looking men waiting in silence around the rectangular table. He took the empty chair nearest the door.

He looked at each squad leader in turn. No-neck Sandrovsky, from the night shift, sporting a newly shaved head. Next to him sat red-haired McGuire from the evening shift, looking dwarfed next to Sandrovsky. McGuire was brandishing yet another black eye, most likely from another bar fight that he'd 'tried to break up.'

And of course, Abraham, from the day shift.

"First thing I'd like to say," Demir said, allowing himself a smile, "they found Cahill alive." He waited until the cheers and whistles died down. "He's been beaten up but not too seriously."

"Did he say what happened?" Abraham asked.

"Unfortunately, he didn't see anything before they knocked him out," Demir said, recognizing Abraham's concern for a member of his squad. He handed each man an e-pad.

"The information we have so far," Demir said. "Dr. Stoddard was supposed to meet some conference delegates for breakfast and when he didn't show up, one of them went to find him. She found his jacket and wallet in the elevator. His money card and ID were still there, so it wasn't robbery.

"The delegate alerted the authorities. Scotland Yard has ID'd the two men that were seen taking Dr. Stoddard out of the hotel. Even though they used facial scramblers to hide from the CCTV cameras, they were identified from trace DNA residue in the elevator. They were able to trace one of them to his work, through traces of mechanic's grease used in high-end sports cars. Both are small time crooks. It shouldn't be long before they're caught. I've included all the names and backgrounds of the scientists staying at the same hotel."

"They must know they took the wrong guy," McGuire said. "Didn't they have a picture of their target?"

"They probably just had the contact info. Name, hotel room," Abraham said. "Didn't want to be caught carrying any evidence."

"You think once they figure out they got the wrong guy, they'll go after Drake?" McGuire asked.

"It's quite probable, that's why I'm ordering 24-hour protection for the scientific staff. I want each member of your units that are on guard detail to draw a weapon from the armoury," Demir said.

"I say once they get those two," Sandrovsky said, "give me five minutes with them. They'll talk."

"Let's focus. Okay?" Demir snapped. Forcing a deep breath and releasing it, he calmly continued, "Scotland Yard and MI5 are on the job, but they'll be casting wide nets looking for someone who'd want to snatch a scientist. With our home field advantage, we might be able to help them narrow their search. If we can figure who'd be interested in the research."

"What about the Vietnamese?" McGuire said. "They were thrown out of the States a few years back for stealing tech."

"That was telecommunications technology," Demir said. "We should concentrate on companies involved in brain research."

"All those companies that are big into neuro or nano whatever research," Sandrovsky began, "they got their own research stuff, so they don't need to steal."

"Haven't you heard of industrial espionage?" McGuire said. "Why waste money and time developing something if you can steal it."

"How about terrorists?" Sandrovsky said.

"It could be something as simple as a kidnapping for ransom of some kind," Demir agreed. "Keep your ears open for any chatter. There are a lot of possibilities to check into." Too many, he thought. India. Russia. China. Anyone. "I've also given you the entire conference delegate list, as well as the organizers. Split it up among you. Once I get more info, I'll pass it on. Make sure your squads are fully briefed." He turned off his e-pad, signalling the end of the meeting. McGuire and Sandrovsky left the briefing room.

"What's this kick butt routine Sandrovsky's got?" Abraham asked.

Demir let out a chuckle that actually relaxed him. "He does take things to a whole new level. How he became squad leader, I'll never know."

"Henderson's choice," Abraham said, as both left the briefing room. "You have to wonder how many other strange decisions our fearless leader's made."

"Who knows," Demir said.

Alone in his office, Demir paced to burn off the excess energy somersaulting in the pit of his stomach. If he'd wanted to make life and death decisions, he would've stayed with the RCMP.

He huffed at the irony of joining the mounted police for excitement. They'd recruited him soon after high school. His easy-going nature and get-in-anywhere ability had made him perfect for undercover work. Fearless in those days as only an eighteen year old could be, he'd worked and studied hard and moved up the ranks in a few short years. Eventually he joined the narcotics division. Again, his hard work had paid off when he uncovered information on a major drug shipment coming into the Port of Halifax. An operation that had taken several months to set up. A landmark case that should have made his career.

He shook his head trying to bury the memory. He knew that it would always linger in the shallow depths of his subconscious where his anger and guilt lived. Rubbing the back of his neck, he picked up the phone to find someone, anyone, who could tell him what was going on in England.

After two hours and little to show for it, Demir checked his watch. He checked voicemail in case Kirby had tried calling while he was on the phone. Nothing. Next, he scanned for any messages. Kirby had sent a quick update on Cahill. Shit! Was the bastard serious? Furious, he needed to take a break.

He knocked on Abraham's office door and entered.

"Ty, you okay?" Abraham asked, as he looked up from the computer.

"Sure," he lied. "What're you doing?"

"Working on the protection schedule. Have a seat."

"Thanks," Demir said. His friend's office was only marginally smaller than his own, but appeared larger thanks to a smaller desk and a two drawer file cabinet tucked neatly in the corner behind the door. He stared at his feet as he asked, "How's the new schedule looking?"

"Almost done," Abraham said, turning back to the screen.

Demir shifted in the chair, an ancient uncomfortable wooden chair. It definitely discouraged long visits. Maybe he'd replace his nice, ergonomic guest chair with one of these. Demir sighed as he checked his watch.

"I've messaged you a copy as well as McGuire and Sandrovsky," Abraham said. "They've almost finished working up their schedules as well."

"Thanks." Demir said. He looked at his watch, then at his feet again.

"Am I boring you?" Abraham asked.

"No, sorry."

"I was looking at the new info you gave us. Why the security alert by Smythe-Williams' name?"

"It just means he *could* be a security risk because, now get this, his mother's grandparents came from Afghanistan. But..."

"But?" Abraham prompted.

"But why take the chance? We should run a full background check. His work is what prompted Dr. Stoddard to message Dr. Jessup and convince her to fly to London. Could be coincidence, I don't know."

"Any more news on Cahill?"

"His injuries are minor. But," Demir paused to rub his eyes. Looking at his friend, he continued, "Kirby tells me that after he's released from the hospital, Scotland Yard will be debriefing him because apparently, they 'find it suspicious that a professional bodyguard' was overpowered so easily."

"Are they fucking serious?" Abraham hit his desk. "Cahill a suspect?"

"They'll figure out they're wrong soon enough." Demir checked his watch again.

"You sure I'm not boring you?" Abraham sounded annoyed.

"Sorry." Demir covered his watch with his hand.

17:20. Kirby had said the rescue team was going in at 16:00. No news was good news. Right?

Mitchell paced in the lobby of the Beacon Hotel in Toronto's waterfront, waiting for Mr. Henderson to return. He liked how spacious this lobby was compared to the two-star hotels he was used to. Eventually he gave up pacing and sat in one of the chairs. Had he known that the cushions would form a comfortable cocoon around him, he would have sat down sooner. Leaning back, he watched the clouds drift by on the holographic sky on the ceiling. Large floor to ceiling windows provided a clear view of the water. It was like being outside on the shore, but without the windchill factor. His wife would love this hotel.

Married just over two years, the honeymoon was still on. Even though she hated sports, her anniversary gift to him had been tickets to see the Yankees play in New York. Of course, she loved musicals and he'd bought her tickets to a Broadway musical. Except for all the singing, the play was pretty good. Not that he'd ever tell her that because then she'd drag him to more cultural things. Growing up in Guyana, the only culture he'd experienced had been Carnival and that was just one big party. Maybe just before the baby arrived, he'd treat her to a weekend getaway at this hotel.

Mitchell checked his watch. 7:30 p.m. Where the hell was the boss? Man, what if he had to wait here all night?

Just then, he spotted Mr. Henderson through the window, sprinting up the steps to open the door for his wife. For a man close to seventy, the boss was in good shape. He worked out at least three times a week.

Once in the lobby, Henderson spotted him immediately and stopped mid-step, his face paling so much Mitchell was afraid he'd pass out. He took a step forward ready to catch his boss if he did fall. Henderson turned to his wife.

"Brenda, I'm sorry, I have to leave," he said tenderly.

She glanced at Mitchell briefly before saying, "I know, there's an emergency and you need to handle it." She sighed and added, "I'll leave with you."

"No, you've been waiting to see this play for a long time. Stay. Visit with your friends. Then tell me all about it when you get home." He kissed her gently, then looked deep into her eyes as though wanting to say more. He caressed her face, then all business-like said to Mitchell, "Where's the car?"

"This way, sir," Mitchell said, heading out the door to the waiting police cruiser. He paused to speak to Mrs. Henderson. "I'm sorry, ma'am."

"I know you are," she said, quietly.

Mitchell wasn't sure if she believed him or not. He forced himself not to think about it. Or to think about that similar smile his own wife always gave him whenever he was called away to work.

At 8:45 p.m., Demir greeted Henderson's jet at the airbase at the Ottawa Airport, relieved to have him home. The chief would know which buttons to push to get information on Matt Stoddard and Cahill. As they drove back to Cyber Labs with Mitchell and the driver in the front, Demir and Henderson in the back, the security chief was brought up to speed.

"And I haven't heard anything more from Kirby," Demir finished.

"Give him time," Henderson said.

"Kirby said the rescue..."

"It's not like a bus schedule. I'm sure everything's under control," Henderson said, lighting a cigarette. He looked at Demir and said, "Sorry, guess this bothers you. I'm down to a couple of puffs a day now." He opened the window and tossed it out.

"Kirby's not keeping us in the loop."

"He's doing his job. National security and all that shit. In fact, if he wasn't around we'd be dealing with the military directly. Trust me, son, you don't want that."

"But..."

"You just need to be patient," Henderson said. "Let the experts take care of things."

"Yes, sir," Demir said. Experts? What the hell was he? Most of Internal Security was either ex-police, ex-military, or ex-something. And each one of them were experts in their past jobs.

"What about Cahill? They want to interrogate him like he's a suspect."

"The term is debrief. Everyone has a job to do and, well, we're in their jurisdiction." Henderson looked at Demir, then turned back to the window.

"Can we insist that we be kept better informed of developments?" Demir asked.

"Sure, I'll mention it to Kirby. In the meantime send the scientists home."

"What about having armed protection for them?"

"What? Oh sure. That's a good idea." Leaning forward he told the driver, "Drop me off at home, please."

"Yes, sir." The driver glanced over his shoulder at Demir.

"Home? Sir?" Demir barely got the words out. "Aren't you coming to the complex?"

"Sounds to me like you've got things under control. I've been shopping all day with the wife. I really need a shower." He patted Demir's arm and said, "I'm sure you'll let me know when the scientist gets back." Then he lit up another cigarette and blew smoke rings out the window.

"Yes, sir," Demir muttered, and cracked open his own window to dilute the smoke with fresh air. Was he the only one worried? Why the hell did he spend all that effort retrieving Henderson if he wasn't planning to do anything when he got back? It was supposed to be the chief's job. Not *his*, damn it!

After they dropped Henderson off at home, Demir returned to Cyber to wait for news about the rescue.

The lead SAS agent, dressed in black from head to foot, studied the 16th century Tudor home. The house sat alone on the hill in the English countryside, the black and white pattern visible in the dawn light. A tall hedge surrounded the grounds, making it a beautiful, secluded home in the Lake District. The light drizzle coated everything a polished silver. The sun would be rising in about an hour, but in an overcast sky, there were no shadows to betray the SAS team to the occupants of the building.

The subject had been missing almost eighteen hours, but new information had prompted a change in plans, delaying the mission. Now, men waited in the hedges around the building as well as a team on the roof. In position all night. The drawn thick curtains concealed any visible movement inside. No drones managed to get closer than one hundred metres before they shut down and fell from the sky. Heat signatures from within the house were inconclusive. The house was well shielded, obviously hiding something of value inside.

Strangely, there had been no movement in or out of the house since the team had taken up their positions last night.

The lead agent signalled it was time. The rest of the team breathed as one, prepared to move in. He could see the two front windows and the agents ready to rappel down, ignite the charge to weaken the glass, and then crash through.

He waited for one minute more before giving the order to move in. His trademark. His good luck charm. Not a single failed mission since that first time that he'd waited that extra minute.

And as before, this mission would be a success. Orders were to get the hostage out, one way or another. Leaving him behind, not an option. Nothing easier than that. He, of course, did prefer getting the hostage out alive.

Ten seconds. He adjusted the earphone in his ear and made sure the tiny microphone was in front of his mouth. He spoke softly into the microphone.

"5 - 4 - 3 - 2 - 1!"

As one, the assault team entered the house through every possible orifice. He followed close behind the battering ram through the front door. Swiftly, the reports came in through his earphone. "All clear." "No hostiles." They moved through the house swiftly. He listened to more reports. "No hostiles." "No hostage."

Was their information wrong? A call from upstairs summoned him and he took the steps three at a time. Followed directions to the second room on the right. He entered.

How? How did they fail?

CHAPTER FOUR

Tuesday morning, a day after Matt had gone missing, Paul Drake opened his office door a crack and peered up and down the hall. Empty.

Before anyone saw him, he started for Laura Jessup's office. He passed the other office and checked around the corner. Still clear. He continued.

She had called for him a half hour ago. And he had tried to get to her office. He owed her that much. But he had not realized that getting from his office to hers at the opposite end of Sub 2 would be so arduous a task.

Those other two kept dropping by unannounced. First, Jeanette Theriault, to berate him for not going to the conference as he should have done. Then, Elton Chan, with his interminable questions that had no answers. And each time it took several minutes before he could make them leave. The worst had been running into Elton later in the bathroom, where he'd endured the man's theories and questions for almost ten minutes.

There had been a time when anger had fuelled Drake's work. Anger at being helpless to do what was needed.

Fifteen years ago, his brother Thomas, a foreman on a construction site in Ottawa, had fallen from a second floor beam and suffered irreparable brain damage. Drake was devastated to see his younger brother in a deep coma with no possible future. Their parents had flown back and forth from England over the course of several months. Their last trip coincided with the doctor's final verdict. Thomas was brain dead.

Drake had stood at the foot of the bed, watching the painful scene unfold before him in a static and painful reality. His once animated brother now lied pale and still, with machinery filling and emptying his lungs. Monitors recording the beating of his heart. His parents on either side of the hospital bed. His mother's audible sobs. His father's wide-eyed disbelief. A scene that refused to fade away.

With nothing more to be done medically, the doctors asked the parents to make the ultimate decision and remove life support. After a full agonizing day of standing vigil over Thomas, his father turned to Drake, his face hard, as the pain hovered just below the surface and asked him to step into the corridor.

Drake tried to block out his mother's sobs echoing in the background; he braced himself to hear his parents' decision. But nothing prepared him for his father's actual words.

"Paul," his father said, placing a heavy hand on his shoulder, his eyes downcast, "I know you have this dream of saving him with your science. But you and I know that any miracle for Thomas is years away. We can't, in all good conscience, let Thomas suffer so. Or become a guinea pig. You must tell the doctors to remove life support."

"Me?" Drake said. Incredulous, he looked at his father hoping he'd heard wrong.

"I'm asking you to do this. For your mother's sake." He paused then, added, "I've transferred power of attorney to you." Without another word, his father returned to the room to take up his previous position by the hospital bed.

At the time, Cyber's research was new and innovative. He was sure that it held the key to his brother's reprieve from death or life with no brain function. It might take years, but there was a chance for him to have his life returned.

Or it might not. His father was right. He couldn't turn his brother into a test subject.

Drake went to the nursing station and asked to speak to the doctor. Later, Drake had hidden in the bathroom crying, unable to face watching his brother take his last breath. His parents had stayed by Thomas' side. Within a few brief hours, it was over.

That evening at Thomas' apartment, while Drake and his parents sat in inconsolable silence, his father beckoned him to follow to the kitchen.

"Paul, since this is your city and you know all of his friends, I'd like you to make the funeral arrangements."

"Of course," Drake said, too numb to even care that he'd been given one more responsibility that should never have been his. He'd make sure everything was as Thomas would have wanted. Since his house was more practical than his brother's apartment, Drake decided to have the wake there. Drake even arranged for a string quartet to play at the funeral. Rather than stress his mother with the details of organizing the food, as he knew she would, he'd hired caterers. Not to further burden his parents financially, especially after the several flights back and forth from England these past months to visit his brother in the hospital, Drake had taken out a second mortgage on his home to pay for everything.

The funeral was dignified. All of Thomas' favourite songs were played, the rock songs beautifully arranged for string quartet. He knew his parents would be pleased.

At the wake, Drake's house was filled with many friends, as well as several relatives that had arrived from abroad. As he walked through the rooms, checking to see that no one was lacking food, or drink, he came up behind his mother talking to a couple of elderly cousins from Bristol. She had finally stopped crying, though a handkerchief peeked out from her sleeve. About to step forward to take her empty glass away, something in her posture and the way she was speaking stopped him. Unintentionally, he eavesdropped on the conversation.

"Oh, my Irene," the female cousin was saying, "I cannot imagine the pain you felt telling the doctors to let your boy go."

"No, it was not my decision," his mother said. Shaking her head, she removed the handkerchief to dab at her eyes. "Paul told the doctors to remove life support."

He felt a sharp pain in his chest. Bile rose up and lodged in his throat. How could she say such a thing?

"It's quite nice to see so many of Thomas' friends here," the other cousin said, looking around the room. "And so many relatives as well."

"But that band playing music," his mother clucked her tongue. "As though this is a party, not a funeral."

Drake felt something climb out of his stomach and lodge in his chest. Band? He'd made sure that the string quartet played quietly so that people could talk.

Confused by his mother's words, he sought out his father. There in the backyard, Drake pulled him aside from the small group of men to question him.

"Well Paul, I have to live with your mother. You don't. What would my life be like if she knew I gave the doctors the word? Living so far away, you're insulated from her moods." His father patted him on the shoulder, adding, "Fine job with all the arrangements." He returned to chat with the men.

His father's words struck him with a physical force that he not thought possible.

Barely a day after the funeral, Drake's parents returned to England. He never spoke to them again. And they never once reached out to him.

Drake took his anger and pain and channelled them into his work. He'd just finished his PhD in neuro-engineering and started work at Cyber, still a fledgling company navigating its way into the field of neurotechnology. When the military took notice and supplied unlimited funding, it also included the inevitable attached strings. Secrecy became a major factor.

Damn them with their cold war mentality, Drake cursed silently. Their research was meant to benefit science in general and medicine in particular. Although it was too late to help his brother, the world was filled with suffering people that could benefit from their work.

For the last couple of days, Drake attempted to bury himself in his work, but his concentration was sabotaged by the incessant reminders of Matt Stoddard everywhere. He'd found Matt's plate with a half eaten bagel from Friday morning in the lab. His notebook with the biofeedback calculations scrawled in his usual messy shorthand. His computer with the simulation of the neural connection to yet a different part of the brain. Drake knew that he should shut it off, or at least re-engage the screen saver, but somehow it felt like a violation.

As well as physical reminders, there was the haunting memory of the look of disbelief on the young man's face when he found out that he would be going to the conference instead. It was the first time Matt had ever stood up to him. Drake had insisted that he was far too busy to take time away from crucial tests using sensitive standards—which he just remembered were still detained in bloody customs. In the end, Drake got his way. As he always did.

Laura Jessup had acquiesced, but then he knew how to persuade her. Of course security simply obeyed orders and adjusted the travel plans. All was arranged as Drake had wanted. But now he couldn't escape the intense feelings of guilt. He quickened his pace to get through the endless, convoluted corridors. Two more twists and he'd reach Laura's office. Once there, their conversation would help remove his focus away from his feelings.

But his anticipation was cut short when Aidan Monette came into view. Aidan's step faltered briefly, though he continued walking to come to a stop, uncomfortably close to him. They hadn't spoken since yesterday.

Aidan remained silent for several moments, his expression unreadable. Drake didn't want to brush past him in the narrow corridor. Laura was waiting but a few more minutes couldn't possibly matter. When Aidan finally spoke his voice was calm and steady. Drake could see that the other man's body tremble as though reining in his fury with enormous effort.

"With all his drug allergies, anything they give him to make him talk could be dangerous. Laura thinks he could be dead," Aidan said.

"She does? How many committee meetings did she hold before coming to that conclusion?" Drake regretted the edge that came with his words, not to mention hating the words he'd chosen.

"She's worried about him, like the rest of us." The voice remained level but his hands clenched into fists. Drake mentally prepared himself for a blow. Instead, Aidan quietly added, "Nothing they do will make him agree to work with them."

"Stop being so naive. Science is meant to be shared, not locked away in a dungeon of antiquated ideals of military supremacy."

"In the wrong hands it could be a terrible weapon," Aidan said.

"Please don't tell me that you share the military's dreams of armies with computer controlled brains." Drake forced a laugh.

"He knows the danger. He won't tell them anything."

"Then he's a fool!" Drake snapped. Why did he answer like that? Forcing himself to make eye contact, he continued in a more reasonable tone. "There is no need for all this secrecy. The chip's inception is medical, not military. It is meant to repair brain damage. Perhaps even revive brain dead patients one day." He broke off with a sharp intake of breath, as his brother's hospital scene flickered in his mind. He found the strength to continue speaking though his voice was strained. "Within a few years our research will inevitably become public knowledge, as so many top secret research projects had done in the past. There is no military value in it. No need for all this secrecy."

Aidan's eyes narrowed into slits as though he was studying him. In a harsh whisper he asked, "What would you do?"

"I have an appointment with our illustrious leader and I'm late." Drake shouldered past. Once around the corner and out of sight, he slumped against the wall, exhaling with exhaustion and relief at finally being alone and for once grateful for the maze of corridors.

He squared his shoulders and continued walking briskly.

Drake rounded the last corner and found the secretary, Edna Esteban, seated at her desk outside the director's office, anticipating his arrival. Barely one and a half metres tall, she had a reputation for being difficult, to the point that even the toughest in security feared antagonizing her.

"Doctor," she greeted. Her bland tone always unsettled him. Everyone else was easy to read.

"Is she in?" Drake asked.

"Dr. Jessup sent for you a half hour ago."

"I had to deal with too many emotional cripples on the way here."

"Really?" She didn't even try to hide her sarcasm.

He bristled at the condescending tone. Then wondered if that was how others felt when he spoke to them. He used his usual tone of authority and said, "I have decided to respect your wish to wait until you announce me. Well?"

She called Laura Jessup, told her Drake had arrived, then hung up. Folding her hands on her desk, she smiled. "Go in."

"Thank you." He nodded as one would to a servant, hoping she caught the subtle gesture. One day she would push him too far.

Alone with Laura, he'd be able to apologize for being late. He'd be able to talk to her, the way they used to. Drake opened the door and entered.

"Where the hell were you?" Laura yelled.

Drake took a step back at her uncharacteristic reaction. She never raised her voice, no matter how stressed she got. And the unexpected sight of Demir unbalanced him further. He'd expected her to be alone. Recovering, he answered, "I was delayed."

"You don't even have the decency to say you're sorry!"

Drake countered quickly, "I say, 'I'm sorry', then you say, 'forget it.' So why say it in the first place? I hate to be redundant."

"I see." She turned her head to look at the seascape picture behind her desk. He could feel her mentally forcing herself to calm down.

"I am here now."

Harsh eyes snapped back to him. "I wanted you here a half hour ago to talk things out with Aidan. But you managed to wait just long enough to miss him."

"Apparently not long enough. I met him in the hall."

"And?"

"We talked." His eyes darted to her seascape to gain his own control over the effect her look always had on him. Of all those he knew, only she could see inside him. Now, he needed to keep her distant. He focussed on maintaining a neutral tone as he returned his attention to her. "I am busy. Was there something else?"

"Yes." Her tone was ice. She turned to Demir. "If you wouldn't mind?"

"Of course not, ma'am." Demir started to leave.

"Do you have any news?" Drake asked, stopping him mid-step. Drake wondered at the security man's hesitation before he turned to face him.

"No, sir, nothing," Demir said, his voice sounding oddly mechanical. Then he seemed to rush out the door, before Drake could question him further.

Laura fumed at Drake's attitude. He had to feel some remorse at forcing Matt to go to the conference instead of him. But Drake hated travel. Hated conferences. Hated people. She sat down behind her desk, deciding on the best approach. Blunt had always worked in the past.

"Look, you're overwhelmed with the workload. As it is, you practically sleep here. So, until Matt returns, I'm assigning Elton to work with you."

"No!" Drake's arms uncrossed and fell rigidly to his sides. "Chan's clumsy, and..."

"And a fool and stupid. As is everyone here," she recited impatiently. "Yes, yes, I know." She stood up, hands pressed on her desk as she leaned forward. Her voice strong, she continued, "No one can measure up to your idea of perfection. But somehow Matt put up with you."

"I never asked him to. I never wanted or needed *anyone*!" Drake finished the last word at a higher pitch.

He did feel guilt, she realized. He'd managed to hide it, even from her. She came around her desk to stand closer to him. Searching his face for a moment, she said softly, "It wasn't your fault. If you had gone to the conference, you'd be the one missing."

"The difference," he whispered, "is that no one would care."

"Please, Paul, talk to me." He turned to leave, but she held his arm. "Do you remember when I first got here, after Dietrich, the previous director left? Everyone was so messed up. You were locked in your lab for days at a time, burying yourself in work, refusing to talk to anyone. I managed to get past your defences and reach you." Moving closer she felt the familiar warmth of his breath on her face. "Please, talk to me." She put her hands on his chest. "I miss you."

Drake held her hands tenderly. But just when she believed that she'd reached him, he gently removed her hands and added quietly, "That was a mistake." And left.

Before the door shut, she sensed that another layer of ice surrounded him.

She hadn't realized how much she'd missed him, until now. When she'd first started at Cyber, her mother had been diagnosed with breast cancer. Within a year, she'd passed away. There'd been a lot of support from so many around her. But only Paul Drake had seemed to truly understand how she'd felt. He listened to her, never judged, offered advice only when she wanted it. Or when she didn't know that she needed it.

They'd shared a brief intimacy. When it ended, what lingered was a different type of closeness. A deep friendship. She was his only friend at work and she suspected, outside of work as well.

As strong as their friendship was, she could never get him to talk about the hidden pain that occasionally peeked out from his galvanized shell. When she did press him, the armour thickened, so she finally stopped. Hoping that he would one day feel safe enough to talk to her.

Some friend she turned out to be, she thought as she glumly returned to her desk. She hadn't noticed the gradual change in his attitude over the past year until it was too late to stop the return to that paranoid isolationist that she'd first met.

When she'd first arrived here nine years ago, she had her hands full of trying to repair the damage the Dietrich had inflicted on morale and on work in general. She studied each individual's potential contributions for the future of the research. She moved six scientists to the surface where security was lower and where they could happily continue their work in micro-circuitry and computer programming.

She'd cut any work that didn't directly contribute to the main thrust of the research—to develop the nanites' abilities. Although Drake's sub-project was one of the ones she'd shelved, he'd willingly participated in the overhaul and made useful and inventive suggestions.

The people were happy. The government was happy to finally see progress on their high risk investment. So happy in fact, that they gave her anything she asked for with no questions. Two years ago, she decided that it was time to endure the security nightmare of red tape and bring in some new blood.

While she searched through recent university graduates, Matt Stoddard's resume had mysteriously landed on her desk. She knew that Drake was also doing his own recruiting search. Matt Stoddard's PhD thesis titled *Nanotechnology Approaches for the Regeneration of the Central Nervous System* had been impressive and Drake had seen the potential in the young graduate.

She still smiled when she remembered the appalled look on Drake's face after she'd assigned Matt to him. That was one possibility that he hadn't anticipated and had fought her decision. Accustomed to getting his way, Drake never suspected that her constant agreements to what he asked for had been very strategic. She gave in on the little things and saved the fights for the big issues. A rocky start at first, but eventually Drake accepted the inevitable and worked with Matt in peace.

Her small team was well balanced between the various disciplines. Elton Chan handled the chemistry. Jeanette Theriault, the software. Aidan's work in hardware required him to frequently interact with physiology, which was Drake's area. After Matt arrived, he became the buffer between Drake and, well, everyone.

Just as Drake had been there for her after her mother's death, Matt had been there for Aidan during his own dark time.

If she was finding Matt's absence painfully difficult. Laura worried about how Aidan was coping.

Demir left before either Drake or Laura asked him any more questions. He shut the office door and leaned against it with a heavy sigh, ignoring Edna's concerned look. He wanted to tell them about the rescue mission, if only to give them hope. But he'd had to lie to them, to Laura, just because Kirby had ordered it. He wasn't surprised when the ever reliable, consistent yes-man Henderson had backed Kirby. Henderson had said that he'd be in early this morning but was still a no-show.

He took the stairs up one flight to Operations to check for messages from Kirby. Nothing. There should at least be news about the rescue. He headed back to his office, rubbing his temple.

"How about some coffee?" Yasmin's voice brought him out of his thoughts.

"Sure," he said, absent-mindedly. He headed for the coffee machine, asking, "How do you take it?"

Yasmin laughed. "No, I mean I'll bring *you* a cup." She gave him a gentle push towards his office.

"Oh, sure. Thanks." He forced a smile. He must really look like hell for her to offer to bring him coffee. Everyone clearly remembered her emphatic statement during her job interview that she 'did not do coffee.' That small comment had been the deciding factor in hiring her.

He sat down heavily at his desk, wondering what he could do next. He tried phoning Kirby, again. It went straight to voicemail. Again. He left a cryptic message, "Call me when everything's finished." Just like the other messages. He debated phoning Henderson at home but what was the point? Henderson was more than happy to let Kirby keep all the secrets and do what he wanted.

Demir punched his desk hard. Damn! Matt Stoddard could be dead before everyone stopped screwing around. And what about Cahill? The only new information was that Cahill was being debriefed by MI5. How long could that take? Why the hell wasn't Kirby expediting it? He was in charge of every other fucking thing!

Demir closed his eyes and cradled his head in his hands trying to control his anger. He was used to following orders that didn't make sense, trusting that his superiors knew something he didn't. But Henderson had never kept him this far in the dark before.

In the distance, he recognized the smell of fresh coffee. Pure, untainted by the faint odour of sugar or warming cream. Coffee was simple. The aroma itself could intoxicate you. And when you took that first sip, you could feel the hot liquid race down your throat to your body's core, which then sent out soothing waves to the rest of your body.

Somehow he felt that this situation should be as simple as coffee.

Dr. Owen opened the medicine cabinet, couldn't remember why, then closed it again. That made what, the sixth time? Why couldn't he concentrate? He brushed back thick grey curls and sighed. Must be old age. Last week he hadn't thought seventy-nine was old. People were working well into their eighties now, thanks to medical advances. However, since he found out that poor Matthew had been kidnapped, he felt like he'd aged an extra decade or two.

He shook his head and opened the medicine cabinet. But all he could see was Matthew Stoddard's face. He slammed the cabinet shut.

If only he had something to keep his mind busy. As staff medical doctor, he had a fairly light workload making sure everyone was healthy. It would have been truly boring if he didn't always find himself giving first aid to Internal Security. Those boys and girls were always exercising too hard or playing some sport too fast. They kept him busy with pulled muscles, tendons, separated shoulders, broken arms, and so on.

But all was quiet now. Nothing to keep his mind off poor young Matthew. The boy was barely thirty-two but had accomplished so much. A genius. Owen prayed the boy was all right. He had so many drug allergies and if they gave him anything...

Owen opened the medicine cabinet and peered inside again, concentrating hard on the shelves of medicines, trying to remember why he'd opened it in the first place.

"Dr. Owen?"

Owen spun around, gasping. "Oh my lord, Aidan!" He clutched his chest with one hand as he leaned his other hand on Aidan's shoulder. "You gave me such a start! What is it?" Tilting his head, he studied him. "Migraine?"

"Yes, and I've run out of pills." Aidan allowed the doctor to guide him to the chair by his desk.

"Son," Owen sat behind his desk, "I told you before that your headaches are from stress, aggravated by lack of sleep. Let me give..."

"No!" Aidan stood up. He paced in a tight circle. Two steps one way, two the other. "I can't sleep. I don't want to sleep. Please."

"All right." Owen went to him, wrapping a comforting arm around his shoulders and guided him to sit on the sofa. Living in a childless marriage, Owen thought of Aidan like his own son. He smiled with a touch of pride as he remembered the number of times the young man had come to him with his problems and not only the medical kind.

"I guess I'm not being very mature," Aidan said.

"I think you're handling things very well." Owen opened the medicine cabinet and retrieved a bottle of migraine pills. "Take one of these, then lie down and rest here until it takes effect. If it doesn't in a half hour, then I want you to go home to bed. No arguments."

"All right," Aidan said, accepting the pill and the offered glass of water. He then lied down on the sofa, while Owen took the nearby chair.

Owen had bought the sofa years ago, immediately after someone commented that the medical offices looked too sterile. After a new coat of pale blue paint, a few scenic pictures, a couple of animated sports posters, and new comfortable furniture, the place had a definite homey appeal.

"We fought before he left." Aidan's voice interrupted the doctor's thoughts.

"About what?"

"I told him Drake was manipulating him, like he always did. Making him work late. Weekends. Do you know that they sometimes worked round the clock and slept in the complex?"

"You weren't jealous?" Owen asked.

"Of course not! Never of *him*!" He covered his eyes as he groaned.

"I'm sorry," Owen said. He really should learn not to blurt out the first thought that came to him. "I meant because they were spending so much time together." Owen broke off before he upset Aidan further. "Here, let me dim the lights."

With the lower light level, Aidan uncovered his eyes and continued, "I didn't mean to yell at you." He gave a weak smile. "I guess I knew what you really meant. It's just that we'd both been working so many long hours that last month, we'd planned a holiday to get away from everything. Just for a week. I'd booked a cottage in BC, in the mountains. He loves skiing. I booked the flights. Then at the last minute, Drake says there's a series of tests that just had to get run. There are *always* tests."

"Perhaps we should talk about this later," Owen said, patting his shoulder.

Aidan shut his eyes against the light and also against the emotions threatening to escape. His entire life, he'd never thought he'd ever care for anyone, until Matt arrived at Cyber. That day, two years ago, was etched securely into his memory...

...His entire world was coming apart, like someone had taken a wrench and loosened every bolt that held his life together. Work had always been his last refuge. It no longer thrilled him, not even the practical jokes aimed mostly at Drake. Yesterday he'd taken apart the transmission electron microscope, claiming it needed realignment, purely for the simple joy of pissing Drake off. Unfortunately, he'd also pissed

Laura off. He'd spent the entire day putting the microscope back together.

Aidan knew something was wrong with him but had no idea what and even less of an idea how to fix it. He needed to travel. To somehow sort out his life. So last month he'd handed in his resignation. But they were in the middle of hiring a new scientist and Laura had pleaded with him to wait until they hired someone.

Reluctantly he'd agreed, but now he had to deal with impatience added to his already full emotional plate. Though he wouldn't disappoint Laura for anything in the world, he could already feel his mental strength fading. How could he wait until they found someone when he wasn't sure he could wait until the end of day?

With each turn of the screw on his repairs, his chest tightened. The last screw secured also meant that the microscope was up and running. Which meant that Drake would be happy. Aidan stood up to stretch his back muscles as his jaw clenched. His only reprieve these last few months that made staying here remotely bearable was finding new ways to annoy the bastard. He threw the screwdriver into the toolbox and started to pack up the rest of the tools, pitching one after another into the box. He could hear voices in the outer lab. One, he didn't recognize. No outsiders ever toured the labs, which meant this one was probably the new scientist.

He vaguely remembered Laura saying that this guy was a genius. Sure, like the ones he'd helped her interview. Most of the men and women boasted boring careers with nothing of significance in their resumes. Some were academics and great theoreticians. Others borderline company employees looking for more money. His favourite was the old man who might have been pushing ninety—well okay, that was an exaggeration—but most of the candidates were near the end of their careers. Frustrated at the lack of scientific talent, Aidan had stopped attending the interviews two weeks ago. Damn, he was in no mood to be sociable and welcoming to some old millennial.

He picked up the red toolbox, bracing himself to meet the scientist Laura had hired. He wondered if it was the man with the potbelly and receding hairline that he'd combed over, resulting in a part near his ear. You'd think he'd at least spent the few dollars it cost to have hair implants. Or maybe just shaved his head. That man's resume was a bit better than mediocre.

Aidan left the microscope room and practically dropped the toolbox at the sight of the man standing next to Laura. Not only was he young, but handsome too. He felt his face warm slightly at the thought, hoping that no one noticed him blush.

"Hi, Aidan," Laura said, "I'm glad I found you. I'd like you to meet Matt Stoddard. He'll be joining us."

Aidan turned to put the toolbox down, trying to get control of himself and his teenage reaction. Okay, he told himself, just because the guy was good looking didn't mean he had to drool all over him. A little dignity was in order. He turned, keeping his face neutral and extended a hand in greeting. "Welcome aboard, Dr. Stoddard."

"Call me Matt, please," he said, as he shook Aidan's hand.

Aidan forced a friendly smile as he tried to pull his hand back. But Matt held it a little longer than necessary, sending a shiver down Aidan's spine.

Laura continued the tour with Matt.

Did he really think Matt was interested in him? Just because he was feeling down and so very alone? It had been his imagination, he told himself, nothing more.

A couple of days later, Aidan went to see Laura to see how much longer it would be before his resignation was processed. She'd given him a smile and asked if he wouldn't mind giving Matt a hand settling in. Elton and Jeanette were both busy running a series of tests on a new electrode they'd developed and Drake was, well, being Drake. So please, would he mind waiting a little longer? How could he say no when she gave him that look of desperation?

He found Matt in his new office, struggling to move a file cabinet across the carpet. Aidan started to offer to help when the other man gave the cabinet a last forceful yank. The bottom shifted enough to start to tip. Rather than move out of the way, the other man tried to catch it and though he was failing, he stubbornly held on. Aidan rushed forward and pulled Stoddard out of the way as the cabinet hit the floor with a deafening bang. Both men fell to the floor.

"Are you okay?" Aidan asked, his heart pounding. He sat up.

"Yes. Thanks," Matt said, leaning back on one elbow. "I probably should have decided where I wanted it before I filled it with files. Then I probably shouldn't have been too lazy to empty it."

"Why didn't you just remove the drawers?" Aidan stood up. He waited for the other man to get up as well, but it didn't look like he was moving any time soon. He just looked up with a smile. Feeling awkward, he said, "I'll give you a hand to stand it back up."

Still smiling, Matt finally stood.

"Okay, on three, we lift," Aidan said.

Together they heaved the cabinet upright. Once done, Matt leaned against the cabinet smiling and stared deep into his eyes. It unsettled him. He cleared his throat and opened the top drawer.

Clearing his throat again, Aidan pointed inside the cabinet and said, "There's a button up here that releases the drawer and it just slides out." When Matt leaned over his shoulder to look, Aidan felt suddenly very warm. He added quickly, "Guess you're not used to using file cabinets and hardcopies. It's partly the security protocols here, so we're sort of used to working with paper reports. But I guess you know that." Matt just nodded but remained silent.

Aidan pulled out the drawer and put it on the floor, as he said, "Makes it easier to move the cabinet around." When he straightened up, he faced that same unsettling smile. "Gotta go." And escaped the suddenly stifling room.

The next morning, Aidan was in the lunchroom on Sub 2 making a fresh pot of coffee when Matt came in.

"Good morning," Matt said. He put a paper lunch bag into the fridge. "Thanks again for the big save yesterday."

"Big save?"

"Pulling me out of the way of the murderous file cabinet." Matt sat at the table.

"Oh, sure," Aidan said, with a smile. Pushing START on the coffee maker, he joined him at the table. "So, no other furniture trying to attack you?"

"No, I learned my lesson." Matt laughed. "It was my fault. I was in such a hurry to unpack and get settled into my office." He paused shaking his head with amazement. "My first real job, you know. But I'm all set to start now. Dr. Jessup said I'll be working with Paul Drake."

"Oh," Aidan said. He hadn't meant for the sympathetic look to sneak out.

"What?" The smile faded.

"Well, he can be a little difficult to work with sometimes, but," Aidan paused. It wasn't fair to let his feelings about Drake taint Matt's opinion. Let him figure things out on his own, like everyone else had. "I'm sure you'll manage."

They continued to chat about Matt's life at university, his thesis, the state of nanotechnology research and how fast it had changed, as well as the work they did at Cyber. As soon as the coffee was ready, Aidan poured himself a cup and excused himself and returned to his office.

The next day, when Aidan came into work he was determined to finish processing the data he'd been working on bit by bit all week. Unfortunately, today his concentration had changed. It was worse.

He shoved the lab book out of the way and slumped back in his chair.

What was happening to him? He really needed to leave and figure out things. Sort out his life. As soon as his resignation was processed, he planned to get in his car and head out of town. The east coast sounded good. There he could watch waves crashing on rocky shorelines. Maybe if he went west and let the mountains help him decide what to do with his life.

A knock at the door interrupted his thoughts. It was Matt. He came in and sat down, placing his coffee mug on the desk.

"Don't you take breaks from work?" Matt asked.

"Not when I've got stuff to finish."

"Sorry, I didn't mean to interrupt you." Matt picked up his cup and started to leave.

Part of Aidan was glad he was leaving. He needed to finish these graphs and organize all the data for whoever took over his work. But part of him realized he was being rude. Antisocial. Too much like Drake.

"No, it's okay, I wasn't ready to start back at this yet." When he sat down again, Aidan asked, "I know you only started working with Drake yesterday, but how'd it go?"

"Yesterday when Dr. Jessup told him I'd be working with him, he basically ignored me all day. When he did talk to me, he didn't ask for things, just barked orders."

"He treats everyone like that."

"And I thought he hated me," Matt said, laughing. Suddenly serious, he asked, "Is it true? Are you really leaving?"

"Yeah."

"But how can you leave this work? All the progress your team's made. Aren't you excited about what's just around the corner?"

"I used to be." Aidan looked away from the unsettling eyes that seemed to bore deep into his soul.

As the silence stretched, Aidan turned back to see an open expression on Matt's face. One that promised he would listen. There hadn't been anyone to talk to for a long time. Without realizing, Aidan started talking. He told Matt all about growing up in a poor section of Montreal. How his father spent day and night working at the grocery store, his mother cleaned houses, while he'd spent his teen years getting into any kind of trouble he could find. His fun ended when the cops brought him home one too many times. His father gave him a choice: go to jail or spend every free moment when he wasn't at school, working in the grocery store. He'd do his homework in the tiny office at the back, then get to work.

That was more punishment than going to prison. He couldn't imagine working in the store for the rest of his life. He took refuge in school, taking his studies seriously for the first time. He earned a scholarship to university and earned a Masters in bioengineering.

When he'd finally admitted to himself that he was gay, during his first year in university, it seemed to take over his thoughts. He wanted to tell someone. His family. Close friends. To tell someone other than strangers in bars. He'd come out to his parents and after a few months of tension, they seemed to accept him. Until he discovered that they hadn't. At least his friends were there, but having a family abandon you just because of who you were...

Aidan stopped talking, shocked that he'd just blurted out his entire life story to a complete stranger. But what really was surprising was when he realized that Matt had listened and understood.

"What about you?" Aidan asked. "What brought you here?"

"My parents never accepted who I really was. I left that dusty little town in Alberta and moved to Toronto. When I got my PhD, they didn't come for the convocation ceremonies. Didn't even phone. But they did send a card with a cheque for $100." He gave an empty, sad laugh before continuing.

"So when the invitation to go for this job basically fell into my lap, I accepted the offer without a second thought, even with the sparse details. And now that I know everything about the research here, I'm really excited. Everyone's been really nice to me. Making me feel like I belong. Something I haven't felt in such a long time. Well, almost everyone."

Aidan said, "When I decided to take a break from my PhD and take the job here, Cyber was just starting out in life. Like me. So I thought it was a perfect match."

He paused for a long while before he added, "It broke my supervisor's heart when I told her I wasn't going back to finish my degree, but how could I give up this research? Besides, no one cared about those three extra letters after my name, except for Drake. And to be honest, I soon realized that I didn't really care about Drake's opinion."

It felt good to have someone to talk to. Someone that understood him and listened without judgement...

...Lying on Dr. Owen's couch, the memory of Matt's first days faded, and Aidan opened his eyes to see the doctor's concerned face.

"I thought with Drake away at the conference, we'd get some quiet time," Aidan told him. "But Drake refused to go, saying 'it was a banal waste of his valuable time.' Matt actually argued with him this time. But in the end, Drake got his way. Just like he always does."

He leaned up on an elbow and whispered conspiratorially, "But you know, it's strange that Drake would change his mind at the last minute. Don't you see, there wasn't time to bring anyone else up to speed to deliver the paper, so it could only be Matt. That's suspicious, don't you think?"

"Just coincidence, my boy."

"Well, it's suspicious to me!"

CHAPTER FIVE

Wednesday morning, Henderson finally came in a little after 10:00 and it had taken almost a half hour before Demir and Abraham were able to meet with him. Unfortunately, the anticipation soon fell flat.

"This is almost like your last mission," Henderson said.

"Sir?" Demir asked. He glanced at Abraham, who mirrored his confusion.

They were in Henderson's much larger office. In one corner stood a four-foot artificial plant, a Canadian flag in the other. A series of framed team spirit posters cluttered the walls. Nestled in their midst, a black and white photo of a very young Queen Elizabeth II hung directly behind the desk. Beside that, a 3D image of King William V.

Under the king's photo hung a framed 30 x 40 cm picture of relay race runners passing the baton, with the caption, IT TAKES TEAMWORK TO REACH YOUR GOAL. There should have been one suggesting, STAY ON TOPIC—YOU'LL GET RESULTS FASTER.

"Sir," Demir said, "I was asking what you thought about four, six-hour shifts. The scientists don't like the idea of being shadowed and are giving their bodyguards a hard time. It's making protection duty more stressful. Shorter shifts would mean fresher security and less chance for mistakes."

"You and Abraham," Henderson stubbornly continued, his tone suggesting what he was saying should be obvious. "That undercover mission that you were on. Which made you both quit the RCMP and join us here."

Demir's back stiffened. He felt that familiar stab in his gut. He stood and turned away to study the inspirational posters on the wall behind him. There was one of a mountain climber, with the caption

YOU HAVE NO LIMITS. He thought about the irony of coming face to face with that particular poster.

Distantly he heard Abraham's voice. "Mr. Henderson? Sir? About the shift schedule. What do you think?" There was the sound of a paper rustling and Demir could imagine his friend waving the paper in front of their boss to get his attention. Abraham continued, unrelenting. "I think you'll agree it works."

Demir looked at another poster appropriately captioned, LEAVE THE PAST BEHIND. LOOK TO THE FUTURE. BUT LIVE IN THE PRESENT. Good advice, though it didn't say what to do when the past wouldn't stay put.

In his mind, he heard the distant lament of a foghorn. The sound of waves slapping. A chain rattling. The faint chime of a ship's bell...

...The strong smell of fish. The taste of salt in the air.

The stars appeared uncannily bright in the moonless sky. The single graphene light bulb on the dock barely trickled light onto the gangway leading up to the freighter *Mesa Grande Queen*. The rotating beacon of the lighthouse out in the bay winked at him.

The huge drug buy was set for 2:00 a.m. at the pier. The endlessly paranoid drug boss had hidden his people all around the pier two hours before the seller was due to arrive.

Demir manned the north side.

He checked his earbud connected to his own RCMP men hidden outside the perimeter. Their plan was to take down both groups simultaneously. Team one would approach the ship from the left. Team two from the right. Team three would charge right up the middle. He would follow team three.

He remembered thinking that the whole thing was a game. The good guys had people hidden. The bad guys had people hidden.

He checked the time display on his night vision glasses. 1:45 a.m. He whispered into the tiny microphone in his collar to his squad, "Hold positions."

"Check." "Check." "Check." Three teams reported from their places around the Halifax pier.

He adjusted the earbud in one ear. With the other ear, he listened for unexpected sounds. A foghorn lamented. He watched the fog on the water, a tumbling wall of grey, silently engulf everything in its path.

He moistened dehydrated lips as his mind worked to adjust the scenario for reduced visibility. Even though his team could adjust the night vision glasses to see through fog, the criminals didn't have glasses. He had to be prepared for the unexpected reactions of the others when their visibility was decreased. He irrationally braced for the impact when the fog hit the pier. He could still see the gangway and surrounding area twenty metres away, so he stayed in position behind the fishing nets and lobster traps.

With the fog arrived a surreal silence. The moist air muffled all sounds. He looked up to see that the stars had vanished.

"Visual, report," he whispered, into his collar microphone to the hidden RCMP officers.

"Clear." "Clear." "Clear."

No need to move them closer.

At 2:00 a.m., headlights ignited the dark haze. A car stopped near the gangway, followed by a cube van. Damn nice of them to be punctual.

Six men dressed in dark bomber jackets and toques rushed out of the vehicles and boarded the ship. They emerged ten minutes later carrying three large crates between them. He ordered his teams to move in closer, staying low and out of sight. Demir moved closer, waiting for the smugglers to clear the gangway.

About to give the word, he thought he heard footsteps behind him and turned, his gun ready. And in that moment of distraction, gunfire erupted all around them...

"Mr. Henderson, sir." Abraham's voice punctured the scene startling Demir back to the present.

A memory. Nothing more. He turned to see Abraham practically wave the schedule in front of the older man's face trying to get his attention.

"Sir!" Abraham repeated, this time succeeding to divert Henderson's attention. "What do you think about making a fourth watch?"

Henderson took the sheet of paper, barely glanced at it before handing it back and said, "Looks fine to me. Let me know if you have any trouble implementing this and I'll have a word with the other squad leaders."

Demir's mind was still reeling from the dredged memory. His tongue felt like cardboard, but he managed to find his voice. "Would you please have a word with Dr. Jessup? Some of her people keep trying to ditch their bodyguards."

"I've been busy since I got back," Henderson said, as he studied the computer screen on the corner of his desk. "I'll try and stop by tomorrow when I get back from Toronto."

"Toronto?" Demir could barely get the words out. "You're going back to finish your holiday?"

"What?" Henderson seemed preoccupied for a moment by whatever was on the screen. Looking up, he added, "I have a lead that I need to check out. I'm flying out in a couple of hours. I'll talk to Dr. Jessup, first thing tomorrow."

"And, sir," Demir said, "about Cahill. They can't still be debriefing him."

"I'm sure they're almost done." Henderson stood and put on his coat. He turned and watched the men silently.

Both men gawked at him. They'd been in his office barely five minutes and they were being dismissed. Demir yanked the door open, using every ounce of self-control not to slam it behind him as he and Abraham left.

"That was a short meeting," Yasmin commented.

"And they seem to be getting shorter," Demir said, shaking his head. "Abe, got a minute? My office?"

"Sure."

"Mr. Demir," Yasmin said, "would you like a coffee?"

"Yes, please. Thanks," Demir said, barely looking up from the floor. In his office, he slumped in his seat, watching Abraham take the guest seat. Yasmin entered and placed the mug in front of Demir.

She looked at Abraham and asked with a smile, "Did you want a cup?"

"Sure, I'd love one."

"You know where the machine is." With a nod, she left.

Abraham laughed, then asked, "There something going on between you two?"

Demir's head snapped up. "Is that the only thing on your mind?"

"Easy," Abraham soothed. "I was just wondering why you get the special treatment." At the glare in the other man's eyes, he added quickly, "Never mind."

Demir calmed down. "She's just being nice." He broke off, taking a sip and burned his upper lip. The coffee tasted bitter. "I'm supposed to be his assistant and he doesn't tell me anything." Demir put the cup down. Pushed it away. "I had no idea that he was leaving again or what kind of leads he's following. He doesn't listen to anything I suggest."

"But he took your idea about the shifts."

"Sure, so he could bugger off on some goddamn adventure."

"You bothered 'cause he's not telling you anything about what he's doing? Which he hasn't done for a long time. Or are you bothered by the memories he dredged up?" Abraham leaned forward, adding, "Ty, it wasn't your fault. On the pier..."

"I was in charge!"

"Nothing you did could have changed things. You won't talk about it, but I can see it on your face. I know that you've relived that moment for more than ten years."

"I was distracted."

"By footsteps behind us, where there shouldn't have been any. There's no way we could have known it was a double cross. It wasn't your fault."

The echo of gunfire erupted briefly in Demir's memory then faded.

Of course it was his fault. He'd been in charge. The result of his lapsed concentration was two dead RCMP officers, three wounded. The dead had been good friends, with families that he'd shared family dinners with. No one had seen the double cross coming. It turned out that the drug boss' paranoia was justified all along. His nephew had great delusions of grabbing the shipment and the title of boss. His reward? To be one of the dead. No one had anticipated the nephew's plans, but it had been Demir's job to have prepared for it. He'd lived with these criminals for months and got to know all of them well. Got them to trust him.

He should have known.

The phone rang. Grateful for the distraction from the memories, Demir answered before the first ring faded. It was Yasmin.

"Major Kirby left a message for Mr. Henderson to meet him at the Dow's Lake Pavilion in half an hour, but he's already left the complex," she said. "I left a message on his sat-phone, which he's apparently forgotten to turn on. Again. Major Kirby also left orders that the meeting not be advertised."

"Thanks." Demir hung up and checked his watch.

"Kirby wants to meet, secretly of course. So, I'm not telling you. If something comes up, call me." Demir stood and took his jacket from the coat rack.

"Ty, it wasn't your fault," Abraham repeated, lamely.

"Tell that to the families of the men I got killed."

Demir arrived at Dow's Lake five minutes late but still ahead of Kirby. He wondered how many clandestine meetings Henderson had had with the old man.

He parked his car by the curb near the pavilion. The upper level housed four restaurants, one that seemed to change names and ownership each time he came here. During the skating season, the lower level housed the skate changing area. Hell of a lot better than changing into skates outside in the cold and wind. Now the Rideau Canal's low water level showed the debris from the winter carnival, Winterlude, held in February. Now, mid-March, all that was left of the magnificent ice sculptures were anonymous lumps of snow. Come to think of it, he hadn't even seen any of the festivities or concerts. Tourists from all over the world came to skate the twenty-kilometre-long Rideau Canal, yet he hadn't even bothered to find the time to do that. He was falling into old habits, just like when he'd been on the force. Work filled most of his days. Off time was just that. Off. Off from work. Off from life.

He couldn't remember the last movie he'd seen. Abraham had managed to get him out to a couple of hockey games, but that was about it.

God, he had no life. How did he let this happen? Other than Abraham, he didn't keep in touch with any other friends. As for women...

God, he had no life.

After thirty-five minutes of waiting and pacing, he seriously considered leaving. He wasn't just impatient, he was also freezing. The wind from the north brought with it a damp cold that seeped through his ski jacket. He'd expected the weather to start getting milder, but just like the rest of his life, it wasn't co-operating.

Blowing into his cupped hands to warm them, he decided to give Kirby a bit more time. The whole point of meeting somewhere other than the complex or National Defence HQ was to keep it quiet. But Dow's Lake was a popular place for walkers and joggers from the several nearby government buildings to spend their lunch hour. And if that wasn't enough, the HMCS Carleton building, which was home to the Canadian Forces Naval Reserve, was only a few yards away. Obviously, their meeting was meant to be secret from everyone at Cyber.

Demir stamped his feet trying to warm them. While he'd waited, the lunch crowd had gone back to work. Forty-five minutes was more than enough. He decided to give Kirby a few more minutes but his generosity lasted only a few seconds.

Just as he opened his car door, a DND vehicle pulled into the circular drive, directly in front of the HMCS Carleton building entrance.

Kirby got out of the car, openly surprised. They met on the sidewalk near Demir's car.

"What are you doing here?" Kirby asked.

"You asked to see me."

"You? I left word for Henderson."

"I'm sorry, sir," Demir said. "I guess he passed your message on to me. He's checking up on a lead."

"Oh, of course." Kirby paused, as though looking for words. After a moment he said, "My fault Demir, I forgot."

"Yes, sir," Demir answered slowly. Perhaps the major was a great military tactician, but you'd make a lot of money playing poker with him. Well, maybe Henderson never told him anything, but it looked like he didn't tell Kirby, either.

"Well, you *are* second in command." With obvious reluctance, he continued. "We just got confirmation that the rescue mission failed. Stoddard had already been moved by the time the team deployed."

"Is he still alive?" Demir asked, his heart feeling suddenly heavy. Good thing he hadn't raised Laura's hopes by telling her about the rescue plans.

"We believe so," Kirby said, though he didn't sound sure. "How's security around the remaining scientists?"

"Round the clock."

"Great. Keep up the good work," Kirby said. "Do you have any issues you need to discuss?"

"Everything's under control. Here." Demir then added, "I need to be kept in the loop more. And when do we get Cahill back? I can't believe they're still questioning him—as a suspect."

"No, he's been cleared. I'll see about getting him sent home, ASAP."

"Thank you," Demir said. "About Dr. Stoddard, maybe if the scientists and I sat down with you, we could come up with some ideas..."

"We've got the best agents searching." He gave Demir a fatherly pat on the shoulder. "You just concentrate on keeping the scientists that we have left, safe. I'll be in touch."

"Yes sir," Demir said. Kirby might as well have patted him on the head and said, 'Be a good boy and let the adults take care of things.'

When Demir got into his car, he started back for the complex, gripping the steering wheel with hands that had been warmed by anger. Sure, he'd take care of the scientists.

And that included Matt Stoddard.

Jeanette Theriault sat in the tiny lunchroom on Sub 2, sipping her tea. The room was simply furnished: a refrigerator, a full stove, and coffee maker. A Formica table surrounded by eight fluorescent orange moulded plastic chairs, someone's lame attempt at retro decorating.

A hanging planter that used to contain a spider plant hung over the sink. Despite its location, no one ever remembered to water it. The dry remains dribbled over the edge of the pot, occasionally dropping bits into the sink and onto the floor. The cleaners took care of that. No one, of course, listened to her when she'd suggested that they get a plastic plant. Dust collector they'd told her. Better than a decaying vegetable, she'd countered. Damned if she was going to throw it out. Or clean up after it. Let the men do it, because it was their pet.

Her musings were interrupted when Elton Chan arrived in the lunchroom. He was a slim man, barely five and a half feet tall. He stopped short in the doorway. She knew he was staring at her dishevelled appearance. Although over fifty, and she refused to admit how much over, she'd always prided herself on looking less than forty. Well, after no sleep and barely any food, did he expect her to look anything but haggard? Her normally neatly styled salt and pepper hair now framed her face in unruly, maniacal loose curls that sat on her shoulders.

"Any news?" he asked.

"Not yet," she answered, exasperated. "You phoned me ten minutes ago to ask. How much do you think might have changed since I came down for lunch?"

"Want to be sure. Okay with you?" Elton shuffled to the refrigerator, opened it, peered inside, then shut it with a grunt. He poured a cup of coffee and joined Jeanette at the table. "Not eating?"

"Don't feel like upchucking right now. What about you?"

"Late breakfast. Where are the others?"

"Aidan looked like he had another migraine and went to see Doc Owen. And I don't give a shit where Drake is." She broke off, blushing, when Drake walked in through the door.

"News?" Chan turned around looking expectant.

"No." Drake poured himself a coffee and sat at the opposite end of the table. "You have any objection to my sitting with you?" He looked pointedly at her.

"Do what you want. You always do," she answered with a shrug.

"Why isn't there any news?" Elton said.

"Stop it!" Drake closed his eyes rubbing his forehead. He looked at Chan. "I didn't mean to snap."

"Sorry. I'm worried."

"We all are." Drake lifted the cup and drank slowly, staring at the table in front of him.

Jeanette and Elton glanced at each other but remained silent.

"Is he dead?"

"No. But he's barely alive."

"I warned you both. He's no use to us dead."

Matt Stoddard listened to the strange voices through a fog of pain and nausea. Was it him? Was he the one barely alive? He concentrated on his surroundings. There wasn't the feeling of speed or movement anymore. The car had stopped. No, he wasn't in the car. He was lying on something soft, taking some of the stress off of his back. He opened his mouth and it moved freely, allowing him to take in quick gulps of air. Thank God for that at least.

He couldn't feel anything on his eyes so he guessed the blindfold was gone. But he wasn't sure. He still couldn't see anything. Was it dark? No, his eyes were closed. But the effort to open his eyelids was too much and he stopped trying.

He wanted to sit up, but it felt like someone was sitting on his chest, making it hard to fill his lungs. What did they say? Barely alive? The pressure quickly became an intense stabbing sensation radiating through his chest and into his left shoulder, leaving little doubt that he was very much alive. What happened to 'passed out from the pain?' It was in movies all the time. Now, each breath felt like knives of flame stabbed him. Vertigo had him constantly on the verge of vomiting. He kept seeing flashes of light even though his eyes were closed. They weren't from outside. They were coming from his brain—or his eyeballs— or—what the hell was it called? Retina? Optic nerve? Why couldn't he remember what it was called?

He focused on the lights, trying to forget that his heart was trying to rip itself free of his chest. A painful pressure pounded in his throat. Another reason he couldn't breathe! His heart seemed to be speeding up with each beat. Yes, it was! Faster! Faster! How fast could it go?

The beats were getting stronger. His heart would burst. He knew it had to. Soon. Long before those fools noticed. Where the hell were they? If they were so worried about him dying, why weren't they watching? He tried to call to them. To get their attention.

Then, another strong beat. A sudden flood of pain washed over him. Finally, peace...

CHAPTER SIX

Thursday morning, Jeanette Theriault came into work early mostly because she was tired of her dachshund staring at her with those big, round, sad eyes. Normally the energy filled six-year-old Puffin was a wonderful companion to someone who loved long walks in the woods. But yesterday evening, Jeanette had patiently endured one soggy stuffed toy or drool drenched rubber one after another eagerly brought to her. After a few minutes of Jeanette's half-hearted throwing and monotone "good girl," Puffin must have realized that something was wrong. She'd joined her on the sofa, curling up into a warm pillow on Jeanette's feet. They'd spent the night with Puffin trying to be warm and comforting, Jeanette hoping to push away her worries about Matt. Both spent the night in vain.

She finally gave up on sleep before dawn. She let Puffin out into the back yard as she showered and dressed in jeans and a baggy t-shirt, covered with an even baggier pink sweater. Giving Puffin a big hug, promising that she'd try to make up being so distant tonight, but also knowing that on some level Puffin understood and forgave her.

She arrived at Cyber just after 7:00 with the sun beginning to cast long shadows. As she signed in at security, she noticed—and not without a little irony—that everyone else was already here. On Sub 2, she headed to her office, hung up her coat, changed her boots for comfortable sneakers, then made herself comfortable at her computer. She planned to lose herself in her work. She'd developed a program to train their neural chip to direct itself to a damaged area of an electrode grid.

Now all she had to do was get their chip to integrate itself into the neural culture and repair it. Yup, that was all. It sounded so easy. If only.

Her concentration at a new high, she was just beginning to immerse herself into the program when Elton Chan burst into her office, shouting, "Did you hear? Did you hear?"

"What is it?" Startled, she spun around so quickly she practically fell off her chair.

"Cahill is coming home."

"Yes," she sighed. Why did he do things like this? She'd never be able to get her concentration back. She was in no mood to be patient with him today. "Don't you remember we were all there when Laura told us? Yesterday?" She turned back to her computer.

"But you don't know everything," Elton added smugly. "I know who took Matt."

She spun around again with renewed anticipation.

"Yamaguchi, the big spy was also at the conference."

"Yamaguchi's a thief. He steals technology. He's not a kidnapper. And besides," she started to turn back to her computer saying, "he's hardly that effective anymore, now that everyone knows about him."

"Maybe that's what he counts on. For everyone to let down their guard," Elton said. When she hrmfed without turning, he added, "He wasn't on the security list. They missed one, maybe they missed more?"

"You've got a point." She glanced over her shoulder and beckoned him over, adding, "Why don't we just check the delegate list?"

"How?"

"This is one of the few conferences that still publishes their delegate list on their website."

"That's not very security conscious."

"Maybe they're so deluded they think an open science conference would never be a terrorist target. Let's take a look and see if anyone else looks interesting." She found the right screen and started scrolling through the list.

"Look." Elton pointed at the screen. "Drake is still listed."

With a "hrmpf," she continued scrolling.

Last night, Demir had tried to phone Henderson at home but was told by Mrs. Henderson that he was out. Vague about where he was, she'd passed on the message from her husband to tell Demir that Henderson would be in on Thursday at 10:00 a.m. And they could meet then. It was almost time. He started to review the notes he'd made, sketchy as they were.

There was a knock at his door. He called, "Come in." He was surprised to see Elton Chan. In the ten years that Demir had worked at Cyber, the man had never once come to see him or anyone in Internal Security.

"Mr. Demir, good morning," Chan said.

"Dr. Chan, have a seat."

"No, thank you. Jeannette and I found the science spy."

"Who is it?" Demir leaned forward.

"Ikiro Yamaguchi. An infamous technology thief. Thank you for your time."

Before Demir could ask anything further, the scientist was out the door. He checked the flagged list and didn't find the name there. He still had ten minutes to go before his meeting with Henderson. Close enough. He gathered the notes in a folder when another knock stopped him. Maybe Elton had remembered another name. Instead, Mitchell came in looking flustered.

"Is something wrong?"

"I just saw Dr. Chan leaving and well, did he talk to you about me?"

"No, why?" Demir's eyes narrowed, worrying that the young security man had done something he shouldn't have.

"I talked to Mr. Sandrovsky and he said I should talk to you."

"And?" Demir tried to be patient with the new guy, but it was an effort.

"Well, I was hoping… I mean it would be easier if he didn't want me…" Mitchell fumbled for words, then blurted, "I've never had to protect someone who keeps trying to dump me at every corner. Can't I get someone else? Please?"

Demir tilted his head to look at Mitchell, trying to decide if his security man was joking or not. His voice had even bordered on a whine. Though he'd been with Cyber about a year, the man handled any assignment he was given, easily and without complaint. Until now.

Finally, Demir told him, "Dr. Chan is the most out of shape, slowest moving of the scientists. Christ, a couple of times I've walked into the elevator and he's just standing there, waiting, because he forgot to push the button. I would think he'd be the easiest."

"Slow moving, yeah sure. But just wait until he wants to move. I swear, under those baggy clothes hides the body of a sprinter."

"And you're a damn good long-distance runner. Adjust!" Demir pretended to turn his attention back to his computer. Noticing the other man was still there he asked, without looking up, "Was that all?"

"Guess so. I mean, yes, sir." Mitchell reluctantly left.

As soon as Mitchell was out the door, Demir indulged in a laugh. Elton was definitely the easiest to tail, occasionally forgetting to start driving when the light turned green. On the other hand, Drake was only assigned to the most experienced. On every occasion, Drake would jump into his car then floor it. His bodyguard always managed to catch up. Jeanette Theriault didn't seem to care and had even suggested that she and her bodyguard carpool, in the interest of the environment.

Shaking his head, he checked his notes in the folder and left for the boss' office, giving the secretary a smile.

"Mr. Demir, wait," Yasmin called to him. "He's not in."

"What?" He came back to look at her, as though in the midst of some kind of nightmare that he couldn't wake up from. Henderson promised that they'd meet to discuss the case and the definite lack of information. But more importantly, he was to tell him what he'd learned from his trip to Toronto. There was no way Henderson would blow him off like this. "Is he in Ops?"

"No, he won't be in and…"

"What the fuck do you mean he won't be in?" Demir slapped the file folder on Yasmin's desk. Paper scattered on the desk and floor.

"Tyler Demir!" She stood, arms crossed tightly. She glared at him for a moment, then snapped, "Don't you use that language with me!"

He caught his lower lip between his teeth as he sucked in a harsh breath. He picked up the file folder and collected the papers. He systematically replaced everything back into the folder, then mentally counted to ten but lost track at three. He asked quietly, "Did he say when he'll be in?"

"No, just that he'd call later to let me know." Her tone still sharp. Her frown deepened.

"Thank you. I'll be in my office. Please let me know when he does get in."

Not trusting his anger to stay in check much longer, he spun on his heel as wooden legs carried him back to his office. With great effort, he quietly closed the door behind him, rather than slam it. Then turned and pitched the folder at the wall. Frustrated at the noiseless impact, he picked up the lamp from his desk and threw it after the file. Slightly pacified by the crash of hollow metal and shattering glass, he marched around his desk.

He took several deep breaths. And sat down. Hands pressed flat on his desk.

So, Henderson wasn't in. Not the end of the world. Demir just realized he hadn't apologized to Yasmin for swearing at her. He would, later. Buy her a gift, dinner, flowers, something. No, a verbal apology would be better.

In the meantime, he had to try to figure things out. Get control of his anger. Losing control was not normally in his nature. It's what had made him an excellent undercover operative. He had to remember that.

Demir had to be honest with himself. For almost a year he'd been covering for his boss; at meetings, with late reports and missed deadlines; being put in the position of constantly second guessing the old man. If only he knew what had made Henderson change from the man Demir had been proud to serve under to this poor excuse for a leader. Could he be burned out after a long career and that made him more ineffectual than usual now? Now when they needed a strong leader most?

They were friends. Not as close as Demir was to Abraham, but they used to be able to talk openly about everything, including life outside of the job. Henderson used to confide in Demir easily. And he had trusted Henderson enough to give him the key to his house—just in case.

He hadn't signed up for this. Demir had taken the job as second in command of security, which meant he didn't have to make any decisions. Not important ones that involved lives. And he hadn't minded sitting around waiting for Henderson to pass on progress reports.

The difference now? Higher stakes. Matt wasn't going to be brought home by luck and Demir was sick of being jerked around by his boss. Bosses, if you included Kirby.

Kirby, with all his resources, still believed that the very British Smythe-Williams, whose only claim to infamy was being on the U.S.A.'s infamous Watch List, was their best lead. In the meantime, Elton Chan, a simple scientist, without any covert connections to covert agencies around the world, had found someone with a history of technical espionage not on any list. Demir sent a quick message to Operations to deepen their checks on all attending delegates. Especially any that registered but were no-shows.

He then called Kirby. It was his turn to call a secret meeting to pass on Yamaguchi's name. And what the hell, he decided, might as well select scenic Dow's Lake for the meeting.

Demir hung up the phone with a smile. Kirby agreed to meet him in a half hour. Demir grabbed his jacket intending to get there first. As he left his office, he found Yasmin at her desk, her back to him. Slowly, he went up to her. Clearing his throat, he waited until she turned around. When she saw him, the smile faded, to be replaced by a stern glare, as she crossed her arms tightly.

"Yasmin," he began carefully, not sure how she'd react. "About earlier..."

She stood, her face transforming into a pleasant smile. She said, "Apology accepted."

"Uh, thanks." Demir looked at her, taken aback by the unexpected change.

"I know you've been under a lot of stress. But don't let it happen again. Deal?" She extended a hand.

"Deal," Demir said, sealing his promise with a handshake, knowing if he did cross her again, he wouldn't get off this easy.

The plane landed at Newark Airport and Henderson looked out the window across the river at Manhattan's distant skyline. He hadn't been in New York for years and he searched his memory, trying to figure out what new buildings had altered the familiar skyline. He unclicked his seat belt and started to stand, then a sick feeling in the pit of his stomach made him slump back into the seat.

Not the presence of new buildings, but the absence of several. Twelve years ago, terrorists had pummelled the city with drone delivered bombs, obliterating four square blocks before the assailants' position was located and neutralized. When the city started to rebuild, tall skyscrapers were no longer desired. This left a prominent dip amidst the tall buildings. The new attacks had also forced the States out of their lingering isolationist mindset and they again co-operated with the rest of the world on everything from terrorism to humanitarian issues to the environment.

How could he have forgotten? Along with the rest of the horrified world, he'd watched the live VidCasts from the safety of his home. The burning skyline. The thousands lost.

Pushing the memory away, Henderson followed the rest of the passengers off the plane.

Inside the terminal, he took out his sat to call, but stopped just in time. All of his effort to use a fake ID and he almost blew it. Last thing he needed was for his location to be identified as someplace other than Toronto. He'd also 'forgotten' his personal tracker at his office, glad he'd switched from the subcutaneous implant to the surface patch a few months ago. Not that he expected Demir to be spying on him, but why risk getting caught by a scheduled security check? He slipped the sat back into his inside jacket pocket and took out the disposable phone.

He thumbed in the number.

"Yeah?" an abrupt voice answered after one ring.

"Just landed."

"Meet you there."

The line went dead. As Henderson passed a garbage can, he flipped the phone into the trash and hurried out to the transportation desk to take a heli-cab into Manhattan. Ten minutes later, he gave the cabbie a generous tip, then got out to walk the last few blocks to Varick Street.

He had planned to come yesterday when he'd told Demir he was going to Toronto. But halfway to the airport, he'd realized that he needed to settle a few things at home first. It took longer than he'd thought and he barely managed to catch an early morning flight.

He should have told Tyler Demir where he was really going if, for no other reason than in case he didn't make it back. But he didn't want to put the young man at risk because Henderson knew that he'd insist on trying to help fix things. He'd never be able to persuade Demir that he had to handle that task himself. Alone.

At Varick Street, he turned left and continued the short distance to the coffee shop. Inside, he scanned the crowded room for any familiar faces. He was early. He decided to live it up a bit and ordered a large mocha with extra whipped cream and chocolate sprinkles.

Tasting it, he couldn't help the little moan of ecstasy at the familiar creamy sweetness that he'd forgotten. Smiling, he wiped the whipped cream from his upper lip with a napkin and realized he shouldn't tell the wife. Brenda had him on a diet and somehow wouldn't understand the sudden need for decadent calories.

He found an empty table at the back of the café and sat facing the door to wait for Smitty.

For years now, he'd been having these clandestine meetings with a member of a Black Ops group, at various coffee shops all over the USA. Their only mission was to find new technologies for the States. It had started several years ago, when the tensions between the U.S. and Canada, well to be honest, with everyone, had grown to a point that there was no longer an exchange of information.

Not officially.

There'd remained an off-the-books agreement between the two countries as Henderson soon discovered when he'd become head of Internal Security. Major Kirby had informed him that Henderson would be responsible for providing progress reports from Cyber, so that the Canadian military could keep on top of the work that they were so generously funding.

In the beginning, he'd submitted his reports without any misgivings. It made sense that the military would want to keep track of the work. Later, he discovered that some of the information he was giving Kirby was being exchanged with the Americans. He raised his concerns, only to have them dismissed. Kirby had insisted that nothing that went out was a threat to national security. And exchanges occurred only when Canada had lots to gain.

But Henderson had enough tech know-how to recognize that Cyber's research gradually surpassed the rest of the world. He continued to submit reports but now he edited the information to leave out key details. Then, just over a year ago, he became the information courier and started making periodic trips to the States. He remembered finding it funny at first that the spy business had reverted to the old, low-tech procedures of dead-drops and in-person exchanges. The humour of it was quickly lost when he was the one making the exchanges.

They gave him total control of the delivery schedule because they knew it couldn't interfere with the daily operations of Internal Security. Deliveries became unpredictable because his own work schedule had become sporadic at best. It's what he told them and they couldn't complain. He had no doubts that when he called moments before boarding the plane, they wouldn't hesitate to set up a meeting.

He wasn't naive and knew that eventually his delay tactics would backfire. To prepare for that inevitable day, Henderson had begun to pull away from his duties at Cyber. He felt bad that for the last year Tyler Demir had been feeling the increasing stress of his growing responsibilities. But it was the only way to keep him out of this. And safe.

Henderson watched for the arrival of his familiar contact. A six-foot, foreboding figure, with a pockmarked face and dark eyes, whose single glance threatened more than a switchblade against your jugular. He refused to give his name so Henderson had named him Smitty. A cliché, maybe, but it made the man more of a regular guy rather than the Black Ops demon persona that he exuded.

Speak of the devil. Smitty swaggered through the door, quickly scanned the room and found Henderson. Detouring to pick up a coffee, Smitty joined him. He hesitated before taking the seat Henderson had left. If the son-of-a bitch had wanted the chair strategically facing the entrance, then he should have hustled to get here sooner.

"It's been a while," Smitty said. "Sure as hell better have one fucking report for me."

"Enough pleasantries," Henderson said, keeping his voice low. "Did you take one of my scientists?"

"You've got some imagination. Maybe you missed your calling and should have been a writer." Smitty gave him a humourless smile.

"You don't get anything until you tell me about my missing scientist."

"Why would we bother when we've got you?" Smitty said.

Undaunted, Henderson leaned forward, lowering his voice further. "Just because it didn't make the news, don't think I don't know what happened to that scientist in South Africa. I better not find out you took Stoddard."

Smitty leaned forward mirroring the severe expression, but tempered with a shadow of cruelty. "Don't forget who *we* are. What *we're* capable of. No one backs out of a deal."

"Give him back."

No reaction but a slight deepening of his perpetual frown. It took a lot of will and a whole hell of a lot of stubbornness for Henderson not to look away from those steely eyes. Henderson continued. "Last I checked, you work for the US government. There are rules even *you* have to follow."

"You really think the government's gonna care how we get the shit to keep up with other countries in weapon development?"

As Smitty stood, he leaned forward to whisper in Henderson's ear, "I'm not gonna ask again. See you soon. *With* the report."

Henderson watched him leave. Smitty was pissed, as he'd known he would be.

Henderson ordered another mocha and moved to a table near the window. Outside there was a busy crowd, each one of them going about their lives. He used to enjoy sitting for hours people watching. But now all he could see were all the tall buildings surrounding the coffee shop. Countless buildings with countless floors and countless windows. A sniper's paradise. From the look on Smitty's face, he wouldn't be surprised if a shot came through the coffee shop window as he sat sipping his coffee. Or maybe as soon as he stepped outside. He half expected it but somehow knew the shot wouldn't come. Not yet. Not as long as Smitty needed information from him.

He left the coffee shop, abandoning his second mocha untouched. Pausing outside the door, he lit a cigarette and took a long, deep drag, feeling the nicotine fill his lungs and invigorate him. He blew smoke rings aiming at various windows, imagining them surrounding the hidden assassin, admiring how the rings undulated then fell apart.

After years of smoking, he was an expert at rings. He smiled at the thought of Brenda's deep frown and crossed arms when she smelt the evidence on his clothes. There was no point in trying to hide the fact that he'd failed to quit smoking from her.

No point in hiding anything anymore. The only reason Smitty's people had been able to keep their hold on him and Kirby was because they'd been allowed to.

It was time for *him* to change the rules.

The meeting with Kirby had been brief and to the point. Demir told him about Yamaguchi, who hadn't made the more infamous Watch List. Demir had suggested, a bit rudely he had to admit, that the list needed to be revisited. Before the major could respond, Demir had checked his watch, announced that he was late, and driven away before Kirby could respond with more than a stunned look.

Back at Cyber, Henderson had finally shown up around 7:30 PM, with no explanation or apology. Demir didn't care what the reason was. And he also didn't bother calling Henderson to ask to see him. Instead, he knocked on the door and entered without waiting to be invited. He told Henderson about Yamaguchi. He told him that Cahill was finally being sent home. Saying he had work to get back to, Demir turned and left. For the first time he felt like he was in control, rather than a whiny little boy tagging along behind the boss, begging for a few scraps of information. He was barely back in his office when someone knocked on his door.

"Come in."

Abraham entered saying, "Got your message that Cahill's coming home tomorrow. About fucking time." Abraham handed him a sheet of paper.

"Yeah." Demir took the offered sheet and scanned the list of names. "What's this?"

"Got it from Doctors Theriault and Chan." Abraham sat down.

"Must be twenty names here."

"It's a list of who they think is suspicious. I think some may just be scientists they don't like. But..."

"But you never know." Demir handed the paper back, saying, "Give it to Ops to carry out a deeper check on these names."

"Haven't seen you since you got back. How'd the meeting with Kirby go?"

"You should have seen the bastard's face when he realized his people missed Yamaguchi. I guess now he knows that we aren't such little kids after all and can play in the big leagues." Demir laughed, but it sounded hollow to his own ears.

"Sounds like everything's going along smoothly."

"Maybe too smoothly." Demir played with a pen on his desk.

"Have you had supper yet?" Abraham asked, checking his watch.

"Man, I just realized I forgot lunch," Demir said. He put on his jacket, adding, "After we debrief Cahill tomorrow, I've got some decisions to make."

"Anything I can help with?" Abraham said, holding the door open for Demir.

"It's time that we become more proactive."

CHAPTER SEVEN

Friday morning, Demir came into work before 7:00 a.m. Cahill would be on the 1:00 p.m. flight. He checked with Operations, checked his messages and voicemail. No new information. With Cahill coming home, Henderson said he'd be in by 8:00 a.m. They'd discuss the case. Then they'd go to meet Cahill's plane.

When 8:00 a.m. came and went with no sign of Henderson, he wasn't surprised. Demir would give anything to know what the hell was going on with the man. Could it be stress because this was the first real security issue they'd had to deal with? Trouble at home?

Whatever the reason, Demir couldn't wait for the man to snap out of it.

He put Henderson out of his mind, got a cup of coffee, then settled down at his desk to call up the daily security reports on his computer. Before the snatch, inspections of the underground complex and pertinent surface facilities were done at random intervals. He felt a surge of relief to see the 'All Clear' confirmed. All the landlines were clear. Satellite or cell phone transmission was not an issue this far underground and was blocked nonetheless, as well as in the surface building, which housed meeting rooms.

Demir had ordered that the security clearances of the two cleaning staff be double checked. Though they both cleared, they hadn't been allowed back into the complex. Not until this was over. All the other security clearances were confirmed and cleared. He'd even had the frequency of the everyone's ID implants and patches changed.

After a sip of his now tepid coffee, he abandoned it and left for Ops. There, he checked out the monitors and noted the several coloured dots on the screen. Everyone was in their expected place. The green dot for Owen hovered in its usual place in medical. The scientists' red dots were sprinkled between the second and third levels. The blue dots of security were mainly on Sub 1, but he could see one dot on each of the other two levels, doing their rounds.

No one was allowed access to the underground facility without an ID tag, no exceptions. He'd even tested the rule himself on several occasions. He'd badgered the guard on the surface to let him pass. Luckily for the guard, he had been denied entry.

Demir felt confident that the complex was secured. He was in control of keeping all the people here, under his charge, safe.

At 1:00 p.m., Demir and Abraham waited for Cahill's plane to clear customs at Ottawa International Airport. The new passenger terminal opened back in the late 2020s, giving the airport a truly international look with its high ceilings, a holographic waterfall, and forest near the luggage carousels.

"There he is," Abraham said.

The frosted glass doors slid open and Cahill emerged from security. His right arm was in a sling. His eyes were sunken and bruised. As he limped towards them, they could see stitches over his left eyebrow.

Demir took his suitcase and said, "Welcome home."

"I'm so sorry," Cahill said. His lips were drawn in a tight line, brow furrowed. Demir recognized Cahill's inner turmoil at his ultimate failure.

"You did your best, that's all anyone can expect," Demir told him. "We'll talk at the complex." He could see Cahill's obvious relief at not talking quite yet in the way his jaw relaxed, his tense shoulder lowered. Yet the drive back to work still echoed with a painful silence.

Back at Cyber, they sat in the briefing room on Sub 1 with Cahill on one side of the table, the other two men facing him. Since Cahill was from Abraham's squad, the other two squad leaders had opted out of the debriefing, saying they didn't want it to look like an interrogation. Demir placed a coffee mug in front of each of them while Abraham turned on the video camera and focussed it on Cahill's face.

"Let's get started," Demir said.

"I shouldn't be coming home alone!" Cahill punched the top of the table and winced. He took a deep breath, keeping his eyes down.

"Just start with everything you did after you landed at Heathrow," Demir said, ensuring his tone was light, not commanding.

"Well, we got to the airport okay," Cahill said. "I turned my back for a minute to get the luggage and when I looked around, he'd vanished." He looked up at Demir. "He'd gone to the bathroom. When I asked why he didn't tell me, he just said he was old enough to go on his own. He refused to take all the security measures seriously. I don't blame him. He's young, wants to go out, but with an old fart like me tagging along... I should have been better prepared. Shouldn't have opened the door without looking who it was."

"Let's back up a bit." Demir coaxed. "Tell me what you did after you got to the hotel."

"We checked in. Then went to the hotel restaurant for lunch. Since we didn't get much sleep on the flight, we went back to the rooms for a nap. He was supposed to call me when he got up."

"Supposed to?" Demir asked.

"I can get by with a quick cat-nap, so I'd set my alarm for half an hour and checked on him, but he wasn't in his room. I rushed down and found him in the hotel bar with this man, Smythe-Williams. They were in a deep technical conversation, so I just took a table nearby and waited."

"What was your gut feeling about this guy?"

"Seemed okay. I know he has a security flag on him, but I didn't get the feeling he was any kind of a threat. And when Dr. Stoddard went missing, he was visibly upset. He even came by the hospital to see me."

"I'd call that odd."

"Not really. He wasn't the only one." Cahill shook his head before continuing. "Dr. Stoddard managed to meet quite a few delegates staying at our hotel. Everyone liked him. They were concerned about him and... me." Cahill choked the last word.

"Did he run into a Yamaguchi?"

Demir smiled when the other man pulled out a paper notebook from his pants pocket. Ex-cop. Old habits. Hard copy couldn't be hacked and if stolen—good luck reading the illegible shorthand. Cahill awkwardly flipped through his notes with his left hand, the right hand in the sling, clenched in a fist of frustration.

"Name's not familiar." Cahill checked through the pad twice, then snapped it closed. "But there was this Japanese guy that came up to us on Sunday. Said his name was Ikiro. When Dr. Stoddard introduced himself, it was like the guy lost interest in talking and left."

"Probably Ikiro Yamaguchi. He's linked to some industrial espionage activities," Demir said.

Cahill whistled. "But he wasn't on the list."

"Sounds like he was looking for Drake, and didn't want to bother with Dr. Stoddard," Abraham said.

"Maybe," Demir said. "How about any of the other delegates?"

They continued discussing everyone that Matt had come into contact with, from delegates to waiters to cab drivers. Two hours later, Demir slid his seat back from the table.

"I think that's enough for today. We'll pick this up again later," Demir said. He nodded to Abraham who shut off the camera. Once off, Demir leaned forward and asked pointedly, "Now, off the record. Anything you want to mention that you didn't think important. Something Stoddard did or said that could be, well, embarrassing?"

"No..." Cahill's voice trailed off.

"Like you said, he's a young guy. London's famous for its nightclubs. Didn't you go to any?" Demir paused, watching the other man struggle to answer.

"Just one, sir." Cahill flushed a shade of crimson that Demir didn't think possible for a human to reach.

"Don't tell me you went in a suit," Abraham said.

"No, I didn't want to stand out too much."

"But you didn't pack any casual clothes," Abraham insisted.

"No." Cahill looked away even more embarrassed. "He lent me a t-shirt and jeans."

"He's about half your size," Abraham said, laughing.

"Let's just say they were snug. Okay?" Cahill fiddled with the sling. "We went to one nightclub, but I never left his side. He chatted with a couple of guys but brushed them off. After a few drinks—I mean he had a few, not me—we left."

"Why didn't you say anything earlier?" Demir demanded, not seeing the humour in the way Abraham did.

"Kind of embarrassing, you know," Cahill said.

"You spent the evening in a nightclub and forgot you were on the job?" Demir said.

"No, sir. I recorded the image of the two guys he spoke to. They checked out. They go to different nightclubs each night. I also recorded as many of the other patrons as I could. No flags."

"Anything else that you're too embarrassed to mention?"

"No, sir."

"Did he get away from you again?"

"No, sir. The conference was starting, and I guess he decided to start co-operating with security protocols."

"All right." Demir said. "Go home and rest."

"Yes, sir. Thank you, sir." Cahill stood. Stoop shouldered with exhaustion and pain, he left closing the door behind him.

Abraham turned off the second recording channel then asked, "What do you think?"

"Once he's had some time to rest, I'll be questioning him again," Demir said. "I think he's holding something back, but it could be he's just tired."

"I'll have the video transcribed," Abraham said, picking up the camera.

They left the briefing room to return to Demir's office. They stopped at the sight of Cahill talking with Aidan. Yasmin sat at her desk, pretending not to listen.

"Do you think they would have hurt him?" Aidan asked.

"He wouldn't have put up a fight like I did." Cahill shrugged the arm in a sling. "I was in the way. He's valuable to them. They'd take care of him."

"Did he get to tour around at all?" Aidan asked. "He was sort of excited about going to see stuff like art galleries and theatres..." His voice trailed off, looking at Cahill expectantly.

"Well, the first day, we were really jet-lagged and didn't do much. On Sunday, he walked through Hyde Park and looked at the artwork that was set up there." Cahill took a deep breath.

"Thanks, Mr. Cahill." Aidan shook his hand and slowly retreated down the corridor.

Yasmin whispered to Demir and Abraham, "He's been waiting here ever since you returned from the airport."

Cahill turned and froze when he saw Demir and Abraham behind him. He stepped closer to them.

"Dr. Stoddard said the club was a mistake and asked me not to say anything to him," Cahill whispered, nodding towards Aidan. "But like I said, I never left him alone and nothing was said that could be considered a security risk."

"We'll talk later," Demir said. "Get some rest."

They watched him trudge down the corridor, looking even more exhausted and dejected than when he'd left the briefing room.

Abraham handed Yasmin the camera to transcribe the video, then followed Demir to his office.

"That Yamaguchi guy is beginning to look good," Abraham said. "Sounds like he might have been looking for Drake, then moved on when he discovered it was the wrong guy. Probably gave it a second thought and decided that Stoddard might be a good consolation prize."

"I think so too." Demir drummed his fingers on his desk for a few beats, coming to a decision. "I've been pretty frustrated about how things are being handled."

"I don't blame you. He disappeared Monday and it's already Friday. There should have been more progress."

"I've been thinking it over. I've still got contacts in England and in the European theatre. I'm going to England to find Stoddard myself."

"I had a feeling you might be thinking of that," Abraham said. "What do you need me to do?"

"I want to keep this quiet for now. If you can check out flight times, for the next couple of days. Don't go through Ops, we'll keep this between us. I want to be ready to leave at moment's notice."

"I've got a bag here and am always ready to travel," Abraham said.

"I suppose we need to find someone to take over while we're gone."

The phone rang. Demir listened briefly and hung up. He looked at his friend and said, "Kirby."

"Another secret meeting?"

"Right. Keep an eye on things till I get back. This saves me calling him to tell him about Yamaguchi actually approaching Stoddard."

Once again, Demir arrived at the meeting place first. Not much had changed since yesterday. It was warmer though and more of the dirty snow in the canal was melting into muddy brown pools. He heard footsteps behind him, then saw Kirby's reflection in the glass walls of the Pavilion. But he was too pissed with all this clandestine shit, so he waited for the other man to speak.

"We get another chance to rescue Stoddard," Kirby said.

Without turning, Demir asked in a monotone, "As good as the last one, Major?"

"They were tipped off. Had to have been."

"Maybe your crack team wasn't as loyal as you thought," Demir said. Not getting a quick retort, he knew the old man had to be after something. He turned and when he saw the smug, entitled look on the old man's face, Demir's defences went up.

"I suppose," Kirby said after a moment, giving an exaggerated sigh. "We don't know where the leak is. All we can do is minimize the risk this time."

"A smaller team?"

"Not team. One man."

"Me." It was a statement. Demir struggled to keep his face neutral in case he gave away that he was already planning to go.

"I realize I have no authority to order you to do this, but you could volunteer."

"That's not something I can do behind Henderson's back." Damned if he was going to mention it to his boss, but he didn't want Kirby to suspect that there as any kind of rift at Internal Security. "Meeting you here when he's unavailable is one thing..."

"I know Henderson should tell you himself, but my job has so few perks." Kirby looked at his watch. "Two hours ago, Henderson resigned as Chief of Internal Security."

"What?" Demir stared at him. Was he joking? Demir suspected retirement might be on the Chief's mind, but not outright quitting. "Why would he resign suddenly this close to retirement?"

"He hasn't been happy here for a long time. You may have noticed this job is not for a family man." Kirby gave him a wide smile. "Upper levels have agreed with his recommendation for his replacement. Congratulations." He extended a hand.

Demir shook it automatically, feeling a strange mix of emotions. Disappointment that Henderson had resigned without talking to him first. Pride that Henderson had recommended him to succeed him rather than go outside to find someone. Trepidation at being in charge. But before all that, he had a lot of questions for Henderson. The main one being why he'd resigned so suddenly.

"You'll need to name a new second, someone you trust with your life," Kirby added.

"No problem there," Demir said. There was only one person that fit the bill. "When do I leave?"

"After a few days, you'll get sick unexpectedly and go home," Kirby added with a laugh, "There's always some kind of flu going around."

"Should I follow you back to your office to be briefed on details?"

"I'll fill you in just before you leave."

"Has Stoddard actually been found?" Demir asked.

"As I said, it'll be in the briefing," Kirby said. "I'll come by tomorrow to officially congratulate the new Chief of Security." Kirby started to leave then added, "Don't skip lunch; you need to keep up your strength."

"There's a fast food place up on Bronson Avenue. I'll stop by, then get right back on the Queensway."

"I know that place!" Kirby gave a dramatic shudder. "You're only supposed to *pretend* to be sick."

"Bye, Major." Despite himself, Demir laughed. The sudden genuine smile on Kirby's face made him seem more human somehow and Demir knew that if he wasn't careful, he'd start liking the old bastard.

Twenty minutes later, Kirby strode into the DND HQ building overlooking the Rideau Canal. He stopped to talk to his secretary, a large, crewcut male corporal. "Is he here yet?"

"Yes, sir," the corporal said. "Arrived right after you left." He gave a wicked grin, adding, "He tried to leave three times but I convinced him to wait."

"I'm glad you're on my side," Kirby said, with a laugh.

"This needs a signature, sir." The corporal handed him an e-pad.

"Well." He paused to read the half page memo, signed it with a thumbprint, and handed it back. "Send it out, right after Henderson leaves. Remember to CC Dr. Laura Jessup at Cyber." He entered his office to find Henderson pacing around the room.

"What the hell, Kirby," Henderson snapped. "You've had me here waiting for almost two hours. And now, thanks to your goon of a secretary, I'm late for a meeting."

"Sorry to keep you waiting, so I'll be blunt." He sat at his desk and stated, "You're overworked. Burnt out and need a change."

"You're firing me?"

"No, I—we're transferring you to another less demanding post, where your talents can be put to better use."

"I've set up everything here. Got security running smoothly, all to *your* specs, for twelve years. Now you want me to just leave it all?"

"You've done a great job. But we think it's time for a change. In fact, why not take a few months? Do some travelling. I know you're not military, but all you need to do is decide where you'd like to go and we'll make it happen."

"Maybe it's time to retire. Got the years in." Henderson sat down absentmindedly examining the arm of the chair. "Brenda would love to have me retire soon. Paint the house."

"Use the time off to think about it. You've got my support, whatever you decide. I've already told Demir the news to save you the trouble. You don't even need to go back to the complex. Your personal effects will be packed up and sent to you." Kirby squinted at Henderson as if trying to focus on something faded. "What happened to the man I knew? There was a time you wouldn't take your work so lightly."

"I've paid my dues. Now this cloak and dagger shit. Time for a younger man to take over."

Kirby leaned forward on his desk, fixing Henderson with a steady gaze. "Why don't you tell me what the hell's really going on?"

Mitchell hurried down the hall to Henderson's office. It was the first time the chief had ever asked to see him. Yasmin started to say something, but he didn't want to keep the man waiting. So, he nodded a quick hello, rushed past and knocked on the boss' door. He heard a muffled, "Come in." He opened the door and stopped short at the sight of Sandrovsky packing Henderson's stuff into two boxes sitting on the desk.

"Uh, sir?" Mitchell tried to speak, but couldn't think what to say.

"Come in. Close the door." Sandrovsky waved him towards the chair.

Mitchell sat down, watching his squad leader move slowly, like each movement hurt. He went through the desk and put things, real gentle, into the boxes. He wondered if he should ask and finally, he cleared his throat. "Sir, what are you doing?"

"Mr. Henderson's resigned," Sandrovsky said, his voice solemn. "Why?"

"Family reasons, I guess. Well, you know how it is. Bet your wife wasn't too happy when I sent you off to Toronto on thirty seconds' notice on Monday. Guess he wants… I don't know." He continued to slowly empty the desk drawers, packing pads of notepaper.

Mitchell studied Sandrovsky. The guy was always a real tough guy that refused to show weakness. Like last year, when he'd broken his wrist. It was a full day before someone noticed and even then, he had to be forced to go to the hospital. But this emotional stuff was really different. Maybe saying goodbye to the boss was harder for him than anyone else. They'd worked together for so long.

Sandrovsky looked up from the desk drawer he was emptying. "He'll need a driver to take him home. So, when I'm done here, take the boxes and go pick him up from DND HQ."

"Uh, sure. I mean, yes, sir." Mitchell watched Sandrovsky put in pencils and pens and then turn around to take down the framed spirit poster of the relay race from under the queen's photo. Then paused, turned around and took the photo of the queen off the wall. "Sir! Aren't you getting carried away?"

"This was the boss' favourite picture. Did you know that?"

"No, sir. Uh, sir, does Mr. Demir know?"

Sandrovsky put the poster on top of the larger box. Checked his watch and said, "Yup."

Demir swallowed the last bite of the NewTofu sandwich and washed it down with weak, tepid coffee. Maybe he should have listened to Kirby and chosen a different fast food place. He crumpled the paper bag and tossed it in the back seat with the rest of the fast food bags. He really should clean out the car before the weather got warmer and things really started to smell. For now it was a question of priorities.

Demir pulled into the complex parking lot thirty minutes later and headed directly to Henderson's office, hoping that the old man would be there, despite what Kirby had said. If he wasn't, then he'd have to get someone to pack up the boss' personal effects.

Yasmin wasn't at her desk, so he knocked and opened the door. He stared dumbfounded at Sandrovsky standing behind the boss' desk. There were two boxes, one already full, one being filled, on the desk.

"What the hell are you doing?" Demir slammed the door shut behind him.

"Hey, Mr. Demir, you're back," Sandrovsky said, pleasantly. He continued to slowly pack the second box. He put the framed photo of Mrs. Henderson into the box, removed the king's portrait from the wall and put that in too. "Just packing up the boss' things. Kind'a sad that he left so suddenly, eh?"

"How'd you find out so fast?"

"Boss called and asked me to pack up his stuff. I'm about done." He reached for the stapler and paused before putting it in the box, then gave a hopeful look. "The chief's gonna come back so we can give him a proper send-off, right?"

"Hope so." Demir studied the other man, surprised at this new sensitivity. "When did you find out?"

"I, I dunno," Sandrovsky stuttered. "Uh, couple of hours, maybe?"

"I see. I'm calling a squad leaders' meeting in fifteen minutes. Unless... did you tell them already?"

"I didn't say nothing."

Demir left him to continue packing up and returned to his own office. He put Sandrovsky out of his mind and sat down at his desk to think about how he was going to break the news to the squad leaders. Without a briefing room large enough to hold all of the security staff, he'd have Yasmin set up a video link to the rest of this level.

He put all his anger and frustrations aside and concentrated on the man Henderson used to be. Despite his recent behaviour, he'd be missed. He remembered how Henderson had welcomed him to I.S. ten years ago. Under that first research director, I.S. had struggled to deal with the director's berserk rules, which had included frisking the cleaning staff as they moved between levels.

Henderson had fought the threatened mass resignations by throwing impromptu staff parties with donuts, an occasional case of beer, and frequent BBQ parties at his home. He'd even arranged for a gym to be built on Sub 1 for I.S. to use. Nothing fancy, just a couple of machines and free weights. The excavation had been a nightmare, but once finished, the new gym had boosted security's spirit tenfold.

The phone interrupted the happy memories and brought him back to the dismal reality of the present. It was Yasmin. The squad leaders were waiting for him in the briefing room and the video link was set up. A briefing room large enough to hold all of Internal Security staff was another thing he'd wished the designers hadn't cancelled.

He opened the door to the briefing room and stared at the ovation that greeted him. Not just the squad leaders, but several others from I.S., including a couple of the tech guys from Operations.

"Congratulations, boss!"

"Well deserved, Chief!"

"Either you've got me bugged or..." Demir said, when the applause ended.

"Edna told us," Abraham said, his voice sombre.

"And you know how she knows everything," Sandrovsky said.

"Does she really?" Demir said. Yes, Laura's secretary did seem to get information before anyone else. Even Yasmin occasionally pulled difficult to find info out of nowhere. He'd always believed there had to be some kind of personal assistants' network that they belonged to. Maybe it was time to consider using that particular skill to his own advantage.

Smiling, he moved to the chair at the head of the table and sat down. The rest sat in the nine available seats, while everyone else stood around the table. So much for worrying about how to break the news.

"I know this is sudden and I'd like nothing more than to take time to settle in and even crack open a few. That'll have to wait. First, though, I'd like you all to join me in wishing Mr. Henderson luck in whatever he plans to do in the future." He waited for the more sombre applause to end. "My first official business is to name an assistant. All of you are deserving." He looked around the room and saw that everyone was smiling or giving knowing winks at Abraham.

"I looked at who was the most experienced, who had the best psychological profile, which by the way came as a hell of a shock to me." He paused to let the laughter die down. "There was only one answer. Abraham." They burst into applause again. Expecting to see his friend happy, Demir was puzzled to see him sitting in silence, frowning. Maybe he should have talked to him first. But who else did Abraham think he was going to choose? Who else did he trust without question?

"Well, I guess this is the shortest meeting ever. Thanks." The men filed out leaving Demir and Abraham alone.

"Abe, it's a promotion. You know, good news."

Abraham just huffed and asked, "I can't believe you're taking Kirby at his word. What's the real reason for the quick shuffle?"

"No idea. I haven't seen Henderson yet. But," Demir lowered his voice and continued, "Kirby has info on Dr. Stoddard's location."

"Shit, about time!"

"But judging from how well the last attempt went..."

"Had to be a leak from inside Kirby's group."

"Just what we thought, eh. Well, Kirby has a plan. Only this time we're limiting the number that know. Him. Me. You."

"And whoever you pick to be in charge while we're gone," Abraham said, matter-of-factly.

Demir kept any expression from his face and used the strongest, most confident voice he could. "You'll be in charge. I'm going alone."

"What?" Abraham stood up to pace in tight circles.

Sighing, Demir knew the news wouldn't go over well. They'd been best friends since RCMP training. They'd had each other's back when working undercover. And occasionally covered each other's ass. They'd left the RCMP together to work at Cyber. The fact that Demir became Abraham's boss had never been an issue. Until now.

They left the briefing room to finish the conversation in Demir's office.

"Look, Abe..." he began as he closed his door.

"Are you out of your fucking mind?"

"Kirby said that they've found Stoddard."

"And details are?"

"Well..."

"No details. What a fuckin' surprise," Abraham said.

"Kirby will have all the details just before I go in."

"Alone. No backup. Since when do you trust Kirby?"

"I don't. Besides, if things start to smell, I still have my contacts.

Come on, are you forgetting? I'm damn good at this kind of stuff."

"That was years ago," Abraham snapped.

"Like riding a bike," Demir said, with a smile. Nothing was going to lighten the mood. There was the old stand by method. Appeal to their friendship. "Abe, I need your help on this end. You know there's a leak somewhere. And, as much as I hate to agree with Kirby, the fewer people that know about the rescue, the better. And I'd rather it be me going after Stoddard than some stranger."

Silent for several long seconds, Abraham glared at him from under hooded eyes. Finally, his tone low and full of resignation, he asked, "What do you want me to do?"

He wasn't happy about it but at least he was on board. "Cover for me and keep things running while I get him out. Be about two or three days, including travel time, I figure. Not enough time for suspicions or leaks to develop."

Just after 4:30, Mitchell pulled into the parking lot under the DND headquarters building, overlooking the Rideau Canal in downtown Ottawa. Henderson was waiting near the door but before Mitchell could get out to open the door for him, the chief got into the front seat of the car.

"I'm sorry I was late, sir," Mitchell said. "There was a lot of traffic. I hope you weren't waiting long."

"Not long. Early rush hour is probably thanks to a lot of people sneaking out of work early. The usual for a Friday." Henderson looked at Mitchell and added, "Thank you, son. I appreciate the ride home." He looked and sounded tired.

"No problem, sir," Mitchell said. "Mr. Henderson, I'm sorry to hear about your resignation. We're going to miss you."

"It was a long time coming, son." Henderson sighed.

"Mr. Sandrovsky asked me to bring your things along. They're in the trunk." He put the car in gear and pulled back out.

"Head towards the Sir John A. Parkway, please." Henderson said, as he snapped on his seatbelt.

"You're not going home?"

"Not yet. I just feel like going for a drive. I always find driving next to the Ottawa River relaxing after a long day. Unless of course you need to get back to work."

"No sir, Mr. Sandrovsky told me to drive you wherever you wanted to go. I'm here for as long as you need me."

"That's fine. How about take it off auto mode? I find it a nicer drive with a human behind the wheel."

"Yes, sir," Mitchell agreed reluctantly. It would also mean the auto-location would be off as well. But he was the boss. So Mitchell switched it off. Not all bad because he loved manually driving.

They drove in silence for a few minutes, headed west on Wellington past the castle-like Chateau Laurier Hotel, then passed the Parliament Buildings and onto the Parkway.

"Son, how's your wife doing?" Henderson asked.

"Real good. She's due any time now," Mitchell said.

"I suppose you were a bit nervous leaving her to track me down in Toronto," he said, putting a hand on the younger man's shoulder. "I'm glad to hear the baby waited."

"So am I," Mitchell said. He hadn't liked the idea of leaving town but there wasn't really the option of saying no. Meesha had been furious and watched in angry silence from the door. But, by the time he got home that night, she'd forgiven him, saying how could she resist that smile? This morning in bed, he'd held her close, revelling in her warmth, feeling the tiny movements of their child. They both wanted to be surprised and hadn't asked the sex of the baby, something apparently no one did anymore, according to both their families. He secretly hoped for a little girl that looked just like his wife, with large brown eyes and silky light brown skin.

"Guess you're getting a bit antsy." Henderson patted him on the shoulder before removing his hand. "But don't worry, babies come when they're ready." He smiled at him then turned to look out the window.

Mitchell continued driving, admiring how close the road came to the water. There were a few parking areas but most had been closed off for the winter and hadn't been reopened. A bicycle path ran along the river, something he hadn't used since he was a teenager. A clump of trees blocked the river from view, but soon they were back to driving close to the water. Mitchell glanced in the rear view mirror and noted a dark blue, generic Honda following at a discreet distance.

"Pull in over there," Henderson said, indicating the Deschênes Rapids lookout.

"Yes, sir." Mitchell pulled into the parking lot, coming to stop near the river. This time of day, the lot was empty. He checked over his shoulder and noted that the other car kept going.

"I always liked to come here. To think," Henderson said, as he got out and walked to the water's edge. Mitchell followed but kept a short distance away to give the chief his privacy. But he was close enough if the boss wanted to talk.

Mitchell thought about his own family. Soon to be three, any day now. And about his job. It was usually so easy going, so relaxing. His squad leader, Sandrovsky, had always been accommodating, giving him time off to go with his wife to doctor appointments. Everyone got along well. And trust was an important part for their little underground community. Now he had to trust that the chief had his reasons for quitting so suddenly. He wasn't sure but Henderson was probably over seventy now. Sure, most people worked well into their eighties, but working security came with stresses most jobs didn't face, and the career lifespan tended to be shorter.

Mitchell turned up his jacket collar against the brisk wind. Lucky it was sunny. He'd come to Canada from Guyana when he was nine years old, but he still couldn't seem to get used to the long winters.

The river's fast flow was hypnotizing and he didn't hear the car pull into the lot until it was close behind him. Mitchell turned to see a dark blue car stop near the parking lot entrance. It was the Honda that he'd seen earlier. Two men wearing three-quarter length black coats and dark glasses got out. Mitchell took a step toward them to find out who they were, when he heard Henderson speak behind him.

"Damn you, Smitty."

Mitchell glanced over his shoulder to see Henderson look him straight in the eye. His face a strange mixture of hate and regret.

"Son, I'm so sorry you're here," Henderson said.

He turned back to the strangers but in that brief moment of distraction, both men had drawn guns and taken aim.

Mitchell unzipped his jacket and reached for his gun.

CHAPTER EIGHT

Abraham tapped his pen on his desk until the sound got on his nerves. He tossed the pen down and got up to pace. He made it halfway around his desk, abruptly reversed direction before he sat down again.

Demir had asked him to recommend one person from his squad to take over as squad leader, but all he could think about was that stupid argument they'd had. Demir had a quiet exterior and understated inner strength. Many called it dedication. Abraham called it stubborn. Too stubborn to know that a solo mission was suicide.

Maybe he couldn't change the man's mind about going after the scientist on his own, but no way was he going in without real backup. When Kirby got his facts together, there'd be enough time to work out the details. And set up a back up plan.

They still had two days. In the meantime, Abraham had to suggest someone from his group to replace him.

He pulled out a deck of cards from the top right desk drawer. A game or two of solitaire always helped him think. No computer could imitate the feel of the deck in your hands or properly mimic the soothing whiffle of cards.

Startled by the rapid knocking on his door, he looked up. "Come in."

"Um, Abe?" It was Friedrich. "I, uh, we, uh ..."

"What is it now?" Abraham asked, impatiently while he continued to shuffle the deck. The man was in almost hourly, double checking everything before he did it. It had gotten worse once the 24-hour protection duty had started.

"The hospital just called. Dr. Chan was in a car accident."

"What?" Mid-shuffle, the cards scattered all over his desk. "And what the hell do you mean the hospital called? You're supposed to be guarding him!"

"Abe, it wasn't my fault. It was near the end of my shift and I was getting ready to hand him over and uh, he snuck out of the complex."

"What happened?"

"Uh, I think they said he hit a tree, or a house or ..."

"You *think*! Is he alive?"

"Uh, yes."

"How badly hurt."

"Uh..."

"Mister, did you get *any* facts?"

"I, uh, guess I hung up when they said he was in an accident."

"Well, why don't you get your ass over to the hospital and find out? And find out if it really was an accident, or if someone helped it along. And don't leave Chan's side for a minute." When Friedrich didn't move, Abraham yelled, "Now!"

"Yes, I will. I mean, no I won't." Friedrich nodded shakily and left.

"Well, at least I can take Friedrich out of the deck," Abraham said aloud as he restacked the cards. Now, he'd have to tell Demir. Add the accident to Demir's already full plate. He picked up the phone to call the secretary.

"Do you know where Demir is?"

"He went to find Dr. Jessup," Yasmin said.

"Oh, that's right. Thanks." Abraham next called Edna, Laura Jessup's secretary. "Can I talk to Demir, please? I heard he's with Dr. Jessup."

There was a long hesitation before she answered. "They're not here. I'll find them for you." Then hung up.

Maybe Edna was mellowing in her old age. He'd expected to hear her usual complaints about doing the work of I.S.'s secretary. Instead, she seemed especially friendly. Good thing the scientists didn't know that their movements in the complex were being monitored by their ID tags. And, he supposed, he could take the short walk to Ops to find Demir, but he had a lot of thinking to do. Let Edna do the work for him.

While he waited for her to call back, he dealt out the cards on his desk.

Sometimes tracking Laura down was like chasing the end of the rainbow. It was never where you expected it to be. He'd never been one for poetic thought, but the image suited her. He'd like it more if he could find her. First, she wasn't in the complex, then she was back. By the time he got to her office, she'd left. Edna insisted that she was in the lunchroom.

He found her in the lunchroom making a pot of coffee. She looked up with a smile.

"I really should cut down," she said, "but I don't think I'd survive without my hourly cup."

"Don't you have a coffee maker near your office?"

"Edna makes it far too weak." She gasped and added quickly, "But please don't tell her I said that."

"Don't worry, your secret's safe with me." Demir laughed.

"Would you like a cup?"

"Yes, thank you." He reached for a mug from the cupboard and placed it on the counter by her cup. Both sat down at the table to wait.

"Anything for the new chief."

She laughed when he gaped at her, his mouth moving soundlessly. Recovering, he smiled and said, "I seem to keep worrying how to tell people but I never get the chance."

"Don't you know you can't keep a secret in a top secret installation? We all want to give you a party." She broke off, then continued, her voice sounding rough, "Right after Matt comes home." She stood abruptly and went to the counter. "Coffee's ready." She filled both mugs and handed him one. "One coffee. Black."

"Thanks," he said, surprised that she knew how he took it. Unsettled by his high school feelings, he focussed on a blue paint spot on the floor. Most of the cheap paint had worn away years ago. Maybe it was time to repaint it. Let the scientists decide on the colour. Feeling like he could concentrate again, he looked up at her. "There is one more thing I'd like to talk to you about."

"Sure." She gave him a smile.

"It's a minor security matter—um, well, sort of minor." What he really wanted to say was, tell your people to stop screwing with their guards. Instead, he said, "I know all this extra security is difficult, but I'd like to emphasize how important it is to co-operate with the bodyguards."

"Everyone knows how important it is." She looked at him with large, unblinking eyes.

Obviously, she hadn't known about the escapades of some of her people.

"Doctors Drake and Chan don't seem to be taking things as seriously as they should."

"Of course," she said, nodding with understanding. "I have a staff meeting scheduled this afternoon. I'll mention it then."

"Thank you," he said.

"Now, I better get back before Edna puts out a yellow alert on me," she said. In response to his raised eyebrow, she added, "Seems I have two bodyguards these days. Every time I'm out of my office, she's one step behind me. Even when I'm home, she phones to see how I'm doing."

"I'm sure she's just looking out for you," Demir said, hearing the annoyance in her voice. As he reached for the handle, the door quickly pushed open and Edna rushed in, crashing into him. He gave a quiet gasp as hot coffee spilled on his chest.

"I'm sorry, Mr. Demir." She grabbed a dishtowel and scrubbed his shirt. "I hope I didn't burn you."

"No, I'm okay." He took the towel from her, figuring it had to be less painful if he cleaned it himself. "I'm fine, really."

"I'll get you another coffee." Edna took the mug from Demir before he could say anything and poured him a fresh cup.

"Looking for me. Again?" Laura asked Edna. He could hear her try and fail to keep irritation out of her voice.

"No, for Mr. Demir," Edna answered smoothly, not reacting to Laura's tone. She handed Demir the new cup, adding, "Abraham's looking for you."

"Thanks," he said and left.

Laura started out the door, saying, "Well, I guess I'd better get back to work. Coming?"

"I'll be up shortly. I just want to make some tea." Edna started to fill the kettle with water. Once Laura was gone, she dumped the water out and returned the kettle to the counter.

"Edna tells me you're looking for me," Demir told Abraham, when he finally tracked him down in Operations.

"Yeah, two things," Abraham said. "First, don't panic, but Chan had a car accident."

"What?" Demir's head reeled. "Is he okay?"

Abraham nodded. "He's alive..."

"You think someone tried to snatch him?" Demir interrupted,

"I doubt it. They wouldn't have left him behind if it was. I've sent Rajan to check into the accident to make sure."

"Good, let me know what she finds out. And who the hell was watching him?"

"Friedrich. Apparently, our scientist gave him the slip. He's on the way to the hospital."

"You said two things?"

Abraham handed him a sheet of paper. "This just came in. They found the kidnappers."

"That's terrific!" Demir took a sip of coffee, then put his mug down to study the sheet.

"Don't get too excited," Abraham said. "They were found floating face down in the Thames."

Demir cursed.

"Anything happening?" A voice boomed behind them. Demir turned to see Sandrovsky leaning on the desk beside Abraham. "I saw

Demir rush in here and thought there's something new."

"There is," Demir said. "They found the kidnappers. Dead." He rubbed his eyes again.

"You look tired, boss. Here, this might help," Sandrovsky said, handing Demir his coffee.

"Thanks," Demir said, taking another sip of coffee hoping to fend off the growing drowsiness. "Why pay them all that money and then just kill them?"

"Probably just tying up loose ends," Abraham said.

"Did anyone trace the money back to its source?" Demir asked. When Abraham shook his head, Demir added through a stifled yawn, "Get someone to follow the money trail, see what we can find."

"While we're waiting for that information," Abraham said, "why don't you take a short break and get some lunch."

"You're always trying to feed me. As a matter of fact, I did eat lunch," Demir said, smiling. It was true, he did sometimes forget to eat. He took a sip of coffee. Damn, it had gone cold. But it was the caffeine that mattered, not the temperature and he downed the last of it.

Sandrovsky took the empty cup from Demir, saying, "I'm gonna go grab a cup myself, so I'll take care of this for you." Then left quickly.

"Thanks," Demir said. To Abraham he added, "It doesn't make sense to hire small time hoods then just kill them."

"Like I said, they're probably eliminating loose ends," Abraham said, as they left Operations.

"You're probably right," Demir said, yawning widely. He guessed the lack of sleep was finally catching up.

Demir wanted to listen, but his friend's voice sounded muffled and he couldn't understand him. He was about to ask him to repeat it when Demir tripped. Abraham caught his arm to steady him.

"Thanks. Getting clumsy in my old age," Demir said, trying to catch his breath. He felt like he'd just finished an intense workout. His legs were heavy, and it took tremendous will to keep walking.

"I always wondered what the assistant chief's job is," Abraham said, with a chuckle. "Hold up the old man."

"Right." Demir started to laugh only to have it turn into a cough. It wasn't until Abraham grabbed him by the shoulders to steady him that he realized he'd stumbled again. He felt dizzy, like he'd had too much to drink. He knew that he wasn't walking right. The old alcoholic two-step his dad used to call it. Sweat dripped in his eyes. A wave of warmth flooded over him. Fighting to draw in a deep breath, he tugged at the collar of his t-shirt. "Remind me to call maintenance to check the air conditioning." He felt an itchy trickle of sweat between his shoulder blades.

"What?"

Looking up, he added, "It looks like we're having a brown-out or something."

"Ty?"

His legs started to tremble, and he leaned against the wall. Panting, he said, "Kirby was right, lunch didn't agree with me."

"Ty, what're you doing?" Abraham grabbed him under the arms trying to hold him up.

"I need to sit down. Just for a minute." He slid down the wall and started to ask if Abraham had any antacid on him when a loud roar filled his ears. Then a stabbing pain in his gut doubled him over.

The lights went out.

CHAPTER NINE

Elton Chan was enjoying the dream when something woke him. Eyes still closed, he tried to recall it, but it had already drifted away as had the feeling of euphoria. He could hear voices all around. Slowly, he opened his eyes and stared at the blurry image of someone leaning over him. He blinked the face into focus—it was that man from security, Fred, no Friedrich, his bodyguard.

"*What happened? Where am I?*"

"Doctor Chan, I can't understand you."

"*What do you mean you don't understand? I asked what... oh.*" He realized he was speaking in Mandarin. Switching to English, he asked, "What happened?"

"You were in a car accident?" Friedrich said, sighing with obvious relief. "Do you remember?" Elton shook his head. "You hit a tree. Did another car try to force you off the road?"

"Tree. I don't remember. My leg hurts." Elton tried to sit up, only to have both the pain and Friedrich push him back down.

"You have a broken leg. They had to put you to sleep to set it. That's why you feel groggy." Friedrich patted him lightly on the shoulder. "Your memory should clear up soon."

Elton looked around and saw that he was indeed in a hospital. He was in one of the emergency room cubicles. There were monitors over his head, opaque walls all around and he knew that in one of the walls was a door. He felt the tingle of the force field on both sides of the bed. As if he was planning to roll over and accidentally fall out. Every movement caused bone splintering pain. He looked down at himself and saw that his left leg was in a cast from the knee down. It was supported on a couple of pillows. His toes were sticking out the end, looking blue and feeling cold.

"Here, how about some water?"

Friedrich brought a cup with a straw close and helped him to drink. Ice water soothed his light-headedness. What did his bodyguard ask? A car try to run him off the road? Did they think someone tried to kidnap him too? He shuddered at the thought and Friedrich, misunderstanding the shiver for a sign of being cold, pulled the blanket up to cover him more. Which was okay, because he was in fact cold.

And the water also cleared his memory. Yes, he remembered the doctors saying that it was a compound fracture, the tibia broken in one spot, the fibula in two. To set the bones, they'd given him a light general anaesthetic. They'd assured him that he wouldn't be out for long. His head and thoughts were clearing up now and he remembered that in the pain and confusion of the accident, he'd given his work number when they'd asked whom they should contact.

He should have given Claudette's number.

"Dr. Chan, can you remember what happened yet?" Friedrich asked, after putting the glass down. "Was there another car?"

The image of a furry tailed squirrel running across the road came to mind. In the summer, he was always on the alert for dogs, squirrels, or children chasing balls across the street. In the winter, the streets tended to be slightly quieter, with the exception of a few cyclists who rode their bikes all year. The unexpected appearance of a squirrel darting across the road startled him. Not sure the auto-drive would swerve to miss it, he'd grabbed the wheel, which instantly shifted the car to manual. He swerved safely, but in a panic, hit the gas instead of the brakes. Last thing he remembered was seeing the squirrel dart away and then a tree getting larger.

"Dr. Chan?" Friedrich patted his shoulder.

The anaesthetic's effect must be lingering, making his thoughts wander. "No car. Just a squirrel."

"Squirrel?" Friedrich looked at him as though he was joking. Eventually the incredulous look faded to one of confusion, then to relief, then finally to a smile and an almost laugh. But just as suddenly, a look of anger, not unlike the one Elton's father used to give him when he discovered he'd been out playing with the children instead of coming straight home from school to do his homework. "A goddam squirrel? You almost kill yourself for a goddamn, fucking rat! Do you have any idea how worried I was?" Even the last line sounded exactly like his father—spoken in Chinese, of course.

"Believe me, I won't do it again."

"And one more thing. What's the big idea taking off the way you did? Drake, I understand him not listening to anyone. But you? Did you forget about Dr. Stoddard? Did you forget the kidnappers got the wrong man? Did you forget there's a chance that they might try for someone else? Until we know it's safe, we need to be careful."

Elton half expected Friedrich to wave a finger at him and continue scolding him. Instead, he just stood there looking at him as though expecting an answer. Was there a question within that tirade? No, of course he hadn't forgotten about Matt. How could he, or anyone, forget? That's all anyone could think of. A depressing pall hung over the complex.

Before Matt started working there, everyone had got into a daily routine of working hard. Though coffee breaks were scheduled so that everyone could get together, in part to keep updated on their progress but also to socialize, they'd become slightly boring and predictable. After Matt's arrival, a new buzz of activity filtered through everyone. There was new work being done. New conversation. Even Drake would occasionally join in the conversation briefly when he came to get coffee. Though as soon as it turned to life outside work, he'd leave. Apparently his own life was so wonderful he couldn't be bothered to lower himself enough to share it with anyone.

Friedrich was still waiting. For what? Weren't they all rhetorical questions?

Obviously not.

"I won't do it again," he whispered.

"And where were you rushing to?"

"Uh," Elton hesitated. That was definitely a question. How should he answer it?

"I promise I won't do it again," Elton repeated, hoping that Friedrich would leave the question alone. Finally, the security man nodded unhappily and reached for the cup of water.

As Elton drank, he wondered how he was going to get in touch with Claudette. He looked past Friedrich and saw the clock. Damn! He'd been here all day. By now, her impatience had certainly turned to worry. They had planned a romantic lunch together. He'd told her despite all that had happened, he still wanted to keep their plans.

He could talk about anything with her: his feelings, his work, anything that bothered him. She was a wonderful listener. Never judged him. Besides, he now realized how short life could be. Further emphasized by his stupid accident. One moment of inattention almost brought complete disaster on him.

Keeping her a secret from Internal Security had been a problem, but he'd managed to do the impossible.

Elton had to get to a phone to explain where he was. But how could he get a message to her? It was late in the evening and her husband would have come home from work long ago.

How the heck did everything get so screwed up? Sandrovsky clomped back to his office. Never thought Henderson would resign so out of the blue. Didn't expect Demir would get that sick. He was relieved when Doc Owen released Demir from the infirmary and let him go home.

He looked around his office. A desk. A sofa. A lamp on one corner of his desk, a fake plant on the other corner with a centimetre of dust on it. He'd clean it when it got to two centimetres. Guess he could'a asked the cleaners, but that seemed to be too much trouble. Cleaning up the chief's office made him think that maybe he should put up some holos, maybe a couple sports pics, to cover the battleship grey colour. But he liked the grey. Helped him relax.

He sat down, saw the blinking message light on his phone, and shook his head. He was tired and just wanted to go home to meet up with that cute honey he met last week. She knew how to make him forget all his troubles. That's what he wanted but knew he couldn't, so he half-heartedly checked his phone messages.

It was Mitchell's wife wondering if her husband was working a late shift. He looked at his watch. 7:34 p.m. Mitchell had picked the chief up hours ago. Sandrovsky phoned her back.

"Hi Mrs. M. It's Sandrovsky. You're not in labour are you?"

"No, I'm fine, thank you. I'm sorry to bother you, I tried to call Darius, but he doesn't answer. I just wanted to know how late he's going to be. He usually phones, but it's already after seven."

"I don't know if you heard but Mr. Henderson's resigned. So, this being his last day, he's probably got a lot of things to finish up. Your husband's driving him around and they probably lost track of time."

"I see," she said.

She sounded angry. But there wasn't much he could do, was there? Mitchell was supposed to stay with the chief until he wasn't needed.

"Don't hesitate to call me. Anytime," Sandrovsky said. She hung up without another word. Mrs. Mitchell was always a little high strung. Overreacting to stuff that most women would let slide. He wondered if it was different because she was a wife, not just a girlfriend. Maybe the baby made her emotional. Thinking about it just made his head spin.

But it sure was weird that Mitchell hadn't called her, or even called in to report. He tried phoning him. No answer. He left a message to call back right away. He phoned Mr. Henderson. No answer either. He left a message asking him to call back when he could.

CHAPTER TEN

At home, Demir curled into a fetal position on his sofa, the only position that seemed to lessen the nausea. He clutched the blanket tightly around his shoulders while Abraham placed a second over his legs. Why bother? In just a few minutes, he'd throw off both blankets and race to the bathroom to puke.

He'd spent the afternoon in the infirmary with Doc Owen fussing over him, then finally persuaded the MD to let him go home to rest. Diagnosing the stomach flu, Owen had prescribed rest and plenty of fluids.

Owen didn't explain how he was supposed to rest if he spent most of the time rushing to the bathroom. And what was the point of drinking when he threw it up within minutes? Through it all, Abraham had been there to help keep his head out of the toilet, then help him get back to the sofa. Luckily, he still had a couple of days before his mission. Plenty of time to recover.

His stomach finally settled enough to let him begin to drift off to sleep only to be startled awake by the doorbell.

Abraham opened the door and stepped aside for Kirby to enter. Demir managed to sit up into a slumped position on the sofa.

"Don't get up," Kirby said, holding out a hand to stop him.

"I wasn't planning to." Demir tried to sound emphatic, but his throat was too raw to manage anything above a hoarse whisper.

"Nice place you have here," Kirby said, sitting in the armchair next to the sofa.

Demir glared at him and the growing wet spot on the carpet under the bastard's snowy boots. Abraham stood behind Kirby in rigid silence, with his arms tightly crossed.

"Just coming by to check how you're feeling," Kirby said, his voice pleasant.

"If I was paranoid, I'd think you had something to do with my getting sick," Demir shouted, then swallowed hard. Getting angry wasn't agreeing with his stomach and he clamped his mouth shut, to stop himself for saying more.

"I just finalized the mission details and came by to update you. You're booked into a bed and breakfast outside of London. Our overseas contact will give you Stoddard's location. Get him to the port at Bournemouth, where a boat will take you to France. From there, a military plane will fly you home. All the details are here." He pulled out a sheet of paper and started to hand it to him, then changed his mind and passed it over his shoulder to Abraham. "You leave at midnight."

"Tonight?" Demir sat forward. The sudden movement was a mistake. His stomach lurched. His head pounded. He barely untangled himself from the blankets in time to reach the bathroom. With nothing left to throw up, he was down to dry heaves. He lay on the floor listening to his heart thump while his stomach burned and spasmed.

Kirby called out as he was leaving, "Just make sure he gets to the airport on time."

"Supposed to be two more days," Demir moaned, struggling to find his feet. "I can't... in time..."

"I'll help you. You'll get there," Abraham said.

That was the last thing he heard as he curled up and gratefully faded into a warm darkness.

Demir arrived at the military airfield, several kilometres west of Ottawa International Airport, just before midnight. He gave the air cab driver his cashcard and vaguely remembered authorizing $60.00 for the $42.00 fare, not willing to even think what a decent tip should be. He tumbled out of the cab and limped into the hangar.

He would have preferred to have Abraham drive him. But despite the late hour, Demir didn't want to risk any more unexpected visitors dropping by, so Abe had stayed at his house for a few hours until well after his plane had taken off. During the early evening, Laura had brought him chicken soup. Edna had stopped by to drop off some lasagna. Even Drake had visited, although Demir suspected it was for some reason other than giving his best wishes.

Kirby might be a jerk and son of a bitch, but he was right that they maintain comm silence. Abraham kept trying to set up a backup plan as he helped Demir get cleaned up and packed. But he could barely concentrate on breathing, so he'd brushed him off with assurances. After all, it was an easy extraction.

Inside the hangar, Kirby paced impatiently near the far wall. Spotting Demir, he marched towards him.

"You're late," Kirby snapped.

"You're lucky I decided to come at all! You almost killed me!"

"A little harmless tranquilizer. You should have just drifted off to sleep."

"What the hell is wrong with you, drugging me before a mission? A tranquilizer doesn't almost fucking kill me. And which of my people did you coerce to do it?"

"It was just a tranquillizer. I wanted your *illness* to look real. So there wouldn't be any suspicions. As for who, just know your people are loyal to you."

"I could have just pretended to be sick." Demir decided to drop the issue of who. For now.

"I couldn't trust your acting abilities," Kirby said. He took Demir's arm and led him to the hangar door. He added, "You are aware how important Stoddard is, don't you?"

"Of course."

"And you're aware of all the secrets in his head?"

"What?" Demir tried to understand what Kirby wasn't saying.

"He knows a lot about Cyber's work."

Demir stopped in his tracks, the brain fog clearing enough for him to ask, "What are you saying, Major?"

"If something goes wrong—I'm sure it won't—but if it does, and you can't get him out..." Kirby paused, and turned to look him straight in the eye. "Don't leave him behind."

Demir thought he'd misheard at first. But he recognized a deep coldness flash in Major's eyes which horrified him. More disturbing was the speed that his eyes returned to a normal pleasant expression.

"The plane's waiting," Kirby said. He took his arm and forced him to continue walking.

"You better have booked me an aisle seat."

"Any seat you want," Kirby said. "You're the only passenger. Look, sorry you got so sick, but this was the safest way to do it."

"If there wasn't so much at stake..." Demir broke off not trusting himself to say any more and followed Kirby outside.

Expecting to see some large military transport, Demir was relieved to find a sleek private jet waiting for him. He'd really have been impressed if he didn't still feel like crap. But one thought did come through clearly as he sat in the plush seat and looked at Kirby on the tarmac: if it was the last thing he did, he'd get even with the bastard for drugging him.

Paul Drake dozed in his armchair, feeling an uncanny sense of tranquillity. He started to drift into a deep sleep when his head rolled forward, then snapped up. He was suddenly awake. He swallowed sour bile and pushed himself upright in the leather armchair. His head ached with exhaustion. Another sleepless night. He rubbed his eyes with one hand and massaged the back of his neck with the other.

He stood. Looked around. Sat back down with a thud. This was *not* his office! It wasn't anywhere in the complex.

The room was lit by a single bright light over his chair. The concrete floor was cracked and water stained. He sat still for several minutes, trembling with fear. He searched deep within himself for the ability to stand. His heart pounded furiously in his chest as he moved towards the light's perimeter to peer into the blackness beyond.

The dark appeared unreal, murky, not black. He shivered as though tiny ice crystals were crawling up his spine. In the smell of dampness intermingled with another putrid odour.

He probed the dark with a cautious toe. Nothing happened at first, then... A flash. An explosion. A scream. Several deafening screams.

Drake woke with a jolt. He had fallen out of the armchair and was on the floor of his office. Nothing more than a dream, he thought with the usual relief. He should have known better than to even contemplate taking a nap. Invariably his dreams transported him to that same horrifying prison cell. He needed sleep. Though not enough that he was willing to visit that cell again or see what was slowly rotting in the dark.

Or who.

His subconscious was trying to tell him that after a week there was little doubt that Matt Stoddard was dead and decaying in some dark corner.

Or perhaps that stench was Drake's own festering guilt.

Drake left his claustrophobic office and headed for the kitchen to make coffee, hoping that whoever was in charge of buying the coffee supplies had done so. He stopped short in the corridor, his chest heavy. This was Matt's week.

Damn him anyway! Matt couldn't leave him in peace when he'd worked with him. And he wouldn't leave him alone now.

Drake opened the door to the lunchroom and was startled at the sight of someone there. Laura Jessup sat at the table resting her head on her arms, apparently asleep. Drake turned to leave, then stopped. What was she doing here at this hour?

"Jessup?"

"Hmm?" Her head lifted slowly.

"Jessup, it's three in the morning. What are you still doing here?"

"Making coffee. Can't get along without my hourly cup."

"Judging from the creases your sleeve made in your face, you missed a few cups." He went to the coffee pot. "You let it get cold." He filled a mug and put it in the microwave for two minutes.

She didn't try to cover a large yawn as she leaned her head on one hand and said, "Pour me a cup too, please."

He poured another, interrupted the microwave to put the cup in and sat down.

"What are you doing here? Paperwork can always wait."

"I do more than paperwork!" she snapped, fully awake.

He touched her arm lightly, sorry for what he'd said. "What is it?"

She pulled her arm away to rub red rimmed eyes. Finally, she asked, "What else can happen? First Matt. Then Elton's in a car accident. Now Mr. Demir becomes seriously ill on the same day Mr. Henderson resigns. Who else are we going to lose?"

"We haven't lost anyone. Demir has the stomach flu. Elton obliterated his car and breaks his leg in order to miss a bloody squirrel."

"I guess you forgot about Matt?"

"Coffee should be hot soon." He avoided looking at her. He didn't know how to be comforting.

"I'm sorry, Drake. I know you were trying to make me feel better. It's just that, well, so much has happened."

"It seems we've had quite a run of bad luck," Drake said. "Did you see Demir today?"

"No, I couldn't get past the front door. Abraham was very insistent."

"Strange."

"Hmm?" Laura asked, half listening.

"It is curious that the chief of security is being babysat by the assistant chief."

"God! I know you're paranoid. But honestly! They're best friends. Who else would you expect to help him out?"

"If he's truly sick," Drake said. The microwave beeped. He brought the cups to the table and joined her.

"Come on, you saw how bad he looked. My God, we thought he was dying."

"There are ways to make someone appear ill."

"You actually believe he'd pretend to be sick and have all of I.S. cover for him?"

"Not all. Just Abraham."

CHAPTER ELEVEN

Tyler Demir blinked the last bit of sleep from his eyes, then sat up slowly, wary of any sudden movement. Just stiff muscles. Those he could live with. He made his way to the window. He opened the shades and clamped his eyes shut at the painfully bright sunshine. How long had he slept? What day was it? He checked the calendar on his watch. Still Saturday. Just after eleven in the morning. He exhaled loudly with relief.

He'd arrived at the B&B on the outskirts of Luton, just north of London, early this morning. Alone on a private jet, he'd been able to rest and recover. The dry heaves had ended on the flight, though a fog of nausea still lingered. Once he'd arrived at Heathrow, he'd cleared customs using a very professional looking fake ID supplied by the military. Using a pay phone at the airport, Demir had called the arranged contact who would give him cash and directions to the bed and breakfast—not really necessary because, as he'd bluntly stated, he wasn't an idiot and knew how to read a map.

But the most important thing the contact supplied was the unregistered gun. The contact also brought Demir a disposable sat phone. He'd left his sat at work. But as soon as Kirby's contact had left, Demir tossed the phone in the nearest trash can and picked up a disposable phone using cash. Then he'd destroyed the ID Kirby had supplied him with and took out his own fake ID from the secret pocket in the bottom of his backpack. He used that ID to book a manual transmission rental, leaving behind the prearranged car already there. He'd made sure the rental wasn't equipped with GPS, or any nav tech.

Demir slowly sat up on the edge of the bed. So far, so good. He stood up and waited to see how his stomach reacted. No reaction. Also good. Sniffing his shirt, he knew it was well past time to shower.

The bathroom was a long, narrow setup with a small shower in the corner near the door. The room widened out at the end to include the toilet and sink, which fit snugly into the corner. He turned on the shower and was about to step in when he realized he was still fully clothed. He peeled off his sweat drenched clothes and stepped into the shower. He leaned his head against the shower wall, letting the water flow over his head and down his back, reviving him. But with renewed life came renewed anger.

How the hell could Kirby take such a big risk and drug him before a mission?

Matt had been snatched on Monday morning, six days ago. According to the best intel, he was still alive. Although intel from Kirby was dubious at best, he had to believe it was true.

The one thing he didn't have a chance to get his head around was Henderson's sudden resignation. When he'd got the news, he'd been so preoccupied with the upcoming mission that he hadn't had a chance to think. Then he got sick and everything happened so fast that he didn't have time to track Henderson down. Now, with the relaxing water and his stomach cramps gone, he began to wonder why the hell Henderson hadn't talked to him about his resignation. As soon as he got back home and the pressure was off, they'd sit down and talk. Like they used to.

He stood in the shower with the water pounding on his shoulders. It was a relief to actually have water pressure. Just before he'd started work at Cyber, he'd returned to England for a holiday. He'd rented a car and driven aimlessly for a month, stopping at several B&Bs along the way. Nine times out of ten, the water pressure was so low that barely a trickle came out of the shower. He'd driven up to the northern point of Dunnet Head. As he'd driven higher into the mountains, he'd enjoyed the scenery of mountainous terrain, blanketed with purple heather, dotted with black-faced sheep until the fog thickened and erased the view. When he broke through the mist, he saw that he'd reached the plateau where the terrain had become flat and barren.

Travelling alone, he'd been free to go anywhere he wanted, stay as long as he wanted. Visited briefly with a few friends from the old days. Even stayed a few days in Newcastle, with a friend. Then Demir had spent the last week in Wales, in a tiny, thatched roof cottage where he considered his future with the RCMP. The security job at the nanotechnology company, Cyber Inc, sounded easy enough with few major decisions which, as second in charge, weren't his to make anyway.

That last ironic thought sent chills through him. Then he realized the water had gone cold without warning and he shut off the taps. Wrapping a towel around his waist, he walked gingerly on the frigid marble floor to the sink. He wiped the steam off the mirror with his hand and checked himself. Not willing to touch his still sensitive head, he opted for the au-naturel hairstyle. The idea of shaving was immediately dismissed. He returned to the bedroom to dress.

And plan his next move.

His job was to get here. He did that. The next step was to wait for the contact. He was doing that.

As though on cue, an envelope whooshed under his door. He grabbed it and ripped it open to read the handwritten note. The message: *wait until Sunday*. Tomorrow? It was barely noon now. What did they expect him to do in the meantime, tour the countryside? He doubted much would have changed in ten years.

He crumpled the note in one hand and the envelope in the other then tossed them both into the waste basket. What kind of emergency rescue was this? Why the hell did he rush to get here if all they wanted him to do was wait?

He slipped the gun into the belt holster, then put on his windbreaker to conceal it. He took out the British money from his wallet, then split the three thousand pounds into three, putting one stack into the front pocket of his jeans, another into the back pocket and returned the rest to his wallet, which he shoved into the other front pocket. He checked the Rolex watch on his wrist and covered it with his sleeve. A habit he'd developed from his undercover days: never use credit slips and always have something of high value that he could sell.

He hooked the visual scrambler on his right ear. Anyone seeing it would think it was just a new sat phone model, not a facial scrambler containing several generic faces. It would hide him from the prying eyes of CCTV and triggering any worldwide security alerts.

Other than the scrambler and his watch, from which he removed all internet or GPS capability, he travelled very low tech. The disposable sat phone could just barely make calls and tell time.

He folded the paper map. GPS devices were great to get you somewhere unfamiliar, but they could also be tracked. So he folded the paper map, slipped the disposable sat into his windbreaker pocket, picked up the backpack and ski jacket, then headed out, locking the door after him. He dropped the key off at the front desk and dashed out to the parking lot trying to remember what the rental looked like. There it was, a grey VW Falcon, four door sedan. Ordinary enough to blend in. Old enough not to have any GPS or auto-drive functions. Totally anonymous. With warm temperatures of ten degrees centigrade, he tossed his ski jacket in the trunk.

He reached to open the door. Damn! Wrong side! Going around to the right side, he got in behind the wheel and started the car. He slipped on sunglasses, reminding himself, "Left side," then pulled out of the parking lot and turned right, making sure to drive on the left side of the road towards the town of Luton. From there he called a friend, well, an acquaintance, who owed him a favour.

Two hours later, Demir arrived at the Pig'n Blanket pub in Brighton. Before going in, he activated the visual scrambler. This time he used his watch to adjust the frequency so only CCTV cameras would be affected, not people. Which meant his friend could easily find him. The last thing he needed was a public argument trying to prove who he really was.

He sat at a corner table, with his back to the wall, and ordered a Guinness. Though it was strange, he'd discovered that beer, especially dark beer, always settled his stomach. It wasn't long before he spotted a short, portly man, wearing a grey pinstriped suit, a little snug around the belly, standing in the open doorway. Demir waved him over.

"Thanks for coming," Demir said. They shook hands.

"My pleasure," Pettigrew said, as he sat down and signalled the waitress for a beer. He looked at Demir. "I haven't seen you in donkey's years. You haven't changed a bit. Still look knackered." Pettigrew laughed. Then leaned forward and lowered his voice. "Why don't you tell me what you need."

"Travel plans. For two. I don't know when exactly. It'll be short notice."

"Short notice is my specialty." Pettigrew straightened up when the waitress arrived. With one swallow, he drank half of the pint. Giving a satisfied smack of his lips, he put the mug down and asked, "Any particular direction you'd like to take?"

"Anywhere out of the country. I can pay you now..."

"No need." Pettigrew took another gulp of beer, reached into his pocket for a folded piece of paper and handed it to Demir. "Name and address of a man outside of Brighton with a boat. You pay him directly."

"Thanks," Demir said with a laugh. He was feeling better already.

"To old times." Pettigrew raised his mug.

"To old times," Demir said. They clinked mugs.

Demir and Pettigrew chatted about the old days for a bit longer. Then Demir paid for both pints, as well as an extra and left Pettigrew in the pub.

On the way back to Luton, he picked up a loaf of whole wheat bread. He managed a few bites of the warm loaf. The rest he saved for the morning. He made a few more stops to buy some supplies, including candles, a blanket, some bottled water, and energy bars. The last stop, the drugstore, chemist as the Brits would say, to put together a first aid kit. By the time he got back to the B&B it was almost 10:00 p.m. He checked for messages. None.

Frustrated at doing nothing, he took off his runners and forced himself to lie down. Dressed and ready to move as soon as the new message arrived.

All Demir needed to do now was wait for Matt's location. Pick him up. Bring him home. How much simpler could it get?

He just wished he could tell Abraham. Now that he was feeling better, he regretted not working out a code, but Kirby was right about maintaining comm silence. Chances were good that Abraham and everyone at Cyber were being watched.

Dozing as the night faded to light, the unmistakable swishing sound of an envelope sliding under his door brough him fully awake.

He tore open the envelope, not even bothering to open the door to try to see who'd delivered it. It would have only been a messenger anyway. A handwritten note with instructions this time. Finally!

At the top was scrawled the message: *In case you are followed, or this note gets lost. Start from current location, turn right and drive...*

The instructions continued with no north or south directions, just so many kilometres one way, turn left at a farm, so many more kilometres. The last line was *Location. Cottage.*

He opened his map on the bed to see if he could find the location, but they were ridiculous instructions. What the hell were they thinking? That he was some rookie? That he'd lose the paper? How about if they'd written an address he could memorize, then destroy the note? He supposed they were worried that the note could get intercepted. He had no choice but to start driving.

Demir shoved his feet into his runners, still laced up from the night before. Checked his gun and put it in his belt holster, shoving the extra clips into his jacket pocket. He packed the supplies he'd bought yesterday into the backpack, including a roll of duct tape, useful for sealing up unexpected bullet holes or stab wounds. He grabbed the loaf of bread and after a quick stop in the bathroom, bounded down the stairs, dropped his key at the desk and paid his bill. With all the driving he'd done yesterday, driving on the left side of the road felt more natural now, leaving him free to concentrate on the instructions.

Note in hand and map on the passenger seat, he started up the car.

An hour and a half later, he drove across Salisbury Plain where the terrain became more undulating and wide open. He turned onto A303, which led him to believe Stonehenge was the destination, but then the instructions took him south. After a few kilometres on the A39, he was guided onto a tertiary road, narrow and lined with tall hedges.

A quick glance at the instructions as he drove around a sharp, narrowing bend, then looked up in time to swerve to miss a black-faced sheep in the middle of the road. However, he didn't miss the drainage ditch under the bushes. The road was full of crossing sheep. Standing and I-don't-care-how-much-you-honk sheep, to be more precise. With solid hedges on both sides of the road, he couldn't see where they could have come from.

He got out to inspect the car. Minor scratches on the bumper and hood. No real damage other than losing the security deposit. But he would need help to get out of the ditch. Damn! He punched the roof of the car, the noise startled a few of the closer sheep but not enough to make them clear the road.

One bold sheep stood its ground, staring at him. He quickly dismissed the idea of tying a rope to the animal to make it pull him out. He didn't have rope anyway, which he should buy at the next store. He looked up and down the road. Since he hadn't passed any houses for the last thirty kilometres, he decided to brave the living barricade and try up ahead. Maybe these sheep came with a shepherd. After having his feet repeatedly stepped on, and once needing to rescue the edge of his jacket out of the throat of one overly ambitious animal, he made it to the other side. He walked for several kilometres before he found a farmer with a tractor that could help pull his car back on the road.

It was noon by the time he got on his way again. But a half hour later, the road ended.

He checked the instructions. Checked the map. Reread the instructions again. He knew he was somewhere north of Glastonbury. With so many tertiary roads hiding in high hedges, he must have missed the turnoff. After a tight three-point-turn, he headed back the way he'd come. As long as he found that last turnoff, he'd be all right.

Famous last words?

"This can't be it," Demir said. He felt like a total failure. Abe was right. It's been too long since he'd been an agent in the field.

He had driven up a long, winding lane and that ended outside iron gates surrounding a large estate. The gate was open and there were several cars parked in front of the estate, as well as a large white panel truck.

Holding the clutch and brakes, he stopped the car outside the gate and picked up the note from the seat beside him to reread the last line. *Location. Cottage.* He looked up at the large two-storey stone mansion. A far cry from any kind of cottage he'd ever seen.

"Damn it." He punched the steering wheel.

In vain, he studied the map again but had no idea where he was.

He'd concentrated on the instructions and stopped looking at the map long ago. With a throaty growl, he slapped the map back on the passenger seat and turned the car around. It took all of his self-control to not peel down the lane. He had few options. One was to go back to the B&B in Luton and start again, keeping better track of comparing the cryptic instructions with the map.

Once he reached the road, he geared down and floored it, enjoying the scream of the tires and the gravel spitting out behind him. After a few seconds, he slowed and continued back to the last village he'd gone through. Other than the dry bread and a bottle of water, he hadn't had anything to eat all day. Now he was actually hungry.

Finding a pub, he chose a table in the corner away from the few other patrons. A beer, the beef stew special and his brain would be ready to figure things out again. The waiter brought his order quickly and Demir picked up the fork to eat. He continued to stare at the map. He really didn't want to go all the way back to Luton. He had to figure out where he'd gone wrong. After so many delays, one more day could make a huge difference between rescuing Matt or retrieving the remains.

"Excuse me, sir?"

Demir looked up to see the waiter looking at him concerned.

"Is there a problem with your food?"

"No, why..." he broke off when he realized he'd been sitting for some time, holding his fork, his food untouched. "No, it's fine. I guess I got myself pretty lost." He indicated the map. "Just trying to figure out where I went wrong."

"Many of the tertiary roads are not shown here." The waiter pointed to the map.

"I thought I'd found the road I wanted, but wound up at this mansion instead. Not the cottage I'm looking for."

"Mansion? Which area?"

"I'm not really sure," Demir said. Back tracking from the village, he added, "I think it was around here." The waiter turned the map around to get a better look.

"There are no mansions there. Unless... The only large building that might look like a mansion to you would be the Saint Mary-Margaret. It's an old cottage hospital, converted to extended care after the new one was built in the city."

"Cottage hospital?" Demir nodded, giving the waiter a smile. He hadn't misunderstood the directions after all. At the bottom of the page, the final destination said *Location Cottage* but when he looked at it again, he noticed the letter *H* under it and had dismissed it as a scribble.

"So, tell me more about this hospital."

Demir made it back in record time and stopped just outside the gate. The white panel truck was gone, and the sign was clearly visible on the lawn: Saint Margaret-Mary Long Term Hospital. If he hadn't had such a defeatist attitude the first time, he'd have checked the place better and seen the damn sign. Then, something in his brain might have pieced together the riddle.

He took in as many details as he could. There was a large circular drive with a small parking lot to the right of it, with eight cars. This being Sunday, he could blend in with the visitors. It was a two-storey building, with simple geometric shapes carved on the sides. Ivy grew on the front and from what he could see, on the sides as well.

A wide staircase of ten steps led up to a set of double wooden doors. A wheelchair ramp snaked up the left of the stairs. On the right stood a very white, obviously new trellis. He'd sworn off climbing them after the incident in Texas. But this one looked solid enough to hold his weight. At least there wasn't a huge cactus waiting to break his fall, only green bushes and what looked like crocuses.

A long-term care facility was the perfect place to hide someone. The waiter had told him that this hospital was being closed down and many of the patients had already been moved to larger facilities in Bristol. With fewer patients came the added bonus of a smaller staff.

Demir pulled out a notepad from his back pocket and made a quick sketch of the layout. He eyeballed a few measurements, including distance from the gate to the front door, distance of drop from the second floor to the ground.

He chewed the end of the pencil as he committed everything to memory. For the first time since he'd arrived in England, he felt the confidence that he'd boasted about to Abraham.

He parked in the last spot in the middle of the small lot. Engaged the facial scrambler and got out of the car. He walked past a few families visiting with their elderly relatives. A few children played tag on the lawn. No one paid any attention as he took the steps two at a time. Inside, he hesitated at the activity paused at the number of people inside the high-ceilinged, large foyer. There were groups of people chatting, drinking from old fashioned china cups and saucers. A few gathered around an oblong table, selecting tiny desserts and finger sandwiches. At least they'd be too busy with their tea time to notice him.

There was a staircase leading up to a second floor. A sign with bold lettering that said WARD, was on the wall at the bottom of the stairs.

As casually as his pounding heart would allow, he strolled around the lobby, taking in as may details as possible. The hospital layout was simple. A large lobby, a kitchen, several offices, and a patient monitoring station at the back, made up the first floor. The patients were on the second floor.

Upstairs, he made a beeline for the window over the trellis and unlocked it. Now to check out the ward. It had a total of six beds, no, eight—two were hidden around a corner. Each bed had curtains hanging from the ceiling that could be closed for privacy. He inconspicuously strolled through the ward, checking each bed. Matt was not here.

Next, he checked out the single rooms. He opened the first quietly. A young woman sat holding an elderly man's hand. The old man was wheezing and seemed to be unconscious. Probably on his last breath, he thought sadly. He continued to check each of the rooms. No luck.

What were the odds of having misread the instructions only to wind up at the wrong hospital? Okay, there was that pessimistic attitude again. He hadn't seen the two extra beds in the ward at first, had he? He just needed to keep looking.

On the second trip through the ward, a group of children started fighting over a stuffed bear and who'd give it to their grandfather. While a nurse rushed by to shush up the melee, he headed for the back stairs. He had to get out of the way before someone noticed him wandering around and offered to help him. He glanced over his shoulder to make sure he was in the clear and that's when he saw the alcove with drawn curtains.

He turned from the stairs and slipped inside the curtain, ready to apologize for the intrusion. No visitors here. Just a patient curled up on his side with a tuft of brown hair sticking out from under sheets. Demir moved a bit closer. His heart raced when he recognized the streak of grey near the hairline.

"Dr. Stoddard," Demir whispered, as he pulled back the blanket to reveal his face. "Wake up, sir. It's Demir." The younger man never reacted. He felt for a pulse in his neck. Strong and steady.

Demir was about to shake him awake when the curtain flew open. He spun around ready to explain his presence, only to find a ten-year-old girl staring up at him with big blue eyes and long red curls tied up in pigtails.

"I'm here to see my grandfather," she said. "Who are you visiting?"

Demir was saved by an irate mother coming after her. The woman looked at him and mouthed, "I'm sorry" before she dragged the girl away, scolding, "Maureen, what did I tell you about behaving yourself?"

The last thing he heard was a slap and an "ow!" from the girl.

Closing the curtain he turned back to wake Matt and tell him that rescue was here. He couldn't exactly get him out now, since he had no idea what the staff had been told or if they knew the value of this patient.

He reached to try to shake him awake when the curtain again swished open. He spun around expecting to see the little girl again. Instead, he faced a puzzled nurse.

"Are you a relative?" She asked.

"No," Demir said, as he tried to steady his expression, and forced a pleasant tone. "I came with my wife to visit her grandfather. I let her off at the door so I could park the car, but somehow I lost her."

The nurse gave an understanding smile, and he knew that his bluff had worked. He spoke before she could question him or offer to help find the fictious grandpa.

"She's probably looking for me outside. I'll get out of your way."

He made a quick escape down the front stairs and out of the hospital.

Demir spent the rest of the day and evening stocking up on supplies, food, water, clothes for Matt, and definitely rope. He found a quiet, secluded area to work on the car. Maybe he could get away with the minor scratches but he'd definitely lose the security deposit, maybe even add an extra penalty when the car rental company found out that he'd rewired the headlights to manual control.

CHAPTER TWELVE

At 11:40 p.m., Demir shut off the headlights at the bottom of the road and continued to the hospital. He backed the car into the bushes near the gate. He put the spare key in the ashtray in case he was on the run and didn't have time to take out the key from his pocket.

No outside lights were on. Dressed in black, including a cap to cover his light hair, face smeared with dirt, he was practically invisible in the moonless night. He tuned the facial scrambler to emit a low energy pulse that would hide his heat signature from the CCTV units. Last, he slipped on a pair of leather gloves and got out of the car.

Easily picking the gate's antique lock, he pushed it open a crack and slid through. Keeping low, he ran across the lawn, the crisp night air making the grass crunch under his feet, and reached the trellis unseen. He tested its strength with a solid yank. It held.

He clambered up to the second-floor window, giving silent thanks that no one had locked it during the day. He slipped inside, landing in a crouch. It seemed too dark. Didn't they have a nightlight for the patients?

He put on the night vision glasses and realized that there was a divider in front of the window. Staying low to the floor, he practically crawled through the ward. There was light coming from under a door at the far end. He carefully moved closer to listen. Voices... no, just a vid show.

Several silent footfalls later and Demir crept through the privacy curtains in the alcove. He pulled the blanket off of the patient's face to confirm Matt was still here. How embarrassing would it be to rescue the wrong man?

Yes!

He knelt by the bed and cupped a hand over Matt's mouth. He

whispered, "Dr. Stoddard! It's Tyler Demir. I'm here to get you out."

Nothing. No movement at all. He removed his hand from Matt's mouth and checked for a pulse. Strong. Steady. He shook Stoddard's shoulder. Nothing. Using the penlight, he examined the scientist's eyes. Pupils reacted to the light at least. But he wouldn't be walking out of here.

Demir could easily carry the smaller man but not down the trellis. No choice. It was down the back stairs.

Demir pulled the blanket back, getting ready to lift him, when the light level suddenly increased. He froze. A foot shifted behind him and the curtains swished open.

Demir turned slowly, wondering how he would sweet-talk the nurse dressed the way he was.

He came nose to chest with a huge muscular male instead. Nurse, orderly, porter, that didn't matter. What mattered was the 20 centimetre knife in his hand. Backlit from the open door, the bulk was a mere silhouette. However, thanks to the glasses, Demir could clearly see the toothy grin.

He wasn't going to talk his way past this mountain.

Grin widened. Demir sidestepped the lunging knife, which grazed his sleeve. He dodged left to barely avoid another lunge. He had to move the fight away from Matt. Towards more open floor.

Demir stepped back. The mountain moved to thrust with the knife. Demir grabbed the knife wrist. Pull forward and down. He used the attacker's own momentum against him. The giant somersaulted. Demir held the wrist and landed on the other man's chest. He released the wrist. Grabbed the head and twisted.

Snap!

Breathing heavily, Demir grabbed the man's legs and dragged him back into the room, sat him in the chair in front of the vid screen, shut the door. On the way back to Matt, he picked up the knife and tucked it into his belt. He had to get out before any other interruptions.

He started to lift the scientist when he noticed an intravenous line. Demir peeled the tape back, slid out the needle and firmly pressed the tape back down. The thin pyjamas would be okay in the short run to the car. He had clothes and a blanket waiting there. He slung the scientist over his left shoulder in a fireman carry and hurried down the back stairs. He paused at the bottom and listened.

Voices echoed from a back room. 'Hope they stay occupied,' he thought and dashed for the front door.

The door was locked with a key that was nowhere to be found. He thought about trying to pick it. Not easy and standing out in the open, despite the dark shadows, left him feeling exposed. All the ground floor windows had bars.

It was the back door then. He reached the back and peered around the corner.

And cursed under his breath.

Two female nurses were in a room with monitors that displayed the vitals of several patients. A glass wall looked into the hall. One had her back to him, but the other faced the corridor. They were both relatively old. One was very overweight. Both easy to outrun, but there was no chance in hell of getting by unseen. Their necks would be easy to snap...

He slumped back into the shadows, horrified at that fleeting thought. A distant foghorn sounded and as the echo faded, he regained control of the present. After a moment, he peered around the corner again. Of course, the patient monitors.

Demir laid Matt down under the back staircase out of sight. Quietly, he raced up the main staircase to the ward and searched for the patients connected to the monitors. Choosing the two that were the farthest apart, he disconnected the leads on first one patient, then the other. The monitor alarm pinged here and downstairs. He hid behind a partition near the back stairs just as the nurses hurried in, moving surprisingly fast.

While they were busy with their patients, Demir rushed down the back stairs. He took off the night vision glasses and shoved them into his jacket. No point leaving evidence behind if they fell off when he picked Matt up. He slung the limp form over his shoulder, not too gently and hurried to the back door. It was locked. No, just jammed. A firm shove and he was out. He silently closed it behind him.

The light from inside lit his path and he hurried around to the front.

He ran across the lawn. Slipped through the gate. And unceremoniously threw his prize into the back seat of the car. Got into the driver's seat and started the engine. He drove away slowly. Once he rounded the corner, he turned on the lights and accelerated smoothly back to the main road. Then floored it.

Tyler Demir sped along the dark snaking road, gripping the steering wheel so hard his fingers started to go numb. His heart pounded in his ears. His stomach was turning. His breathing—he remembered to breathe. Then he remembered to calm down. Five kilometres and no sign of pursuit, he pulled over.

Demir kept his foot on the clutch, the car in first gear, then leaned his head on the wheel for a moment. He hadn't felt a rush like this for years. Panting. Pulse racing. Adrenalin pumping. A natural high.

He still hated it.

He reached into the backseat to check for a pulse. Alive. That was something at least. He resumed driving, this time more sanely, towards the port just outside of Brighton.

Demir let out a long, deep sigh as he pulled into the port at 3:50 in the morning. The rescue mission was almost over. The feeling of success vanished when the contact met him.

"I wasn't told one passenger would be sick," Gareth snapped.

"We can hide him in a crate," Demir argued.

"And have him die? No. The trawler captain wouldn't hesitate to kill the second passenger rather than deal with complications."

"I can take care of myself."

"I'm sorry, no." Gareth raised his right hand to stop any more argument.

Demir looked at Matt curled up in a comatose sleep.

"Just get us another boat." Demir turned back to Gareth, his voice commanding. "I can pay more." He slipped the Rolex off his wrist and offered it to him.

"There *are* no other boats in port that I can trust." Gareth pushed the watch away.

There was no point arguing, he realized. Demir took a few steps away, turned his back to Gareth, keeping an eye on Matt, and pulled out his phone.

He was sure Pettigrew wouldn't mind a call at this hour if it meant getting a tidy bonus for setting up different travel plans. The phone was answered after one ring.

"Hello?" A young male voice answered. Probably Pettigrew's son.

"Hi, is your dad home?"

"Just a tic."

Demir heard the boy cover the phone and call, "Ma!" Soon a woman answered.

"Hello. You're asking about my husband? Are you a friend?"

"Yes..." Demir said.

"I'm sorry. But he was in an auto accident yesterday."

"What? Is he all right?"

"He's still at the hospital. The doctors aren't sure if he's going to..." She broke off sobbing. The line went dead.

Demir listened to the silence on the phone, his head spinning with questions. Could it have been an accident or had someone known Pettigrew was meeting him?

Now what? Show up at a boat with Matt slung over his shoulder and ask to book a sightseeing tour. Damn. He really didn't want to risk using Kirby's plans, which so far left a lot to be desired.

Only one option left. He closed the phone, pocketed it and turned to face Gareth.

"How about another favour instead?" Demir asked.

"If I can."

"I might be traced through this car..." He didn't get to finish before Gareth had his own car keys out. Demir traded them for his. "Thanks. I'll leave word where you can pick it up."

"Keep it. It's my brother-in-law's and I don't like him much. He's on the continent for another month. Oh, and don't worry. It's too old for any nav type thing. So you won't be tracked."

"Thanks," Demir said.

"I'll give you a hand," Gareth said.

They moved Matt to the other car. With Gareth's help, they quickly dressed him in sweatpants, a pullover, and socks. Demir slipped a pair of runners on him, sighing with relief when they fit. Gareth rolled up the pyjamas and tucked them under his arm to get rid of them. Demir put his backpack, the map and a couple bottles of water on the passenger seat, thanked Gareth and then headed north to his last chance.

Newcastle. Where Anton lived.

CHAPTER THIRTEEN

Drake admitted to himself that he had been avoiding everyone lately. So immersed in his own issues, he hadn't realized how distant he'd been until he'd run into Laura in the lunchroom yesterday. It wasn't that long ago when they would easily talk about anything and nothing and he actually enjoyed it. Although he didn't crave the company of others, she did. And he had always tried to be available for her when she needed to talk over an idea or a problem.

Friday, in the middle of the night, more precisely three in the morning on Saturday, he'd hoped to make up for his absence in the course of a few scant hours over coffee.

As they returned to their offices, he suggested that she go home to sleep or at least take a nap on the sofa. He doubted she would.

In his own office, he'd tried to concentrate on work but found his mind wandering to Matt, to the project, even to hopeless Elton Chan and his ridiculous accident. Perhaps the change in view might help him. He went home.

After sleeping very little during the night thanks to the dreams that inevitably returned to test his sanity, he finally gave up on sleep and got out of bed mid-morning Saturday.

Might as well get up do some housework, especially laundry, since he was down to his last clean shirt.

He washed, finger combed his hair and dressed quickly. He wondered what his co-workers would say if they saw him wearing paint splattered sweatpants and a red t-shirt with a faded UBC logo on the front and a hole in the armpit. Barefoot, he went downstairs and into the kitchen. He filled the kettle with water and plugged it in to make instant coffee. While waiting for it to boil, he went to the patio door off the kitchen.

Most of the spring snow was gone in the south facing backyard. Soon he'd need to start doing yard work. He made a mental list: rake up the detritus from the decaying leaves that he hadn't removed last fall; trim the hedge; set up the table and chairs on the deck. Maybe this year he'd add flowerpots on the deck to make the backyard more appealing. More cheerful.

Once, in another life, he used to be sociable. Enjoyed having friends come to his home at least once a month for dinner. Then they'd either spend a quiet evening listening to music, watching classic movies, or going out to see some of the recent blockbusters. He'd considered his taste in music eclectic, ranging from old Celtic and English folk songs to new-age jazz. He was even beginning to enjoy electro rap, but could never quite manage to tolerate grunge rock or country music.

Then his home became a house after his brother's death.

He'd wanted to sell the house. He should sell it. He had even approached a real estate agent but backed out just short of listing it. The idea of strangers going through his house, identifying design and decorating weaknesses was intolerable. Or was it more? Could it be remembering sitting in the family room, the fireplace ablaze with golden red warmth as he and his brother roasted chestnuts, laughing at the cliché as they listened to Christmas carols?

Or maybe recalling the night that they'd planned a BBQ and after a few too many pints of ale, he and his brother had decided to arm wrestle. To this day Drake couldn't figure out how they'd managed to knock over the BBQ and spill the coals all over the deck. Miraculously, they'd managed to retrieve the coals before the deck caught fire. He looked out the patio door at the numerous round dots of blackened wood. He'd refused to replace the burnt wood planks. Instead, he re-stained the deck with a clear varnish so that he could always see the scars that reminded him of a happier time.

He hated this place and the happy memories locked into every crevice. For they mingled with the painful memories of that damnable wake after his brother's funeral. Memories of his father's betrayal, portraying him as an impatient, cruel, and pitiless man who had rushed to organize a funeral, then host a party. Perhaps he should consider himself lucky knowing the exact moment that he realized how alone he truly was.

He'd refused to talk about his brother, afraid that verbalizing those memories would make the pain even more intense. He should at least tell Laura. She didn't even know that Thomas had existed, and that was wrong. Perhaps by talking about him it might make the pain of missing him not go away but at least be less prominent. More bearable.

He forced himself away from the patio door and went to the side closet to pull out the upright vacuum cleaner. After one bad incident with a previous robo-vac involving a pair of shoes, he'd gone back to the old-fashioned manual style. He had the cord unwrapped and was about to plug it in when the doorbell rang. He glanced at his watch. Who the devil would be at his door at 8:42 in the morning?

Opening the door, he stared at the sight of Jeanette on his doorstep.

"Good morning," she said, with a slight smile.

"Uh, good morning," he responded. It took a few moments before the cold breeze on his feet registered and he invited her inside. He stepped aside, then shut the door against the cold. She had her boots off and had removed and extended her coat to him. He hung it up in the closet and motioned for her to go ahead into the living room. He took a deep breath, then followed.

She paused to look at the bookshelf and saw her eyebrows rise in surprise at the variety of books and music CDs. She probably assumed he'd have everything digitized and only listened to classical music and read Charles Dickens or Shakespeare. But he'd always like the smell of books and the sound of a music disc slipping into a player, then music coming out of every speaker in the house.

"I was boiling water to make coffee," he offered.

"No, thanks." She glanced over his shoulder at the vacuum. "Looks like I came just in time."

"Excuse me?" He looked behind her in confusion.

"I saved you from house cleaning." She sat down on the sofa facing the fireplace.

He took the armchair facing her.

"How're you doing?" she asked.

"Has there been some development?"

"Not that I've heard." She paused to look around the room. It seemed that it was simply to avoid his gaze. "Look, Drake." She turned back and looked him directly in the eye. "I want to apologize for what I said the other day." When he didn't respond, she added, "When I said I didn't give a shit where you were."

Drake was completely taken by surprise and realized too late that he'd let it show on his face. He didn't even remember the comment. But that was the norm. He rarely listened to anything they said unless it was directly related to work. This had two results: he didn't need to bother with their inane mindless chatter and their insults were rarely heard.

"Quite all right," Drake said, seeing that that was what she wanted to hear.

"We've all been under a lot of pressure since, well, since, you know. Then Demir getting so sick and then Elton breaking his leg in his car accident. He's really upset, being stuck at home with only his thoughts to keep him company."

"I see, and you would like to borrow some books or music?" he asked, not sure what she wanted from him, wishing she would get to the point or to leave.

"No, he has a large collection of books, music, and movies on file. But the problem is being at home all alone." She paused, as though expecting Drake to say something. When he didn't, she continued, "Like I said, he's alone with his thoughts and um, well, he came up with an idea. And, well, he'd like to discuss it with you."

"What idea does he have?" Drake said.

"Well, I think it's better if he talks to you himself," she added.

"I'm sure that he doesn't need me," Drake said, as he shifted to the edge of the chair as though intending to stand, expecting her to take the hint and leave.

"No one *needs* anyone. But no one can be completely alone. We have to work together. We need to get along. We don't have to like each other. But we do need to support each other, especially now."

"Then when you go, please feel free to give him my regards."

"I promised I'd get you there. A few minutes out of your life isn't going to kill you." She settled back into the sofa, looking like she was getting comfortable for a long stay. Looking him up and down, she added, "I'll wait here while you change."

He couldn't understand why she was so insistent. Why was this so important to her? Drake started to say how he was far too busy to go today, perhaps tomorrow. He started to say many things, but knew that she wouldn't leave until he agreed. And other than physically picking her up and carrying her outside, it did not appear as though she would change her mind.

"Very well," he agreed. He hurried upstairs to change. He returned, dressed in jeans and his last clean shirt calling, "Ready."

"Good." She joined him at the front door, as both put on their coats and boots.

Holding the door open for her, he locked it behind them and followed to the driveway. He stopped short as he watched her get into her bodyguard's car.

She smiled saying, "So much easier when we're both going to the same place. Why don't you and your shadow join us, and we'll all go together."

"No, thank you," Drake said as he pointedly turned to the carport and got into his own vehicle. He waited for them to back out of his laneway, then backed out onto the street himself. He watched his own bodyguard back into the lane across the street, ready to pull out in either direction. Drake allowed himself a wry smile; like rats in a maze, the security man had learned quickly and was prepared for Drake's unexpected route changes. Which meant he'd have to come up with some other ploy to annoy his bodyguards.

Arriving at Elton's home, Drake let Jeanette and her guard park in the driveway first, leaving himself an open path of escape. Jeanette got out of her car, carrying a potted African violet and a wrapped present. She headed up the path to the front door with Drake trailing reluctantly behind. She rang the doorbell, then opened the door and walked in calling, "Knock, knock. We're here to visit."

"Hello," Elton called.

Drake and Jeanette took off their boots and after she hung up her coat in the front closet, she reached for Drake's. He hesitated.

"Don't worry, no one expects you to stay long. But let's not make it obvious."

With a sigh, he reluctantly surrendered his jacket. She picked up the present, handed it to Drake as she picked up the plant and led the way into the living room. The room was small, but the large picture window made it bright and—yes—cheery. There was a low table under the window with a variety of plants, though most were various types of African violets. Obviously his favourite plant.

"Welcome..." Elton began, but broke off at the sight of Drake.

"No, don't worry, hell didn't freeze over," she said, with a laugh.

Drake watched Elton's face flush slightly. Drake wanted to assure him that there was no need for embarrassment. He was quite aware that they said things behind his back and that he didn't care. He remained silent.

Jeannette went to the window, shifted a few pots around then added the new plant.

"Thank you. It's beautiful," Elton said.

Drake started to hand the gift to her, when she added, "And Drake brought you a little something too. Chocolates, didn't you say?"

She looked at him, with an innocent smile. Caught off guard by the comment and the smile, he silently handed the box to Elton, who ripped it open immediately.

"*Turtles*! My favourite!" Elton gave Drake a wide smile as he said, "How did you know?"

"Maybe," Jeanette said, as she sat on the facing sofa, "when you don't talk much, you listen more? A lesson you could take."

"I don't talk a lot," Elton said, sounding indignant. Then more sheepishly, added, "Maybe."

"Yes." Jeanette looked at Drake, who was still standing. She patted the sofa beside her and said, "Have a seat."

"Yes, please make yourself at home," Elton said, as he opened the box and offered it to his guests. After Jeanette took one and Drake declined, he sampled one piece, eyes closing in ecstasy as he chewed it slowly.

Drake was amazed at such a reaction for a small piece of chocolate. Maybe he should have tried one.

"Tea. I'll make tea," Elton said, as he started to get up, wincing with pain as he reached for his crutches.

"Sit down!" Jeanette said, pushing him back into his armchair and adjusting the pillow under his cast. "I'll make it." She left, mumbling, "Some people just don't know how to be take care of themselves. Always trying to do too much. Always bugging the crap..." her voice faded.

"The bones are responding to the meds," Elton called after her. To Drake he said, "I reacted to the usual drugs they use, so they've had to go to the older type. It'll take a little longer for the bones to heal, but should be back to normal in a couple of weeks. Three at the most."

"That's very good to hear," Drake said, feeling so uncomfortable left alone with Elton and his open and friendly smile. But she'd moved so quickly that Drake didn't have the opportunity to volunteer to make the tea. He just was not good at chitchat for the sake of talking.

"Thank you for the gift," Elton said, offering him a chocolate again.

This time Drake couldn't resist taking one. Partly from curiosity but mostly to have something to do other than talk. Though his reaction was somewhat less dramatic, he had to admit that the chewy and crunchy combination was delicious. Elton's openly grateful smile made Drake explain the real source of the gift.

"It was Jeanette..."

"I know," Elton interrupted. "She knows me so well and gave you the idea."

"No, she bought..."

"She does love to shop," he interrupted again. "Another?" He extended the box.

Drake sighed. There was not point trying to correct the misconception. It was Jeanette's fault anyway. What was she trying to do, make him appear more human? He liked his inhuman, isolated personality that he'd spent years and great effort setting up.

Noticing the box was still extended, he sighed again and took another chocolate. As he enjoyed the taste dissolving on his taste buds, he wondered if perhaps he could be returning to his old sociable self. He looked around the room. It was simply decorated with a sofa and armchair. There was a built-in floor to ceiling shelving unit with a variety of sculptures ranging from the Ming Dynasty to the modern era by the popular artist, Genomyte. And of course, the table with the numerous African violets. Drake had never imagined there were so many varieties and colours. One looked like a climbing ivy, while another was reminiscent of the decaying spider plant over the sink at Cyber. Those two, as well as the strange coloured ones, were probably genetically modified.

He turned back and noticed Elton watching him. Clearing his throat, Drake said, "Nice place you have."

"Thank you," Elton said.

To Drake's relief, Jeanette came out of the kitchen just then. She set a tray with three mugs, milk, and sugar on the table and handed a mug first to Elton, then picked up the other two, handing one to Drake as she sat down beside him. All three took their tea black and Drake wondered why she'd bothered with the milk and sugar. Habit, perhaps? That was what he used to do when he had company over, knowing how each took their tea or coffee but always putting out the condiments.

Yes, the memory of entertaining friends was coming back. Could he get used to this? He realized he was only half listening when a phrase broke through his daydreams.

What did they say? Elton's accident wasn't an accident?

"How many times do I have to remind you that squirrels get out of the way?" Jeanette was saying. "They always do."

"Beg to differ."

"Like I said, it wasn't an accident. It was a moment of stupidity."

Ah, Drake thought, no great revelations of espionage. Just Elton's idiocy getting him into trouble, just as he'd told Laura Jessup. He started to drift back into himself, mentally calculating the impedance across a cell membrane when Matt's name tore him from his sanctuary.

"I know the military thinks Yamaguchi is the prime suspect," Jeanette said, "but like I said before, he's not into kidnapping. It has to be someone else."

"Who'd want to hurt Matt?"

"They won't hurt him. Not on purpose," Drake said. He'd spoken without thinking. No harm done. Only now, he had their attention. "They want his knowledge, they will take care of him to protect the information he possesses."

"Who do you think took him?" Elton asked.

"Many countries have engaged in industrial espionage," Drake said. "At the moment, the Chinese seem to be the most likely. They are expanding their technology by stealing or bribing what they can." He paused and looked at Elton, adding quickly, "No offence."

"No offence. I know," Elton said. He waved his hand dismissively.

"But is it likely that they would kidnap someone?" Jeanette asked.

"Not usually," Drake said, "but this research may have actually been too good to pass up, since we're in an underground facility with limited access. Which meant theft wasn't an option."

"So how would anyone know what research we're doing?" Jeanette said.

"But why take Matt? He doesn't have that much experience. Not like the rest of us."

"Don't forget it was really Drake they were after," Jeanette said.

"Yes, let's not forget," Drake said, his voice monotone. This was his cue to leave. Putting his mug on the coffee table, he stiffly got to his feet. "Thank you for the tea. Hope you feel better soon, Chan."

"Wait!" Jeannette stood and blocked his escape. "I know—I mean we both know that you feel bad. And I wasn't trying to make you feel worse."

Drake stepped around her, but she grabbed his arm with surprising strength.

"We didn't invite you here just to visit Elton."

"But it's nice that you came," Elton added quickly.

"Why am I really here?"

"Okay," she said, taking a deep breath. She let go of his arm and continued. "You were the original target. And, uh, well, we were thinking that you would be the best one to help us find out who's responsible."

"How?" Drake's curiosity held him in place.

"Well, if you were out walking around. You know, maybe in the south end market. Browsing in all the shops, then maybe who ever was responsible, well, they'd try again."

Drake blinked at her. His mouth opened to speak. When no words came to him, he looked at Elton. He was shocked to see an expectant smile on the other man's face. Finally, he found the words he needed.

"Are you serious? You want me to be a target? Allow myself to be kidnapped?"

"But there's no danger. You've got your security guard. And we'd be there, with our guards, right?" She looked at Elton, who nodded eagerly. "So that means you'd have three guards there. To watch you."

He wanted to scream at them. Ask if they were crazy. Ask if they really hated him that much. Instead, he took a step back. Kept his voice calm.

"I hope you feel better soon, Chan. Thank you for the tea." Then he calmly walked to the front door.

He put on his boots, grabbed his jacket and carrying it in his hand, was out the front door before they could call him back. He revelled in the icy wind cutting through his shirt as he hurried to his car. So that was the new idea that Elton had come up with. He thought it had to do with work. As he got in, the ache in his heart turned to anger.

This was why he never listened when others chattered on about their lives. Jeanette had caught him in a weak moment today. Fatigue and guilt at what he'd done were beginning to exact a price.

He turned the ignition and slammed the control into reverse and squealed out of the driveway. He sped down the street, away from the happy people inside that had each other to get through this hellish time.

He slid around the corner before his bodyguard had even started moving. He glanced in the rear-view mirror and for a fleeting few seconds, he was alone. Free. Then, all too soon, the other car fishtailed into view and closed the gap between them.

So, the rats in the maze had not learned their lessons after all.

Drake allowed a shadow of a smile on his face.

After Laura had run into Drake in the lunchroom a few hours ago, she had thought he'd returned to his old self. He seemed more empathetic than usual, and they'd chatted, or sat in silence with a familiar comfort of two people who were very close. She could see him trying very hard to cheer her up and get her mind off of everything that had happened.

It was almost six by the time both had left the lunchroom. She should have taken his advice to go home, but by that time the caffeine buzz had kicked in.

This was the time to get caught up on reading. Almost every flat surface in her office was home to stacks of files, scientific journals, and papers. One of the jobs she had was to keep on top of all research and that was helped by the library doing a monthly literature survey for her. Scanning the abstracts, she would then order hardcopy papers that looked promising.

She picked up one journal at random: *Developments in Neuroscience and Nanotechnology*. It was four months old. Judging from the mess, there was more than four months of surveys here. The library kept trying to get her to work with the abstracts online, but she preferred the hardcopies. Having everything spread out helped her see things more clearly.

She spent the day scanning the journals and organizing them. And Edna had spent the day supplying her with coffee, snacks, lunch, as well as taking away the sorted stacks that held no valuable information.

Starting on the last stack on top of the file cabinet, Laura paused when Edna came in with a fresh mug of coffee.

"Nice and strong the way you like it," Edna said, handing her a cup.

"Thanks," Laura said, taking a sip. It actually was strong. She gave her a proud smile as she waved her hand with a flourish at her office. "So, what do you think?"

"Impressive."

"And after I finish this pile," Laura put her mug on the desk and reached for the top journal, "this will look like an office again instead of a storage room."

"I think the rest can wait," Edna said, taking the journal from Laura and replacing it on the cabinet. "It's after 5:00. You've put in more than twelve hours. Two days, if you count spending the night. Time to go home."

"Oh my," Laura said, looking at her watch. She'd completely immersed herself in what she was doing, never noticing the passage of time. "Thank you so much for helping out. I doubt I could have done so much without you."

"That's my job. Now, as your friend, how about I take you out for dinner?"

"Thank you, but I think I'm just going to go home. I'm sure my plants miss me," Laura said, with a laugh. "Besides, it's the weekend and I think I could use some alone time. Recharge my energy. How about you, any plans?"

"Oh, the usual," Edna said, heading out the door. "See you Monday."

Laura smiled as her secretary closed the door behind her. Hands on hips, she admired her office with a great feeling of accomplishment. And to think she'd spent the entire day completely immersed in the science she loved and never once thought about Matt Stoddard.

Her arms fell limp by her sides as the smile vanished. Damn. How could she have so callously forgotten what might be happening to her colleague and friend? She slipped on her boots, shrugged into her coat, grabbed her purse and left.

At home, she warmed up some leftover stew and ate in silence in her kitchen, trying to mentally wind down. Three quarters of the way through supper and more than halfway to a feeling of calm, the sharp ring of the phone startled her. She'd have to change that ring tone.

"Hello?"

"Hello, Dr. Jessup." It was Edna.

"Did something happen?" Laura asked, as she braced for bad news, but hoped for good.

"Just checking to see that you got home okay," Edna said. Her voice sounded tinny and far away.

"Yes," Laura said, relaxing but feeling annoyed at the interruption that brought empty hope for a brief moment.

"How about I come over? We can make popcorn and check out the latest movie releases on the net."

"What?" That, she wasn't prepared for. She answered politely, "Maybe some other time. I was just about to call it an early night. See you Monday." And she hung up before Edna could say anything more.

Of all the daily phone calls at home this week to check if she needed something, this one was the strangest. Normally very perceptive, Edna seemed to have forgotten about her plans to have a quiet weekend of alone time. Appetite gone, she put the last of the stew in the fridge and got ready for bed.

Slipping in between the cool sheets, she fluffed the pillows behind her and sat up pulling the blanket up to cover her legs. Reading in bed usually relaxed her, so she scanned through the tablet for something. She passed on the mystery novel, she had enough questions right now; passed on the romance, why remind herself what she was missing; and settled for a nice quiet science fiction novel dealing with the discovery of new worlds devoid of any of the reality of her life.

The first paragraph dealt with the intrepid space travellers landing on a planet and being slaughtered by the war-like alien inhabitants. She shut off the tablet with a grunt.

On Sunday morning, after a fitful night of vivid nightmares, Laura got out of bed. She pulled back the curtains to find the sun rising out of its own bed. She took a long, leisurely shower, then dressed in comfortable jeans and a baggy t-shirt. Barefoot, she padded downstairs to put on coffee and toast. With the radio tuned to a classical station, she ate her breakfast.

Once finished, she made an executive decision not to clean up after breakfast. She'd spend the morning in the living room listening to music and relaxing. Getting comfortable on the sofa, she tuned her wall screen first to a majestic waterfall. The roaring crashing water wasn't inspiring the mood she wanted. After scanning through the nature selections, she settled on a view of aerial flight over snow capped mountain. She remembered how she used to ski and should make time for those activities she used to love before becoming absorbed in work.

The doorbell woke her from a sleep she hadn't realized she'd drifted into. She glanced at her watch and was impressed that she finally did get some dreamless rest. It was almost 12:30. She opened the door expecting to see one of the neighbours or maybe even her bodyguard. Instead, she found Edna, carrying a large casserole dish, standing at the door.

She stared at her secretary for a moment. She finally remembered her manners and invited her in.

"I made a vegetarian lasagna for you." Edna slipped off her low-heel pumps and carried the box into the kitchen.

Laura shut the door and followed to the kitchen as Edna put the dish on the counter.

"You've been looking a bit pale lately and haven't been eating properly," Edna said. She took off the lid. "Still hot. These new casserole dishes are amazing."

"I've been eating." Laura was always amused at Edna's maternal ways.

"Drive-through doesn't count."

"You following me or something?" Laura said, with a laugh, remembering yesterday's lunch.

Edna's smile flickered for a moment, then brightened as she answered, "No, I just know you well. Would you like some?"

"It does smell wonderful. As long as you join me," Laura said. She took out two plates from the cupboard as Edna took out a large knife and serving spoon from the second drawer.

Laura set the counter with napkins and glasses, as Edna placed two small portions in the plates. Edna then got the milk from the fridge, smelt it, and wrinkled her nose.

"How about wine instead?" Laura asked.

"Sounds good," Edna said, returning the milk to the fridge. Before Laura could get around her, Edna opened the pantry, pulled out a bottle of red wine, placed it on the counter, and opened the third drawer to get the bottle opener.

Laura sat on one barstool, realizing for the first time how at home Edna was here. In the past, it had been a comfort, but now it felt strange. Out of place. A bit creepy. Pouring the Merlot, Edna took the other barstool. They clinked glasses and Edna sipped, while Laura drained her glass without meaning to, only to have it refilled before she even put it back on the counter.

Edna started chatting about the weather and how once the snow was gone, cleaning up the backyard was going to be a big job. Then she continued on saying things like "We'll have to rake the lawn well, to stimulate the roots," also, "We'll turn the soil in the garden, get it ready for planting," and "We'll have a big job cleaning all those windows."

Annoyed, Laura tuned out the list of chores 'we' had to do. Yes,

Edna seemed to be trying very hard to reassert herself back into her life. The old maternal instinct kicking in perhaps. And while she'd been grateful for Edna's support when she'd truly needed it years ago, she was a stronger person now.

Noting that Edna had long since finished the minuscule lasagna portion on her plate, Laura ate quickly and had barely put the fork down before Edna scooped in another serving. Out of politeness more than hunger, she managed to eat about a third of the serving. Her second glass of wine she left on the counter.

With help from Edna, the counter was cleared, dishes stacked in the dishwasher, lasagna covered and put into the fridge.

"Thank you, it was delicious. I'll get the casserole dish back to you this week."

"No hurry," Edna said picking up the wine bottle. "Some more?"

"No, no thank you. I'll just work on this one. But help yourself."

"Thanks, but I'm driving," Edna said.

"Driving?" Laura laughed. "I've never seen you even touch the controls."

"That's true." Edna laughed and poured herself a third of a glass before corking the bottle and returning it to the cupboard. Raising her glass, she said, "Here's to whoever invented self-driving cars." They clinked glasses and both sipped a bit more wine. Then she turned to face Laura with a clap of her hands. "How about I give you a hand with the house cleaning?"

"There really isn't much to do. I have a service come in every couple of weeks."

"Really?" Edna asked.

"I work long hours and really don't want to clean when I'm home," Laura said. She was irritated by that one word. She resented feeling that an explanation was necessary.

"Relaxing is much nicer," Edna said, giving her a smile. She looked at the pile of laundry in the armchair. It had been there so long that Laura had stopped seeing it days ago.

"You relax and I'll fold the laundry for you," Edna said.

"Really," Laura began, "that's not necessary..."

"I don't mind helping you. Besides, it's been a tough week for everyone, and I hate seeing you this way. Let me help, please?"

"Sure," Laura agreed, reluctantly. She had to admit that she'd been on edge this week. If anyone could see it, it would be Edna.

As Edna worked, they chatted, this time with Laura joining in, about the newest movies coming out and whether or not they'd bother making time to see them. They even talked about the environmental cleanups going on worldwide that were managing to hold back the worst effects of climate change. Though snowstorms late into the spring were becoming normal.

Laundry folded, Laura remained on the sofa guilt free as Edna went upstairs to the bedroom to put the clothes away.

Taking a small sip of wine, enjoying the quiet, Laura's mind drifted to Matt and to Demir. She drained the glass without noticing. It wasn't until she saw the empty glass that she realized what she'd done. She put the glass down and stretched her legs out on the sofa. If she wasn't careful, she'd be drunk before supper time. She closed her eyes, trying a deep breathing exercise to help her relax. It was working until she realized the passage of time. Edna had been upstairs a long time.

She got up to see if Edna needed help finding where things went. Part way up the stairs, she called out to her. Almost immediately, Edna appeared at the top of the stairs, a stiff smile on her face, as she smoothed her sweater with both hands.

"Sorry, I just had to use your bathroom," Edna said, coming down the stairs and pausing when she met up with Laura.

"That's okay," Laura said, as she turned and went back down the stairs. Heading towards the sofa, Edna stopped by the door.

"I should get to the grocery store," Edna said.

"Oh." She returned to the door. "Thank you for dropping by with lunch. And for helping with the laundry."

"Of course, anytime. Would you like me to pick up something for you at the store?"

"No thank you," Laura answered, a little too quickly. She tried to cover her tone with a smile.

"All right then," Edna said. She put on her coat and shoes. Gave another smile then opened the door to leave.

"Thanks again for lunch," Laura said. Edna waved as she got into her car.

Shutting the door, Laura retrieved her book, put on a fresh pot of coffee and settled back on the sofa to finish reading. The last thought she had as she turned on the reader was that she'd have to speak to Edna on Monday. Sure Edna's maternal instinct was running at top speed since Matt Stoddard disappeared. As much as Laura appreciated her concern, she really didn't appreciate the constant invasion of her personal time. First thing Monday morning, she vowed.

Edna started up the car, backed out of the driveway a bit faster than she'd planned, then drove away, a bit more sedately. It was a nice afternoon: sunny, mild, the snow was melting. The perfect day to have spent it outside, not cooped up the first half of the day cooking lasagna. Then a good part of the afternoon engaged in lame conversation. She'd rather have spent her time off, doing her own stuff.

But it couldn't really be helped, could it? Laura had been growing more distant. There was a time when she confided everything in her, thinking of her as more than a secretary. Considering her a friend.

Edna had almost blown it with that slip about eating fast food, but Laura hadn't been too concerned by it. Now more than ever, Edna had to work on getting that closeness back because she knew Laura wasn't confiding in her about the little things anymore.

And definitely not the big things.

She reached into her sweater pocket, pulled out the e-pad and tossed it on the seat. If Laura hadn't interrupted her, she would have finished searching through the pad for something of importance. Not a problem. She'd go through it tonight, then sneak it into Laura's office tomorrow. Considering the stress Laura had been under this week, she knew that the young woman wouldn't even remember that she'd taken it home.

Sunday evening and still no word from Demir.

Abraham paced a trench in the carpet outside Kirby's office. He knew the major was in the building because that's the only thing the beefy corporal, seated outside the office, would admit.

He'd been waiting since 7:00 p.m. It was now 8:37. To work off the growing anger, as well as the urge to pick a fight with the secretary who had fifty kilograms and several centimetres on him, Abraham waited. And paced. And cursed. He even chanted a quiet mantra of "I won't yell or punch Kirby when he finally arrives." But he also wasn't leaving without answers this time.

"What an unexpected pleasure," Kirby said, coming up behind him. He took a message e-pad from the corporal, then ushered Abraham into his office.

Abraham's barely controlled anger snapped at the smug smile. "Where is he? It's been almost two days and he hasn't checked in. What's gone wrong? And don't try to give me the run around this time!"

"I was just coming from the communications room in fact. There's been a delay. He's still waiting at the hotel for our overseas agent. Everything's fine."

"Fine? God damn you! I spent most of the night keeping his head out of the toilet while he puked his fucking guts out, thanks to you. And now you expect me to believe you?"

"It was just a tranquillizer that his stomach reacted to. Your doctor thought he had a touch of food poisoning. It all worked out in the end."

"I want to talk to him myself."

"You know that's not possible." Kirby finally looked up from the messages. "The plan is…"

"Simple, yeah, I know. I want to talk to him myself!"

"As I was saying," Kirby continued, sounding impatient. "The plan is for him to send out a coded message when he gets Stoddard. Do you really want to jeopardize the entire mission just to satisfy your curiosity?"

"Damn you." His voice barely escaped through clenched teeth. Abraham took a step forward, fists clenched, then stopped. Kirby's only reaction was a slightly straighter posture.

"You're not worth the energy," Abraham said. He turned, slammed open the door and charged out.

It was his own fault. He should have worked out their own method to stay in contact. But everything had happened so quickly.

He stopped mid-step on the way to the elevator. Kirby said that Demir was to maintain comm silence and only send out a message when he found the scientist. So how the hell did Kirby know there was a delay and that Demir was still at the hotel? He considered going back and beating an answer out of him. Other than an extreme sense of satisfaction, it wouldn't get him any answers—not before the corporal rushed in. Abraham would get his own answers through his own sources.

He punched the elevator button, grumbling all the way down to the parking garage, where he stormed out to his car. There were a lot of things to be taken care of when he got Demir back home. Top of the list, get rid of Kirby and his control over Cyber's security.

Around the corner from the elevators hidden in the shadows, Sandrovsky waited until Abraham's car squealed out of sight. He took the elevator up and asked to see Major Kirby. The corporal waved him in.

"Why are you here?" Kirby asked, frowning.

Obviously Kirby wasn't pleased to see him. He wouldn't have come at all if he hadn't really believed it was an emergency. He took a deep breath before speaking.

"Well," Sandrovsky said, hesitated for a couple of seconds. "I've been trying to get a hold of you, you know. So, when I overheard Mr. Abraham saying he was coming to see you, I followed."

"Why are you here?" Kirby repeated. His frown deepened.

"Well, Mitchell hasn't called in and when I called Mr. Henderson's house and…"

"You have a reason for bothering his wife at home, worrying her?" Kirby's voice was low and even, but it sure as heck felt like he'd shouted.

Sandrovsky thought about finishing his sentence. He wasn't military.

And he knew he wasn't smart. But he knew when to keep his mouth shut.

"All I asked you to do was have someone drive him home. Now you're trying to turn this into some big case." Then Kirby's tone turned polite. A bit too polite. "I can tell you this much. Henderson is out of town, on assignment. His wife's already been told, though she doesn't know details—for reasons of national security. It sounds like your man has gone with him. I'll check into it. Now, do you remember what I told you yesterday?"

"To not tell anyone?"

"That's right. Thanks for coming in."

"But sir," Sandrovsky insisted. "What about Mitchell's wife? She's pregnant. Due any day." Sandrovsky waited for a reaction. Nothing but a couple of blinks. He was being dismissed. Had he done the right thing not telling Abraham that Mitchell was overdue? But he was just following orders, right? Reluctantly, he said, "Thank you, sir."

Outside the office, he watched the corporal give him the same blinking gaze. Must be military lingo for 'No comment.' Or maybe 'Get the heck outta here.'

No, he knew that there was no doubt it really meant, 'You've been fucked, so leave.'

Once Sandrovsky had left, Kirby called for the corporal.

"How's the search for Henderson and his man going?" Kirby asked.

"We've been trying to find out why they were on the River Parkway. Nothing so far."

"Damn," Kirby said, rubbing his forehead. "Keep me informed of any developments." When the corporal left, closing the door behind him, Kirby rested his head in his hands trying to think.

There was a chance Henderson was going to meet someone. But who? And where the hell was Demir? They knew that he had the scientist and a nameless goon had been killed. But they never made it to the boat. Kirby wasn't too worried though. When the chips were down, he knew Demir wouldn't leave Matt Stoddard behind with all those secrets in his head.

CHAPTER FOURTEEN

Abraham grumbled as he passed the security check on the surface, then again while waiting for the elevator. On Sub 1, he growled something unintelligible at the man who tried to ask how he was. He slammed his office door shut behind him.

No one with any sense of self-preservation would think of bothering him when he was in a foul mood. And he was sure he looked more foul now than he had ever been in his life.

He tried to pace some of the fury out but thanks to the small office, four steps in each direction didn't calm him. No amount of pacing would change the fact that he'd let Demir go off with only Kirby's word that he'd have proper backup. His instincts had screamed not to let him go alone. Too late to change the fact that he'd ignored his instincts, but maybe not too late to save his friend.

Demir would never approve of his contacting the FBI. But Henry was a friend. More importantly, he could be trusted. They'd met by accident, early in both their careers: Abraham working a money laundering operation that he'd tracked to Detroit; Henry working the same case but from a different angle. Rather than fighting over jurisdiction, they'd shared information and brought down the perp on the harsher charge of murder—it made Henry's case and career. He sat down and dialled the old familiar number.

The call was answered on the third ring.

"Hi Henry, it's Abe."

"Son of a gun. How the hell are you?"

"Can't complain."

"I hear you lost one of your egg-heads. And you think it's got something to do with Yamaguchi."

"You hear anything else that I *don't* know?" Abraham asked. Apparently, the other man was damn good at finding out facts. Or maybe Kirby's security just plain sucked.

"Forget Yamaguchi," Henry said. "His game is to try to bribe to get what he can then steal the rest. He's not into kidnapping."

"We figured one of our senior scientists was the actual target."

"Yup, Drake was on his shopping list. He figured with Drake's dislike for all the secrecy, he'd be easy to recruit."

Abraham bit back an audible reaction. How the hell would anyone know about that?

Henry continued, "But Yamaguchi was willing to settle for the young guy. Word is he was really pissed when someone else got to Stoddard first and actually *took* him."

"Any ideas?"

"I put out a couple of feelers and came up with a very short list. Got a pen?" He asked but didn't wait for an answer. "There's Leung from China, Prud'homme from France and Thakar from India. Hell, who wouldn't be interested? Who wants doctors opening up your skull then poking around in your brain when you can have one tiny chip put in with a simple injection?"

"I see," Abraham said, managing to keep the surprise out of his voice. No one should have known exactly what the research at Cyber was. Shit! No one, not even Henderson, knew details about the work. Just generalities. But Henry mentioned it as though it was common knowledge. Looked like he needed to keep in better touch with Henry. Apparently, it was the best way to find out what secret activity was going on in Canada.

"Seems the Chinese are the best candidates," Henry continued. "Our sources indicate that someone was selling Drake to the highest bidder. But too late, they discovered they got the wrong guy. Your boy might be smart but I doubt he would have brought in the same price as Drake. Just doesn't have the years in or the experience."

"Any idea where Stoddard is now?" Abraham asked.

"Last anyone heard he was hidden away at some private hospital, though the staff didn't know who he really was. Actually, we're not sure why he was there in the first place. But someone took him out of there recently. Only casualty was a guard. All interested parties are keeping their ears open and are still looking for him. Looks like we have an outside player on the scene."

Abraham knew the outside player had to be Demir. The dead guard meant Demir got away. So where the hell were they now?

"You need to check out that list. I'd put my money on the Chinese," Henry finished.

"Thanks," Abraham said, and hung up.

If something went wrong with Kirby's plans, Demir would take the scientist, run for the nearest shore, and hitch a ride on anything that could float. He'd send word when they were safe. Which meant that he wasn't in the clear yet.

Abraham started tapping his pen on the top of his desk. Where the hell were they? He abruptly stopped tapping and tossed the pen down. He checked his watch. Almost ten at night. He hoped it wasn't too late to call Cyber's medical doctor at home.

"Hello?" The voice was groggy. Guess it was too late.

"Doc Owen, sorry I woke you, it's Abraham."

"Has he been found?" Owen sounded fully awake now.

"I'm sorry, no. I just wanted to ask you a question. With all of Dr. Stoddard's drug sensitivity, if he reacted to some drug and it didn't kill him, would it take time for him to be able to—let's say—travel on his own?"

"Umm..." He could visualize Owen rubbing his eyes, trying to make sense of the question. Finally, the doctor answered, "Matthew has the most problem with anaesthetics. They could put him in a coma at the best, stop his heart at the worst. So yes, being given something like that would incapacitate him for several days. Why are you asking?"

"Thank you. Sorry I woke you." Abraham hung up, cutting off the doctor as he started to ask a new question.

They were probably laying low until Matt recovered enough to travel. What if he needed medical attention?

Damn it! Why didn't they work out their own backup plan? Why did Abraham agree to stay at his house—in case of visitors? Who the fuck was stupid enough to come by and visit at midnight? He should have gone with him to the airport and on the way forced a plan to be made. But Demir had insisted he stay at the house. As he'd practically crawled into the cab insisting that he still had enough contacts there that could help out in a pinch. "Don't worry" were Demir's last words before closing the cab door.

Don't worry? What good were those out of date contacts going to do now?

No wait. Not all the contacts were out of date.

Demir had told him a story years ago about something that had happened on his first overseas undercover mission, when he'd run into a Russian scientist fleeing with his young daughter. He'd helped them reach England. As far as he knew, Demir had kept in touch. It was a long shot.

Abraham booked the next flight to the UK, which unfortunately was the red-eye to Heathrow. He would have preferred going straight to Newcastle, but by the time he factored in the driving, he would still arrive several hours before the direct flight. He had two hours to get to the airport. More than enough time.

He jotted down a few notes then left for the squad room, in search of someone to leave in charge. The most senior was Sandrovsky, but damned if he'd leave him in charge of his cat's litter box, even if he owned a cat. And McGuire was too volatile, among other things. Besides, he preferred to have someone from his own shift. He knew each of them well. In the squad room, he looked around at his people. There, working on a computer terminal in the corner, was the right person for the job. Level headed and tough. He went over to her.

"Hi, Wallingford," he said.

"Hi, Abe." She looked up at him, her blue eyes full of concern. "How's Demir doing?"

"The same." At close to six feet tall, Wallingford was an imposing woman. But she was also very empathetic. A lot like Demir, in fact. There was no doubt. She was the best choice.

"I need to be away for a few days. I'm placing you in charge till I get back."

"Sure, Abe, I can keep the squad in line," she said, with a grin.

"I mean of all of I.S. Listen," he leaned closer and lowered his voice. "I'll be out of touch. I need you to keep things running and make excuses.

Say what you need to. You'll be on your own. Clear?" He handed her the notes he'd made.

She looked at him for a moment. He could see understanding in her eyes. She said, "You bet."

Straightening up, he announced, "Listen up, everyone." They all stopped what they were doing and paid attention. "I'm leaving Wallingford in charge of I.S. till I get back. If I hear about anyone giving her grief, you'll answer to me and also Demir—when he gets better." Seeing everyone nod, he turned back to Wallingford and added, "Good luck!"

She stood up to watch him leave, concern on her face. As he slowly closed the door behind him, he listened.

"Hey, Wall, congrats."

"So, you giving us the day off?"

"Don't forget, you buy the first three rounds."

"Okay, fun time is over," Wallingford said. She sounded commanding as she added, "Get back to work!" A short pause and she said, "And the rule is only *one* round of drinks."

Feeling comfortable with her in charge, Abraham returned to his office. He sent a quick note to Yasmin to make the temporary transfer of command official. From the top right desk drawer, behind a fake panel, he pulled out a credit card with the name Manny Kline and a passport with the same name.

He got a backpack from the bottom drawer of his file cabinet. Inside he had a change of clothes and some ready US cash. From the top drawer of the cabinet, he took out a Rolex watch and replaced the durable Shinrai he wore. It could be useful in a quick trade. Before he closed the drawer, he grabbed the roll of duct tape and tossed it into his backpack. Duct tape, the undercover man's first aid for bullet holes. He hurried to the elevator.

When the elevator doors opened, he came face to face with Sandrovsky.

"Abe," Sandrovsky began, as he stepped out of the elevator, "can I talk to you…"

"Later, when I get back." Abraham pushed past him and repeatedly hit the close door button, cutting off Sandrovsky's protests.

CHAPTER FIFTEEN

Twenty years ago, Demir had been on his first overseas assignment: following the money trail of a drug shipment to Norway. There he discovered Anton and his teenage daughter hiding out near the docks. An electrical engineer, Anton had paid all he had to have people smuggle him and his daughter out of Russia, only to be abandoned at the port in Norway. Penniless, they had no choice but to hide and figure out their next step.

Always a sucker for abandoned strays, Demir had put them up in a hotel until after his mission. Then, with the help of a friend with a boat, had got them safely to England and a new life.

Demir kept in touch with occasional letters and phone calls. The last time he'd visited Anton, his daughter, and her twin boys was five years ago. He shook his head, realizing that that was also the last time he'd taken a real holiday. Anton had constantly reminded him that he owed Demir everything. And Demir had always shrugged off the gratitude. But now, he'd call in that debt. They needed a place to hide while Matt recovered.

On his route north to Newcastle, Demir used his disposable sat to call Anton, saying he'd be there by noon. He kept the details sketchy, saying only that he had a sick companion that needed medical help. Discreet help. Anton assured him a trustworthy doctor would be there.

After driving almost two hours, he thought he heard Matt gasping for breath. He exited the M1 and pulled over on a quiet road to check on the unconscious man in the back seat. Demir pulled him into a sitting position, noticing the slight muscle tension as he sat up. He wasn't as limp as before, which had to mean the scientist was gradually waking up. Ignoring first aid basics of not giving liquids to an unconscious person,

Demir grabbed a bottle of water from the front seat and trickled a few drops of water into the other man's mouth.

Relieved to see the younger man swallow, he trickled in a bit more. This time, Matt swallowed most of it, while the rest dripped down his chin. At least he wouldn't die from dehydration, he thought, wiping the dribble with the corner of the blanket. He checked the pulse. Strong, but fast. He didn't know what that meant but at least it was beating.

"Just hang in there a little longer," he whispered, as he lay the scientist back down and adjusted the blanket around his shoulders. Still six hours from Newcastle, he got back on the M1 and continued north.

"Almost there," Demir called over his shoulder, not actually expecting an answer. Crossing the River Tyne, Demir sighed at the prospect of finally ending the marathon journey of practically driving all around the country. The overnight drizzle had ended a couple of hours ago and as soon as the sun peeked out the clouds vanished. He had a clear view of the city of Newcastle growing closer. He double checked that his face scrambler was on, then chose a swarthy European type. No worries about being picked up by CCTV now. And this time, it would also project the same image to anyone that saw him. With luck, they'd reach Anton's house in a half hour.

Crossing Tyne Gorge, he remembered the last time he'd seen that magnificent view from the bridge. Proud of all his new home had to offer, Anton had taken Demir and the boys on a walking tour of Hadrian's Wall. Demir knew its history, but no book did it justice. He'd been amazed that the stone wall, built to protect England from attack from the north, was still standing after 18 centuries. Demir had built a deck in his backyard but it had barely lasted two years.

He glanced in the rear-view mirror at Matt. Maybe the sound of his voice would help to wake him.

"So, we took the boys to play along Hadrian's Wall and stopped for a picnic near a wooden gate overlooking the valley. There were sheep grazing in the field near us and in the valley on the other side of the Wall. The boys didn't leave one rock unclimbed and it was great to see such innocent fun. A nice change from..." Demir broke off, not wanting to start reminiscing about money laundering and drug shipments. He cleared his throat before continuing.

"Then one sheep on our side starts baaing at the sheep down in the valley. Then, he turns around and baas at the sheep in the field and they all start heading towards us. I was worried the boys were going to get trampled, so I picked them up, one under each arm, and got ready to make a run for the car. But the sheep calmly walked around us to gather in front of the gate. Next thing I know, a sheepdog's bringing the flock up from the valley, followed by a tractor. As soon as the driver opens the gate, the new herd blends in with the old and they go off to graze in the field. The sheepdog hops onto the tractor beside the driver and they drive back down into the valley. Isn't that just remarkable?" He laughed, looking in the rear-view mirror. No reaction. Well, he'd thought the story was amazing. Who knew sheep were smart enough to communicate like that?

They soon reached the edge of Newcastle. Traffic was light and they were making great time. He rounded a corner and screeched to a stop.

"Shit!" Demir's bright mood vanished at the sight of a detour and road construction ahead. Which meant he'd have to detour through the downtown area during the lunch hour. He reached back to pull the blanket over Stoddard's head, saying, "Don't want any nosey pedestrians seeing you."

After forty-five minutes of false starts, long stops, and old ladies waving umbrellas, Demir was on his way to the residential area. He came to a fork in the road and turned left. A few more minutes and he pulled into Anton's driveway. Demir shut off the face scrambler and started to get out of the car when Anton rushed out the front door.

"Tyler you're here, finally!" Anton said. He came around the car and pulled Demir out of the open door into a surprisingly strong embrace for elderly, thin arms. "Why are you so late?"

"I'm only an hour late, barely that," Demir said, escaping from the hug with a laugh. "Same old Anton. You worry too much."

"Worry?" Anton said. "You said noon. You are so punctual, Big Ben sets his time by you. Don't laugh! It's true!"

Demir quickly sobered and asked, "Did you get a doctor? One you can trust?"

"Yes, he's inside. A friend of the family. You can trust him to be discreet. Where is..." Anton broke off when he looked in the backseat. "Bring your car into the garage." He pulled the garage door open, waited till Demir drove in, then shut it quickly.

Just then, a man in his early forties came into the garage from the house. Anton's reassuring hand on Demir's arm kept him from pulling the gun.

"This is Dr. Patrick Ryan," Anton said.

"Bring him inside," Patrick ordered, after checking Stoddard's pulse and pupils. Not waiting for an answer, the doctor went ahead.

Demir paced in tight circles in the narrow hall, pausing every now and then to listen at the door of the living room. Patrick had thrown him out for "loitering" and getting in the way. Last time he'd seen Matt, he was lying on a sofa-bed, hooked up to an IV and heart monitor, wearing a respirator.

"It is time for tea," Anton called, from the kitchen. "Come. The doctor doesn't need your help."

Reluctantly, Demir obeyed. He sat in a wooden chair that creaked in protest when he slid it closer to the wooden table. Anton took the boiling kettle off the gas stove, shut off the flame, and poured the water into a teapot to let it steep. He brought it to the table and set it near a plate of sandwiches.

"How well do you know this doctor?" Demir asked.

"Since we arrived here." Anton sat, folding his hands on the table.

"Patrick used to always come around after school to work at the store. He put himself through medical school. After Eliza's marriage ended, he remained a good friend and an uncle to the children. He's a good boy."

"Do you miss the store? I never thought you'd sell it."

"Ah, I was getting too old to be repairing electronics." Anton took the tea bags out of the pot and set them in a small dish. "Yes, in Russia I was a wonderful engineer. In England, I was a wonderful electronic repair man."

Demir watched him laugh, with no hint of bitterness. He'd been forced to give up his old life for criticizing the government one too many times. But the new life he started here, over twenty years ago, had always completely satisfied him.

Anton poured a little hot cream into Demir's cup before filling it with tea.

"I remember you like the warm cream. Very odd in tea but you have had a hard day. So I will allow it in my house."

"That's right," Demir said. "I'd figured if hot cream was good for coffee, then why not tea?" He'd never had the heart to tell him that he didn't like tea and the cream just made it easier to swallow. "The look of horror on your face when I held out my tea cup." Demir faked a Russian accent adding, "Hot cream is for coffee. Milk is for tea." They both laughed and Demir felt a release of tension. "We had a lot of good times. I'd forgotten them."

"Because the bad times were so strong, they remain more vivid for you. I understand. When I escaped, I never thought I could ever rest. For twenty years, we've been safe. No one knows who we are. My mind selects the happy memories, buries the bad."

"The tea smells good," Patrick Ryan said, from the kitchen entrance.

"How is he?" Demir asked. He was on his feet and ready to see for himself.

"Sit down, old boy," Patrick said, pushing him back into his chair. "He regained consciousness briefly. He'll be fine. He is asleep now, which is something he needs more than anything at the moment. By morning, he'll be fully awake. After a couple of days of solid food, he'll be strong enough to travel." He sat down as Anton poured him tea. He added, "By the by, he called out a name when he came to. Drake. Is that important to you?"

"Not really," Demir said, thin lipped. Then he added, "Thank you for bringing him through." He rubbed his eyes briefly. "I can't believe it's finally over. You're sure he'll be all right?"

"I'll keep an eye on him tonight. He'll have a headache in the morning but nothing a couple of analgesics can't fix."

"I was sure I'd killed him," Demir said, shaking his head.

"You almost did," Patrick said. Then softened the edge of his words with, "You had to remove the intravenous to take him out of the hospital."

"I suppose..."

"Of course I'm right. Now finish your tea. Eat one of these fine sandwiches Uncle Anton is famous for. Then you go have a lie down." Patrick smiled. "Doctor's orders."

"I *am* tired," Demir admitted, more to himself than the doctor. He chose an egg sandwich and bit into it. He hadn't had a normal meal since lunch in the pub yesterday and come to think of it, he hadn't eaten it. In fact, he'd had nothing other than the loaf of bread and some water since he left Canada. He ate the first, then the second sandwich in a few large bites. He drained the tea, wiped his mouth with the back of his hand and only then noticed he was being stared at. Patrick in amazement and Anton with amusement.

"I guess I was hungry," Demir said, with an embarrassed shrug. He stifled a yawn then added, "You do make good sandwiches."

"I'm surprised the food was in contact with your taste buds long enough for you to tell," Patrick said, with a laugh. "Now, go rest."

"You can have my room," Anton said. "The bed is more comfortable."

Demir picked up his backpack from the back of the chair and followed him to the front hall. Anton took Demir's arm to keep him from following the doctor into the living room.

"Not to worry. I will stay with him," Patrick whispered, then closed the door.

They climbed the stairs, with Demir barely hearing the old man's chatter through his exhaustion.

"Yes, Eliza and Patrick have grown close over the years. Both have the same interests. He loves the children, so much. As a matter of fact, he started to take more of an interest in her not long after your last visit.

And this week, he asked her to marry him. In fact—" he paused when they reached the top of the stairs saying, "I put on fresh sheets. Clean towels are in the bathroom. Everything is where you remember." Leading to the end of the hall, he continued, "In fact, Patrick proposed to her and the children together. I think that was very touching. Don't you?"

"Yes, very touching," Demir said. The words echoed in his head. He felt like he was standing in a fog. And now that he could see the bed, so close, so soft, so inviting...

He was barely aware of the old man removing Demir's shoes and socks, then gently covering him with a blanket. He had a faint sensation of floating. Feeling relaxed for the first time in a long time, he allowed sleep to catch up and overtake him.

Demir jolted awake. His head spinning. The old man was gone. Looked at his watch. He'd slept only an hour. Something had woken him...

Patrick had known about the hospital!

Demir hadn't told Anton anything other than he needed a doctor for a friend.

Demir opened his backpack. He took out the knife. The one taken from the dead guard at the hospital.

Barefoot, he crept down the stairs. He listened at the closed living room door. No sound. Cracked it open slightly. Matt was asleep. The heart monitor blinked calmly.

Demir closed the door. A muffled voice from the kitchen.

He padded softly down the hall. Paused near the kitchen door.

Patrick stood with his back to the hallway, keeping an eye on the rear entrance. He clutched the sat phone in both hands, speaking in a harsh, impatient whisper.

"No, you have to interrupt him, I can't wait. No! You don't understand. The old man will return shortly. The agent's upstairs asleep. I've drugged the scientist... What?... I know I haven't reported in before. I never had anything to report... Wait, don't put me on hold again. Bloody hell!"

Demir moved forward swiftly and silently.

He clasped a hand over Patrick's mouth. A single thrust of the knife, up between the ribs. Demir let the body fall, grabbing the phone before it hit the ground. He listened till someone spoke.

"Hello, sir," Demir said, a perfect imitation of Ryan's English accent.

"Did they show up at the old man's home?"

"No, sir," Demir answered, struggling not to react to the question. His mind spinning, he managed to add, "The agent called to say he's going to Wales instead."

"You're sure? Why didn't you persuade them to go to the old man's house?" The voice was gruff, with a heavy European accent that Demir tried to place.

"I never spoke to him myself." Demir replied.

"Good work," the man said, and hung up.

Numbly, Demir clicked off the phone. He looked at the body on the floor and the growing pool of blood silently screaming at him.

Anton would never forgive him for this.

CHAPTER SIXTEEN

Monday morning, Laura stared at her computer screen, considering turning it on. She wasn't even sure why she'd come into work. She should have taken the day off to relax at home instead.

When she'd first woken up today, she'd planned to give relaxation another try. But who was she kidding? She would have done nothing at home except pace and frequently check to make sure her phone was working. When she did arrive this morning, everyone was already in. Jeanette, Drake, Aidan, and even Elton had hobbled in on crutches, ashen faced, obviously in pain.

After a week, there still was no word about Matt. If there'd been a ransom note, it could have been proof that he was still alive. Now all she could do was worry in ignorance.

A knock at the door.

"Come in," she called out, grateful for the distraction.

The door opened and Edna entered carrying a bag from Tim Hortons and two cups of coffee. She stopped short in the doorway and said cheerily, "Good morning."

What the hell? Laura thought. She forced a smile and echoed back, "Good morning." Then, trying to keep her voice pleasant, asked, "What are you doing here at this ungodly hour?"

"I thought you might come in early today. It seems like everyone else had the same idea. Anyways, I took the chance and got your favourite. Chocolate dipped doughnuts. And I know you hate my coffee so here's some I know you'll like." She placed one cup and the bag of donuts in front of Laura, then perched on the arm of the sofa.

Laura motioned towards the coffee table They settled into the two plush armchairs. She extended the bag to Edna. "Doughnut?"

"No, thank you. I brought them for you," Edna said. "And don't tell me you're watching your weight. Everyone knows calories don't count on Mondays." She chuckled.

Smiling at the joke, Laura selected one and took a bite, loving the fresh, decadently smooth chocolate icing. Tim Hortons was enjoying a resurgence in popularity ever since they started baking their doughnuts on-site again. They'd also wisely resumed buying coffee beans from Brazil, instead of the cheaper gen-mod beans.

As she watched her secretary sip at her coffee, she tried to remember the woman who had become the wonderful support system when Laura's mother had died. With no other family close by, Edna, though basically a stranger, had stepped up to help with the arrangements. She'd got her through the painful funeral, where everything moved in nightmarish slow motion. Edna had kept her functioning at work until the pain faded to a dull ache.

She'd been grateful to have someone else's strength to draw on during that horrible time. Edna had always looked out for her. She'd definitely been annoying this past week and her constantly checking up on her. How could she fault her for something that had helped so much in the past? She should talk to Edna about how she felt now. Assure her that she was grateful for the concern but occasionally needed to be alone. Unfortunately, in the face of the generous doughnuts and coffee, now wasn't the right time.

Laura enjoyed the companionable silence until Edna broke it.

"You know Demir likes you," Edna said.

"He likes everyone," Laura said.

"I mean, he thinks you're special."

"Well, everyone thinks he's special too."

"No, I mean, he really *really* likes you," Edna repeated. At the lack of an answer, she sighed and added, "No wonder you're still single."

Laura just couldn't understand why her secretary was making such a lame attempt at matchmaking. It was obvious that there was nothing between her and Demir. How could there be? He was like a brother to her.

"Mr. Demir tells you everything," Edna said. "Things he wouldn't tell others. Things he would only tell you." She paused. "About Matt?"

Laura fiddled with her cup. Why did Edna's innocent sounding words put her on guard? Was it the tone? Was it the way she seemed to stare into her eyes? Did she believe that Demir knew something about Matt's situation and had confided only in her? Was it that special bond created after the funeral that led Edna to believe that all she had to do was ask and Laura would tell all?

Pretending to look in the doughnut bag, Laura answered in a quiet voice, "If I hear something, I'll let you know."

After a few more uncomfortable seconds of being scrutinized, Laura took a bite of the second doughnut and slowly, almost lazily, stood up to return to her desk. True to form, Edna got the hint.

"Well, I have some work to do," Edna said.

Mouth full, Laura gave her a closed lip smile, mumbling, "Thanks for the treat."

After Edna left, Laura continued to sip at her coffee and nibble on the doughnut, her mind in a state of numb confusion.

Maybe she was being too sensitive. Edna could see she was stressed and was trying to be nice. She had to stop being suspicious and just take it for the friendly gesture it was meant to be. But trying to set her up with Demir and fishing for information... That was just simply wrong.

She jumped at the sound of a knock at her door. She called out, "Come in." She smiled at Aidan Monette.

"Aidan, how are you doing?" She came around the desk to talk to him. He looked exhausted, his hooded eyes lifeless and dark.

"I was working on some energy calculations for the chip interface and got stuck because one of the calculations uses data from the physiology department which Matt was working on at home and with the rush of leaving for the conference—I think he left his notes there." He got everything out in one breath and only wavered a little near the end.

"Can't you continue without them until Matt gets back? I'm sure..."

"It's been a week. How much longer do I wait?" Aidan broke off, combing his fingers through his hair, untangling some of the curls. "Sorry, I didn't mean to snap." He looked at her. "I just need the notes so I can continue to work. I need something to concentrate on."

"Then you should go get them if it'll help you."

"That's just it. I drove by his place yesterday but the thought of going in there, with all those memories, I couldn't even get out of the car. Would you…"

"Of course," Laura offered, knowing she didn't want to go to Matt's home either.

"Thanks. Here," he said, handing her two key cards. "The blue one's for the lobby door. The other's for the apartment."

She watched him leave, looking like the whole world was crumbling around him. She worried about him slipping back into a depression similar to a couple of years ago. She had to do what she could to keep him out of it until Matt got back.

She put on her boots and coat and took her purse from the coat rack. She opened the door and peeked out, feeling a sense of irrational relief when she found Edna's desk empty. She hurried to the elevator.

Not sure of her courage to make the trip alone, she decided to call on an escort and she knew just where to find one. She took the elevator down to Sub 3, the laboratory level.

Laura fumbled with the door key. Tried swiping. Turned the card around. Swiped again. She looked up at the door. 4807. This was the right apartment, so what was wrong with the damn key?

"Here, let me try."

She handed Drake the card and stepped aside. *His* hands seemed steady. *He* didn't look on edge. Why couldn't she be more like him?

With one swipe of the key, a push of the door, Drake stepped inside. Laura took a deep breath and followed closing the door behind her.

"I don't see why you could not have come alone," Drake said, sharply.

"I already told you." Laura paused, sighing. "You're the best one to know which are his recent notes. I'd have to either read everything or collect every piece of paper and bring it back."

"What's he doing with notes here anyway?" Drake muttered. Laura wasn't sure if he was talking to himself or her. She answered him anyway.

"And you don't work at home? I'll give you a hand looking..."

"I don't need help," Drake interrupted. "Why don't you water these plants? Some are beginning to wilt."

"Should have thought of that myself," she said, looking around the living room. How would it be for Matt to come home and find that his plants had died? As Drake went off in one direction, she walked slowly around the sunken living room.

The whole condo was spacious and airy. The solarium style windows made every nook and cranny a plant's haven. She paused to look at the spectacular view of the city from forty floors up, fondly remembering Matt's housewarming party. She'd commented that she could never trade in her home that cuddled warmly among the trees, even for a view like this. He'd countered with "nothing could compare with looking down at the world at your feet." She smiled at the nice memories and clung to them.

She continued to the spacious kitchen with beautiful mahogany wood cabinets. Real wood was a rarity in construction these days, but for a little extra fee, Matt had been able to personalize the unit. Under the sink, she found the usual cleaning supplies but nothing to water the plants. She checked another cupboard and found a coffee pot. The spout would be perfect.

She filled it with water, having to make several trips back to the kitchen sink before she finished all the plants in the living room.

On the other side of the living room was the master bedroom, with its solarium that had been turned into an office. Drake sat at the desk, his back to her. There was only a climbing vine that wound its way along a bookshelf and a large, flowering cactus. She went into the master en-suite bathroom to get more water. She climbed the two marble steps to the large oval tub to sit on its wide edge and filled the pot. She could only imagine how relaxing it would be to soak in a whirlpool after a hard work day.

Finished with the plants in the master bedroom, she called to Drake from the office doorway.

"How's it going?"

Drake literally jumped to his feet, scattering papers on the floor.

"Sorry," she said. He haphazardly scooped up papers. Usually meticulous, Drake didn't seem to care how many papers got crumpled in the process. She quickly watered the two plants, giving the cactus a dribble then said, "Did you find what Aidan was looking for?"

"Uh, yes." Drake's voice sounded hoarse. She was surprised to see he wasn't as calm as he pretended.

"Is something wrong?"

"No, I was just—concentrating too hard," he answered.

"I didn't mean to rush you," she said. "I'll wait for you in the living room. Whenever you're ready."

"Sure." He didn't look at her, but turned to straighten the papers on the desk.

Laura went back to the kitchen, dried the coffee pot and put it back. She was about to sit on the sofa when Drake came out of the office. Shocked by his pallor, she asked, "Are you all right?"

"Yes, are you ready?" When she nodded, he said, "Let's go then."

This time her hands were the steadier ones as she locked the door. The silent trip to the elevator and down to the car made her regret not coming alone. She knew he felt guilty about forcing Matt to replace him at the conference. She should have been more sensitive and not forced him to accompany her. After all, how many papers could there have been? She could have brought them all.

"You sure you're okay?" Laura asked, as she put the car on auto.

"Yes," Drake answered, then turned his head to stare out the window.

The entire trip back to work was painfully silent. Drake kept the case on his lap, gripped with both hands. She wanted to ask again what was wrong but knew that it would only make him withdraw into himself even more.

Laura had barely stopped the car before Drake was out, splashing through slush towards Cyber's entrance, the briefcase clutched to his chest. She sighed, turned off the ignition, then got out, shutting both her door and the passenger's. She waved to the Internal Security men that had shadowed them, then shouldered her purse and followed in Drake's wake. Annoyed that he hadn't waited for her, she stabbed the elevator button and waited for it to return.

On Sub 2, she rounded the corner to her office and nearly crashed into Aidan Monette.

"Aidan, sorry. I didn't see you. Are you looking for me?"

"I was just coming to see if you were back yet," Aidan said. "Did you find the papers I need?"

"Drake has them..."

"But I told you *I* need them!" Aidan snapped.

"Aidan," Laura said, putting a gentle but firm hand on his shoulder. "Drake is just carrying them. He's probably already dropped them off in your office by now."

"God, I'm so sorry," Aidan said. He ran his fingers through his unruly curls. "I should have gone to Matt's place myself. Not acted like an immature..."

"Come into my office." She patted his shoulder. "I'll phone Drake and have him bring them."

"No, I'll go find him," he said, giving a weak attempt at a smile.

Laura looked at his beaten down expression and his sad, lost eyes as he nodded thanks and walked away. She continued to her office and was startled to see Edna pacing.

"Where were you?" Edna snapped.

Taken aback, Laura could only gape at her. Recovering, she said, "I went out for a drive."

"With everything that's been going on, why didn't you tell me? I was very worried."

"Well, I'm sorry you were worried," Laura began, as she went to her office door and opened it. Recovered from the shock of the greeting, she turned to look at Edna. Her voice steady, she added, "But did you forget I have a bodyguard watching me everywhere I go?"

She went in, shut the door and leaned against it. Maybe she was needlessly suspicious of the generous act of bringing her coffee and doughnuts. But no one could convince her that Edna's angry reaction was normal.

Drake leaned heavily against his office door, out of breath from his rush to reach the safe haven of his office unseen. The briefcase was still clutched tightly to his chest. He reached behind his back to lock the door. Trembling and a little light-headed, he rushed to his desk. Cleared the surface with a swipe of his hand. He put his briefcase on his desk. Took out the papers. Tossed the briefcase to the floor. Quickly sorted the papers into two piles. He took the larger of the stacks and went to the machine in the corner of his office. One more check of each sheet before he passed them through the shredder.

"Monette is not getting *these*," he told the shredded papers in the basket at his feet.

Three hours after returning from the condo, Laura stared at her computer, planning to get to work. Not from a sense of duty, but rather self-preservation. She tried to concentrate but the only thing that came into her mind was the image of Matt's empty condo.

She'd been there last month to celebrate his thirty-second birthday and tried to think about that happy occasion, only to have her mind wander to Drake. She wanted to go to him, to apologize for dragging him there, though truthfully, she just wanted to talk to him. She hadn't realized how lonely things could be when Drake was hidden deep in his lab. She was the only one who understood him and was truly saddened by everyone's attitude towards him. The others never noticed his absence but his presence was always resented.

She scanned her messages for something interesting. Aidan had cc'd her on a message to Drake. He still didn't have the papers. So much for getting her mind off of Drake. Her first thought was that this was the perfect excuse to see him. Her second thought was that he would be insulted that she was checking up on him and end any chance that he'd ever open up to her again. It was wiser to stay out of it and to let them try to work it out on their own, at least for a little while. She'd get involved after Aidan sent the next message.

She considered starting the dreaded monthly report and chose instead to look through the files of inactive projects that she'd shelved after she'd reorganized Cyber Inc. Every few months, she reviewed them to check if any were worth resurrecting or if any portion could be used in their current work.

She selected one file and began the frustrating, tedious procedure of entering one password after another to open the specially encrypted document. Security had insisted on the extra precaution, but it was a big pain anytime she just wanted to look at one of them.

When the file opened, the message that flashed on the screen surprised her.

PREVIOUS ATTEMPT TO OPEN FILE FAILED

She opened several more and found that all seven files had failed to open. She might have forgotten one failed attempt, but seven? And all these failed attempts had happened within the last month. She knew that she hadn't looked at any of these files for over six months.

She remembered that the encryption program also had another function. A few more keystrokes and a new message greeted her.

FILE COPY SUCCESSFUL

Her heart sank. Her computer had been hacked! From outside? No, that was impossible. Their entire network was self-contained. It would be a herculean task for someone to get past the military firewalls installed on their internal network. That left only one possibility.

Someone inside the underground complex was responsible. The sense of violation stunned her. She checked through the rest of her files but it seemed only the cancelled projects had been copied. It probably wouldn't take one of *her* people —she choked a bit at the thought— long to figure decrypt them. But why? There was nothing in those files of value. And, if someone really was interested in looking at them, all they had to do was ask her.

She tried to think. Tried to figure it out. But her mind just kept whirling like a leaf caught in a tornado. She should report the breach to Security. But if Security got involved, then they'd be in control. And so would the military. The research and the scientists were her domain. Once she discovered the person responsible, then it would be her decision whether or not to involve Security.

She needed her favourite sounding board, but he was busy avoiding life somewhere. However, he'd never turned her away when she needed to talk. This mystery could even be the driving force to get him to talk to her about what was going on in his mind.

She left her office, snapping some inane answer to Edna's question about where to find her, then continued down the hall.

She stood outside Drake's office, waiting. No chance of an invitation to come in if she hadn't knocked yet. Of course, he couldn't refuse to see her if she didn't give him the chance, so she barged in.

Damn. Empty.

She decided to leave him a note asking, no, demanding that he meet with her. Today. She searched his desk for a paper to write on. Everything seemed to have some note or calculation on it. She decided to retrieve one from the recycle bin. A surprised "oh!" escaped when she found it was filled with shredded paper.

The rule was to shred any papers that you were planning to throw out, but Drake usually refused to be consistent about it. Seeing the filled can, she was pleased to see that he was finally obeying the minor inconvenience. She turned back to the desk and started looking through the drawers. Could it be possible that the man didn't have a blank sheet anywhere? She was about to give up and decided to simply message him when she heard a sound outside the door. She looked up with a smile when Drake returned, carrying a cup of coffee.

Her smile faded when she saw his expression. He paled visibly when they made eye contact, then an expression that she could only describe as anger coloured his face.

"What are you doing here?" He said, his voice almost a hiss.

"I came by to talk to you. I was looking for something to write on to leave you a note." Her words tumbled out with the guilt of being caught red-handed. Going through the man's desk was unforgivable to Drake. To her as well.

"What do you want?"

"I needed to talk to someone..." she broke off. What was she going to say? She suspected a fellow scientist of going through her private files? And what was she just doing?

"It can wait until you have time," she said finally.

"All right." His voice was low. His eyes darted from her to the shredded paper in the recycle bin.

"Aidan's been wondering if you found the papers he needs."

"I'll send them shortly."

Feeling very uncomfortable, but not quite sure why, she took a shallow breath and said, "I need to return to my office. Please let me know when you have time to come by. Today or tomorrow. There's no hurry." She rushed past him.

She had barely stepped into the hall when Drake pushed the door closed. She tried to tell herself he hadn't meant to slam it. But there was no mistaking the sound of a lock engaging.

She returned to her office and was greeted by a question from Edna, wanting to know where she'd been and if she was okay. She ignored the questions and locked herself in her office. She didn't want any concern from her secretary. No advice. She just wanted peace.

And to overcome the horrible sense of violation.

Who could have hacked into her computer? With a complex full of geniuses, it was like asking who knows how to use a pen.

She still didn't want to involve security. In fact, all she needed to do was figure out who had been in during the days that her computer had been hacked. Not wanting to involve Edna, she called Yasmin directly and put in a request for access to the records. She used the excuse of needing the attendance records for a new monthly report that was due. Fortunately, Yasmin bought the lie and promised to get right back to her. Unfortunately, barely two minutes later, Yasmin called back to tell her that access to any security records couldn't be granted without the chief's authorization.

She could ask Edna to bully security, but with the way her secretary was behaving, that didn't seem to be a comfortable option. No, there was only one person left. She quickly got dressed to go out. Again, barely out of her office door, Edna questioned her.

"Where are you going, in case I need to get a hold of you?" Edna asked.

The violation of her computer and the stress of the past week, combined with Drake's cold reaction, made Edna's routine question unbearable.

"You know something?" Laura paused to place both hands, palms flat, on Edna's desk as she leaned in close. A part of her knew she wasn't being fair, that she should back off. And a part of her knew she didn't care. "We should think about investing in a tracker for you to watch on your screen. Would that make your little micro-management mind happy?"

"I'm sorry. I'll wait here should you need me," Edna said, her voice subdued.

"Fine." Laura turned and left before she buckled under the stress of guilt and apologized for being so rude. Despite the subservient tone, there was no mistaking the defiance in Edna's eyes.

Aidan drummed his fingers on his desk. Thinking. He wasn't exactly afraid of Drake, but he didn't want to confront him and ask for the notes. Why hadn't Drake just brought them to him? Why was he nowhere to be found? He didn't answer the phone and he hadn't answered the door. He wasn't even sure Drake was locked inside.

There was no reason for Drake to refuse to give him the notes.

Until he got the data from physiology, all he could do was fiddle with the schematics for the neural connections, but he'd already modified them countless times. He needed that data, damn it!

Sure, he could just sit here and whine, or grow up and do something useful. He stood, forcing heavy legs to walk to Matt's office at the other end of this level. A brief hesitation and he opened the door, entered and turned on the lights. Matt was such a neat freak that seeing files scattered all over the desk unnerved him for a moment, until he remembered that this was the aftermath of the last minute preparations for the conference.

Taking a breath, he sat behind the desk and put his coffee down on the coaster. Aidan started to tidy up the files, closing folders and stacking them neatly on the corner of the desk. He wondered if there might be copies of the data calculations somewhere here. Even preliminary data would be helpful. He checked out these files and the ones in the file cabinet. Nothing. He searched through the desk drawers for something. No luck. As he searched the bottom drawer, he noticed a sheet of paper caught in the top of the drawer. Careful not to tear it, he pulled it out.

Just some gibberish, or...

...a computer access code. But it wasn't Matt's, that one he knew. Maybe, just maybe, it was Drake's. When you worked closely with someone else, there'd have to be open access to information. Unless that someone was Drake. But Matt had a way with people. If anyone could persuade Drake to give up his computer password, Matt could.

Aidan picked up his mug and left, taking the paper with him.

Drake had gone to find Jeanette Theriault and Elton Chan. He'd managed to get them out of the lab on the pretext that Laura needed to see them. That would give him five minutes, ten if he took into account Elton's slow hobble on the crutches. More than enough time to go through their computer records. He quickly found the files. Erased them. Then emptied the Trash folder.

Next, the hard copies. He pulled out the seven folders, shuffled the others in the drawer so the gap wouldn't be readily noticeable and left the lab quickly.

He had to hide or destroy as much of the evidence as he could.

Laura turned the last corner and parked in front of Demir's house. She hoped that she could get him to authorize access to the records using the same excuse of a new type of monthly report. But if he didn't accept that reason, then she hoped she could get him to promise not to do anything official until she had a chance to talk to the person.

She got out of the car, noting that her I.S. bodyguard had parked a few car lengths behind her. She smiled at her, then walked up to the front door and rang the bell. No answer. She gave him a few minutes to get to the door; after all, the man was sick. Knocking on the door also produced no result. Shamelessly, she peeked in the window to the living room. Empty.

About to leave, she looked for the I.S. car. Hmm, her guard's first mistake. Not following her from the car. The bushes near the door kept her conveniently out of sight, so she hurried around the side of the house, struggled through the snow that came to her knees, ignoring the snow flooding into her boots, but she won the fight to reach the back of the bungalow.

She peeked in the first window. Bathroom. The second was a patio door to the kitchen. The last window was a guest bedroom, she guessed from the size. Another room had been turned into a mini-gym, with a bike and treadmill. Around the side, she peered into the master bedroom. Bed was neatly made. No one was in there.

She returned to the front in time to see the I.S. woman coming into view to check on her. She gave her a smile and called out, "Miss me?"

She waved back with a smile and waited until she got into her car.

Where could the allegedly sick Tyler Demir be? Unless he was in the basement, which she knew was unfinished, he wasn't in the house.

It looked like Drake's theory was right after all. Demir wasn't really sick. She smiled, thinking that she'd have to compliment Demir on his acting performance of a man deathly ill when he got back. Didn't she always tell him all those years with the RCMP would come in handy here at Cyber?

This would explain his distant attitude just before he got sick.

She made a silent vow to keep his secret. It would be hard to not show the renewed feeling of hope. He'd gone to find Matt himself.

No, the relief wouldn't show. Because with that one concern taken care of, she could now devote all of her energy into finding out who had violated her trust and taken those files.

Drake took forever to leave work. As soon as he did, Aidan had broken into his office to search for Matt's notes. Where the hell could the cold hearted asshole have put them? Thinking the data was entered into the computer, Aidan used the passwords that he'd found in Matt's office.

He did a general search and found nothing. Actually, there was a lot but not what he was looking for. About to log out, he had another thought. There could be something else related to the data that would help him complete his calculations. If he got caught, that's the excuse he'd give to justify the deeper search. Also, how could he pass up the once in a lifetime chance to ransack Drake's private world that he guarded with manic possessiveness?

Buried deep within a program directory, he found eight encrypted files, which Aidan would never have dug up without his own manic obsession. He copied them to a memory slip, logged out and left.

CHAPTER SEVENTEEN

A gasp. A cry.

Demir wasn't sure which sound brought him out of his shock. He blinked and was embarrassed to feel tears on his face. His vision was clear now and he could see the backdoor entrance to the kitchen. A bag of groceries lay scattered and broken on the floor. How did they get there? Demir looked down at his feet and saw Anton hugging and crying over Patrick Ryan.

Whom, Demir realized, he'd made a lifeless corpse.

"My dear boy. My poor dear boy," Anton chanted, and rocked back and forth. The sound began to echo in Demir's head.

"We have to get rid of the body," Demir said, his voice calm. His mind a blur. His heart numb.

"Why? Why?" Anton screamed. He stopped rocking to hug the body protectively closer and glared at Demir.

Demir recognized the pain, the confusion. The hate. He'd once promised himself that he'd never see that look on anyone again. But a job needed to get done. A helpless victim's life depended on him. He hated those words every time he looked into the eyes of the innocents caught in the crossfire.

"He betrayed us," Demir said quietly.

"Why!" Anton screamed, as he leapt for Demir's throat, yelling something—curses—in Russian. He allowed the old man's fists to strike him in the face, in the chest. He supported the old man when the fight was gone.

"Listen to me." Demir was amazed at how calm he actually sounded. He'd never wanted to kill again. And now, two in 24 hours. He couldn't believe that he'd done this. "He was turning us in. I didn't have time to think…" He cradled the sobbing man and tried to make him understand something he barely understood himself.

"Do you think that once Patrick's friends came for Matt, they'd leave witnesses?"

"Eliza!" Anton pulled away, looking directly into Demir's face. "The children! Are they in danger?"

"No, I stopped him in time."

"He was like my own son. Why would he do such a thing?" A pitiful question.

"I can't answer that, I'm sorry." Demir thought for a moment then added, "You said you met him here soon after you escaped from Russia. It's possible he's a sleeper. An agent assigned to keep an eye on you. And he took an interest in your daughter to make sure he stayed close. And," Demir paused, thinking. "When did you say he proposed?"

"Uh," Anton shook his head and Demir wasn't sure if he was trying to remember or erase the image of the man on the floor. "Oh, yes, it was Tuesday evening."

"The same week Stoddard is kidnapped. Anton," Demir put his hand on Anton's shoulder, "he may have been keeping an eye on you all this time. Knowing your connection to me. My connection to—other things." He stopped short of mentioning his current job.

"Oh, how can I tell her?" Anton looked at Ryan.

"You can't tell her anything. Not yet," Demir said. Seeing Anton wasn't listening, he shook him by the shoulders. "Anton! I need to clean everything up here. Then hide the body in the recycle ponds."

"But they'll never find him in there."

"Anton," Demir said, with a sigh of exhaustion and frustration, "that's the idea."

Demir rubbed his temples with tight fisted knuckles before opening the door to the living room. Anton was still sitting in a chair near Matt. Watching him with eyes that Demir knew were seeing images of a dead friend that he'd once trusted.

"Anton," Demir whispered. The old man looked up. "Everything's taken care of in the kitchen."

"I remember agents in Russia," Anton said, turning his attention to the heart monitor. "The successful ones were always the one that everyone liked. They knew how to trick you into liking them. Patrick was using me all along. And my daughter." He looked at Demir and continued. "I'll tell her that he had to go abroad, for a family emergency. He wasn't sure when he'd return. I will suggest she put her engagement on hold. She's young. In time she'll forget."

The man seemed to age before his eyes. But when he stood, his back was straight, his shoulders pulled back. He showed that same strength that Demir had seen twenty years ago when he'd first found them huddled behind some crates in the dockyard.

"Perhaps a cup of tea would be nice," Anton said, as he left the room. Demir went to Matt's side and removed the IV line. Quietly he said, "There wasn't time to come up with a plan. It isn't just your life at stake. It's Anton and his family." He pulled the blanket back, sighing with relief that he was still dressed. It would make leaving easier. Soon he'd be driving with a body in the trunk and an unconscious man in the back seat.

He started to put the scientist's runners on when Anton returned.

"The kettle will boil soon. Oh," he paused, as he came around to look at Demir. "Please don't feel you must leave. Stay until the young man is better."

"Thank you," Demir said. "But it's better that I leave now. Don't worry, you're safe. Patrick was only supposed to report in if he had something." Remembering a detail, he added, "There'll be questions when he misses work."

"I'll call the medical clinic and give them the same story as I will give Eliza." Anton paused, a flicker of sadness, then it was gone. "In a week, I will again call and give them his resignation. He has me listed as a contact, since he has no one else here. There won't be questions."

"I'm so sorry to bring this down on you."

"Would it have been better to remain ignorant and have my daughter marry a... a criminal?" He calmed and added, "Where will you go?"

"I need to find someone who's willing to take us on a boat to—anywhere." He shrugged, adding, "There was someone who lived in Scotland. We've lost touch, but I might be able to track him down."

"No concerns, my friend," Anton interrupted, with a gentle hand on his shoulder. "I know someone closer that will help with no questions."

"Thank you," Demir said. "For everything."

"Ah, no need." Anton dismissed the words away with a wave. "We are friends who help each other when needed." Anton gave him a sad smile. This time, Demir believed the man had forgiven him.

After several weather delays, Abraham's commercial plane finally landed at London's Heathrow Airport at noon, instead of five in the morning. Wearing the facial scrambler, he used the credit card with the name Manny Kline to book a rental and was finally on the road to Newcastle an hour later.

He'd debated trying to phone the old man, but he didn't want to take the chance that Anton wouldn't believe it was really him and Demir might panic, take the scientist and run. No, the only way was to show up unannounced on the doorstep.

Just when he thought this rescue was finally on track, the motorway turned into a parking lot. Trapped in the inside lane, there was nowhere to exit. Early afternoon traffic should have been light, which meant there was an accident up ahead. He tried to calm down. Turned on the radio to find something to listen to and finally settled on an electronic classic grunge rock station.

The hard beat drowned out the pounding frustrations growing in his head.

At 9:15 p.m., Abraham arrived in Newcastle and pulled to the curb to wait and watch the house. All the lights were off, giving the house a dark silhouette against the grey clouds.

Careful not to slam the car door, Abraham went up to the house. He could just break the door down, but how embarrassing would it be to get shot waving hi? He knocked quietly at first, then a bit louder. He waited and listened. Silence. This time, he tried the doorbell. Once, twice. A third time. Either they were really sound sleepers or there was no one home.

Or something could be wrong.

To avoid any nosey neighbours peering out of their windows, he went around to the back of the house. Easily picked the lock on the back door and slunk into the kitchen. He slipped down the narrow hall and cautiously opened the living room door. It had been converted to a makeshift hospital room. There was an EKG monitor, an IV stand, an open medical bag on a coffee table with a variety of medical supplies. A blood pressure cuff lay draped on the back of the still open sofa bed, along with a stethoscope. Someone had been here recently. But where the hell were they now?

He crept up the claustrophobic staircase. A small bathroom on the left. Linen closet next. An empty bedroom on the right and what appeared to be a master bedroom at the end of the hall, also empty though the bed looked like it had been slept in. The slanted ceiling reminded him of the house he'd lived in when his son was still alive. Frowning, he pushed the memory away and checked the dresser for some clue of where they might have gone. He checked the night tables. Photos of a smiling young woman and two small children in front of a pier. He searched everywhere. Nothing helpful.

Back downstairs, he carefully went through everything. Again, no hint of where they could have gone. The house was neat, with few knick-knacks or clutter, which made it easier to search than some of the pigpens he'd seen way back in the good old days. But with clutter came the hope that you'd eventually find something.

He looked around the 1950s style kitchen, with a sleek ceramic-top stove looking strangely out of place. He gave a low whistle, admiring the good condition of the room that was almost a century old. A quick search through drawers and cupboards and he found what he'd expected to be there. Kitchen stuff.

Mounted on the wall near the door was a landline. Below the phone was a narrow counter with several papers in neat piles. Among them lay an open notebook handwritten with neat penmanship. It was an address book open at the letter 'P'. There were only a few entries: Cally Pond, the cleaning woman; Benji Plymouth, the butcher; and Dwight Parker, with no notation of who he was.

With no way to tell how long it had been sitting open like that, Abraham examined the papers, surprised to discover that they were hardcopy mail: household bills and personal letters. Come to think of it, there was little tech in the house. Not surprising for someone not wanting to be easily monitored. He scanned all the letters. Nothing that would help. He methodically began to replace the stacks exactly as they'd been.

He slipped the last letter back into its envelope; he looked at the phone book again. Wait a minute. He picked it up and looked at the entry for Dwight Parker. It was a Tyneside address. Near the coast. A lame clue, finding a coastal address in a country that was an island. Still, it was the only clue he had. He wrote down the address and phone number. He left, locking the door behind him.

He did have to admit to himself that Demir seemed to be doing just fine without him, so far. He was probably already on the boat and headed for safety.

But, whether it was needed or not, Abraham planned to provide backup.

Demir peered through the dark, trying to see Matt curled up in the back seat. Why hadn't he remembered to bring a blanket, he asked himself as he turned up the heat? They were in Anton's car, with the older man driving.

Before they left the house, Demir arranged to meet with another contact from the old days, this one a bit shadier. In exchange for having all debts paid in full, the contact agreed to make Patrick Ryan and the car belonging to Gareth's brother-in-law vanish.

Demir turned to look at Matt again.

Anton clucked his tongue and said, "You need to stop worrying."

"He should be awake by now," Demir said, turning back to face the front.

With Anton driving, Demir had nothing to do but look at scenery, invisible in the dark and fog. And worry.

And check on Matt Stoddard.

"My boy," Anton said, clucking his tongue again. "You make me worry now."

"I just wish I knew what Patrick gave him. That he was going to be okay. Why he's still unconscious. If I should risk taking him to a hospital..." Demir broke off at the even louder tongue click from the driver's seat. He turned to watch the fog scatter in the headlights, imagining that they were speeding through a field of stars. That entertained him for a quick count of three.

"Aren't we there yet?" he asked. At the sound of laughter from beside him, he realized how much he sounded like an impatient child on a long trip. Damn it, he *was* impatient. The drive to Tyneside was less than a half hour, but his journey had started three, almost four days ago.

"In answer to your question," Anton said, "we have arrived."

Demir came fully alert as they turned off the road into the car park of the marina. There were floodlights and music coming from a boat where a party was under way complete with bright lights, loud music, dancing, and laughing people. There was no way Demir could get past them unseen with an unconscious body slung over his shoulder. He asked Anton to pull around in the car park and stayed in the shadows, shutting off the car.

"If you wait here, I will find Dwight," Anton said. "He will tell me what is going on."

"Be careful," Demir said. "If you feel anything's wrong, signal me."

"Yes, yes, this isn't my first picnic," Anton reassured him, as he got out of the car.

Demir watched the old man pass the party boat and board the *Maureen McKenna*, a 40-foot fishing boat. It seemed sturdy enough to take out in open water. He just wanted to get out of England and would have settled for a skiff. He watched Anton come around the deck of the ship and enter the wheelhouse to meet with the ship's captain. The two men greeted each other with a warm handshakes and hugs. After a brief exchange, Anton returned with quick, long strides.

"It's a teenager birthday party," Anton began, breathlessly. "With school tomorrow, they should be finished by 10:00."

"That's over an hour," Demir said, looking at the clock on the dash.

"I know of a quiet place we can wait," Anton said, starting up the engine.

A few kilometres from the port, Anton parked in a secluded area hidden from the road by some bushes. He shut off the engine, then reached into the back to retrieve a small cooler from the floor and handed Demir a sandwich. Mechanically, Demir took a bite, chewed and swallowed. He stared at the bushes. Nothing much to see, but he stared at them just the same. What was he going to do if he couldn't get Matt on that boat? He knew what his orders were.

Don't leave him behind—alive.

No secret was so valuable that a man's life was expendable. Though life was looking kind of cheap on this mission.

He took another bite of his sandwich as he turned to check the back seat. The young man's breathing wasn't as deep as it had been. He hoped that meant that whatever drug Patrick had given him was wearing off. Demir put his sandwich on the dash, then got out and opened the back door.

"Doctor?" He whispered. He shook his shoulder lightly. No response other than a slight tensing under his hand. He shook a little harder, his voice a bit more insistent. "Try to wake up. I don't know what he gave you but try to fight it." Still no real reaction. He took both shoulders and lifted him to a sitting position, supporting the scientist's head as it rolled back and tapped his cheek lightly, "Doctor?" A harder tap. "Doctor?" His voice louder, demanding, almost a full slap. "Doctor!" The eyes fluttered. "That's it. Fight the drugs."

He felt the limp muscles under his hands tighten. Finally, the eyes opened and he did seem to be focussing on the world around him.

"That's good, my friend!" Anton said. "This will be much easier to get him aboard the boat should those teenagers still be there."

"Just what I was thinking," Demir said. He pulled out a water bottle from the cooler and helped Matt drink. A few good swallows. "He's alive and I plan to keep him that way." Whatever his orders were.

Matt's eyes closed again, so Demir laid him down. The night air was crisp and refreshing but not for someone who was sick. He took off his jacket and covered the scientist, then closed the door.

He leaned against the car, his head swirling with exhaustion and relief. Anton came around to him.

"We still have time to wait," Anton said. "You'll feel much better if we walk around in the fresh air." Before Demir could object, he quickly added, "Naturally, we'll keep the car in sight."

"Sure," Demir said. He smiled when Anton shoved his sandwich into his hand. He'd probably starve without Anton always reminding him to eat. Just like Abraham. He hoped everything was okay back at Cyber. With Abraham there, that was one less thing he had to worry about.

Demir finished his sandwich, only now realizing it was salmon. He hated salmon. Usually he hated salmon. He gave Anton a smile saying, "Never thought canned salmon could actually taste good."

He gave a dramatic gasp. "Canned? Oh my, never! It is fresh. I baked it two nights ago."

He chuckled, thinking that maybe he should start cooking meals himself after he got back home. Whatever his skill level, it would be healthier than fast food, the major part of his diet. They walked and chatted about their lives since they'd last been together. The pleasant conversation and cool air cleared Demir's head and he was ready to continue his mission.

Checking his watch, he said, "It's been almost an hour. By the time we get back..."

"Why not?"

They drove back into the parking lot by the pier, both relieved to see the party boat deserted. All the boats were quiet and dark.

Anton parked close to the *Maureen McKenna* and both men got out. Demir pulled his jacket off of Matt and put it back on. As he reached in to lift him out, he noticed that his sat phone had fallen out of his jacket. He stuffed it back in his pocket, then gently lifted Matt into a sitting position. He lightly slapped the scientist's face. No reaction.

"So much for being easier to wake him a second time," Demir muttered.

With the older man's help, he lifted the scientist over his shoulder, then followed Anton, who rushed ahead to tell his friend that they were back. Partway up the gangway, Demir slowed down. He felt the hair prickle on the back of his neck. The feeling in the pit of his stomach felt like a snake unravelling. Something wasn't right.

Halfway up the gangway, he realized what it was. *All* the lights on this boat were off. Sure, they needed cover of darkness and he wasn't expecting floodlights, but why was the wheelhouse dark too?

He could try to make a run for it but doubted he could get Matt safely back to the car. And he wasn't about to leave Anton to fend for himself. He rushed the last few steps up the gangway and unceremoniously dumped the scientist onto the deck.

He turned, his hand halfway to his gun. He froze when he saw a man holding a gun to Anton's head. How the hell did they find them?

"Just give me that bloke there and you and your granddad here can go home all safe and comfy like," the gunman said.

"How about I double whatever they're giving you? And you just say you didn't find us."

"Well, how about I take your money and think about it?"

With the dim lighting from the parking lot, he couldn't see the man's face clearly but the tone said that he had no intention of letting them go. And Demir wasn't going to let him take Matt, even to save Anton. He also wasn't going to obey orders and kill the scientist. He wasn't sure how the hell he was going to do it, but he refused to sacrifice either one of them.

Brave words. There was a slim chance he could save them both, but he had to try. Looking at the gunman shielded behind Anton, there was a chance he could hit the gunman's head. But in the dark...

Letting his shoulders slump a bit, as though he was giving up, he turned fully around to look at Matt as he reached for his gun. His hand on the weapon, he prepared to turn and fire, when he heard a scuffling noise and grunts from behind. Somehow Anton had got free. Demir spun around, his weapon drawn, and saw instead a larger man struggling with the now disarmed gunman. Anton leaned as far away as possible on the deck railing, trying to avoid the melee barely half a metre from him. The newcomer took a punch to the face and was knocked to the ground. Demir charged forward, grabbing the gunman in a chokehold. Within seconds the would-be kidnapper went limp. Demir kicked the gun out of reach and let him drop.

He turned to see who the good Samaritan was, his gun ready in case this was another buyer interested in getting his hands on a high tech scientist.

He held his gun steady as the other man rolled onto his back and looked up at Demir.

"Abe?" Demir asked, incredulous.

"Man, I am just too old for all this wrestling shit," Abraham said, with a wide and bloody grin.

Demir extended a hand to pull him to his feet.

"How the hell did you find us?" He picked up the assailant's gun, tucking it into his waistband.

"I found the open phone book at Anton's place. Went to the address where your guy Parker has a sign advertising boat rentals from here." Abraham said, wiping his bloody lip with the back of his hand. "When I found all the lights off and you're supposed to be setting sail soon, I figured something was wrong. I snuck on board to check things out."

"Oh my God. Parker!" Anton remembered in a panic. "He's not..."

"No, he's okay," Abraham said. "I found him and the deck hand tied up below." He handed Anton a knife. "I didn't have time to free them."

"Thank you," Anton said. He took the knife, carefully stepped over the gunman, then rushed below.

"I wonder how this guy knew where you were," Abraham said.

Demir bent down to check on the slowly reviving ex-gunman.

"Maybe when Patrick called to turn us in, they got the message and sent someone to confirm the story. They probably followed us here from the house. God damn it, I should have been more careful." This guy didn't seem to be a pro. Damn. Used to be he could go for days without sleep before he started making stupid mistakes like this.

"Where's this Patrick now?" Abraham asked.

Demir's glum expression gave his friend all the answer needed.

With Abraham keeping an eye on the now conscious gunman, Demir hurried back to check on Matt. Still alive.

"So," Abraham said, waving his gun at the stranger, "What do you want to do with this one? Dump his body in the ocean?"

"Here, now," the stranger spluttered, "no need for all that."

"Then maybe you should tell us who sent you," Abraham said, his voice low.

"They just ring me up and give me my work orders. Don't know who they are. Honest, guv, don't know."

"Abe, we need to get going in case he has friends close by," Demir said.

CHAPTER EIGHTEEN

Standing by Abraham's rental, Demir and Abraham watched as the *Maureen McKenna* pulled away from the dock with Anton waving from the stern. Parker would keep the boat out until Demir called to say they were safely away, then release the gunman. He should've taken the money, Demir thought. Now all he could do was report that they got away and not be any richer for it.

He and Abraham started to drive towards Edinburgh. Demir turned to check on Matt.

"He okay?" Abraham asked.

"He's alive," Demir said. Facing forward again, he leaned his head on the head rest. He listened to the car engine's voice change in pitch, then settle down as Abraham shifted into sixth gear. The road was bumpy but he imagined it was smooth and that they were making perfect time and that the mission had been perfect from the start. The car hit a large pothole, which erased the dream. He sat up straight to watch the road in the headlights.

"What kind of plane did you get us?" Demir said.

"Cargo." Abraham gave him a smile and added, "It's not exactly first class, but it has wings! It's waiting for us at a small airport outside of Edinburgh. Used to be RAF, not anymore."

"Can it be traced? Where'd you get it?"

"You're not the only one with contacts, you know."

Demir smiled, then asked, "How the hell did you figure out I came to Newcastle?"

"I may be getting old, but I ain't dead yet. I figured you'd say fuck Kirby's plans and head out on your own. But when you didn't show up or call in, I really started to worry. According to my FBI contact—remember

Henry?—Stoddard hadn't been recaptured, so I knew you were out here somewhere. Then I remembered your friend up north. Flew over in case you needed help."

Demir nodded, glad he'd shown up when he had. He asked, "Your buddy give you any ideas who might have snatched him?"

"Just a list of names, nothing concrete. I have Wallingford checking them." Abraham added before Demir could object, "No one knows where I am. All she knows is that I'd be out of reach for a while."

"I can't believe we still have no idea who took him," Demir said.

"Well, I've been thinking about that. Remember that Drake was supposed to be going. Right?" Abraham answered. "And he's never tried to hide how much he hates being muzzled about the research. Maybe he decided to sell out and the best way was to sell young Stoddard here. That would explain his cancelling at the last minute."

"You really hate Drake, don't you?" Demir said.

"I just call 'em as I see 'em."

Thanks to no traffic and Abraham taking it off auto-drive, they reached the airport in less than two hours and parked on the tarmac next to the cargo plane. Two men brought a stretcher to move Matt from the car to the plane. Abraham tossed the car keys to a third man, then boarded the plane. He stopped at the cockpit to talk to the pilot, while Demir double checked that the stretcher had been secured to the floor, then took one of the two airplane seats that had been bolted to the floor.

Abraham joined him, taking the second seat asking, "Comfy?"

"You were right, this isn't exactly first class," Demir said. Nodding towards the cockpit, he asked, "Good man?"

"Extremely trustworthy. He's also the best pilot around." Abraham handed him a pair of earplugs. "You'll need these."

The engines fired up and both men put the earplugs in their ears. The drone blended in with the buzzing in Demir's head. He shut his eyes, trying to block out the world around him. The lives taken by his own hands. Taken quickly. Silently.

He just wanted to go home. Sleep in his own bed.

Before the thought was complete, Abraham was waking him. Blinking dry eyes, Demir squinted out the window. They were back in Ottawa, the engine drone winding down and finally silent. There was a swirling snowstorm outside.

"You sure this is Ottawa?" Demir said. "Looks like the arctic."

"Guess it's just winter giving us one last goodbye."

"What time is it here?" Demir asked, yawning.

"3:17 A.M. and it's still Tuesday."

Demir looked outside again and he saw the flashing lights of an ambulance drive towards them, coming to a stop at the back of the plane. He looked at Abraham with a questioning expression.

"I radioed ahead to let Internal Security know we're on our way home and to have an ambulance meet us."

"You announced us?" All this effort to keep things secret only to have their arrival broadcast.

"Relax. I used a secure channel. And I never mentioned Stoddard. Just said we need Doc Owen and an ambulance to meet us."

Demir began to relax when a loud clank and the sound of gears turning startled him. He reached for his gun, then realized that it was only the back of the plane opening. A slap of frigid air gushed in and he breathed deeply, revelling in the smell that said home. He looked out the window and watched as two attendants, bundled in toques and thick jackets, jumped out of the ambulance; tiny snow tornadoes whirled around their ankles.

He bent to help the attendants unclamp the stretcher when he saw someone in a parka rush up the ramp. Once inside the relative warmth of the plane, the newcomer pulled back his fur-lined hood. Cyber's medical doctor smiled at Demir.

"Tyler, my boy," Owen said, "so glad to see that you've recovered from your bout with the flu. And I see that you found our young Matthew." Owen checked the motionless form under the blanket, then signalled the attendants who whisked him away. Owen gave Demir a pat on the shoulder, then followed down the ramp and into the back of the ambulance.

"Time to get you home too, old son," Abraham said, stretching his back muscles.

"No, I have to follow to the hospital." Demir mirrored the stretch. Zipping up his jacket, he thanked the pilot and disembarked.

Demir gasped when the frigid air slapped him and he finally

understood the expression, 'takes your breath away.' Quite a difference from England's damp cold, where a windbreaker and sweater were more than enough and occasionally too much. He held his collar tightly around his neck, wishing he had his ski jacket, but he'd left it in the trunk of the rental when he'd swapped cars in Brighton.

Wallingford, from Internal Security, met them with a car. As Abraham climbed into the back seat first, Demir stopped to look at a car parked at the edge of the tarmac. Even from this distance, he could tell it was military. Who would be watching their arrival at three in the morning? Kirby. How the hell did he find out so fast? He really wanted to go over there, drag the bastard out by the neck and beat the crap out of him. Instead, he settled for giving him a curt nod before getting into the car.

Demir settled into the back seat, rubbing his hands together to warm them. He watched the swirling snow outside, knowing he wouldn't trade a lingering winter for any tropical paradise. This was home.

As the car started moving, he heard someone clear their throat and looked expectantly at Abraham, who was looking at the driver.

"Wallingford," Demir said, "did you say something?"

"Well, I'm not sure how to break this to you," she said, accelerating to catch up to the ambulance.

"Just say it," Demir demanded, really getting tired of people forgetting how to express themselves. And do it quickly.

"Well, we've got a situation here." She hesitated, then all the words gushed out. "Mitchell was driving Henderson home and that's the last time anyone's seen either of them. Both their wives think they're on assignment and that's why we didn't figure there was a problem when he didn't come in for his shift Saturday."

"Saturday? When was the last time anyone saw them?" Demir asked.

"Friday, when he picked Mr. Henderson up at DND."

"Friday?" Abraham interrupted, leaning forward. "You mean no one's done anything since then?"

"No, sir, Sandrovsky was trying to find you on Sunday when you were, you know, out of the complex for a while," Wallingford said.

"Sunday..." Abraham sat back, looking at Demir. "He did try to talk to me, but I was in a rush to make the flight and blew him off."

"What about their sats?" Demir asked.

"No signal, from either of them after Mitchel picked up the chief," Wallingford said. "They cut off together, almost like the signals were being jammed."

"So what *has* been done?" Demir asked, trying to ignore the guilt he could feel from the man beside him. He had his own share in that guilt.

"Abe, when I told him you'd be out of touch and I was in charge, he finally spilled it Sunday evening," Wallingford said. "We've called the police and RCMP. And our own people are looking as well."

"That's something, at least," Demir said. He pulled the phone out of his pocket and turned it on. Damn, he forgot it was the phone he'd picked up in England. "Abe, you got your sat with you?"

He shook his head. "Sorry, I left mine in my desk. Didn't want to be tracked."

"Use mine," Wallingford said. She held it up for Demir to take.

He phoned Operations at Cyber. "It's Demir. Any word on Mitchell or Henderson?"

"Glad you're back, sir. We're working with the Ottawa police, but nothing yet. Couldn't get Major Kirby on the phone, but his assistant still insists Mr. Henderson's away on assignment."

"You believe that?"

"Not for a moment, which is why we're still looking."

"Good," Demir said. "Dr. Stoddard is on his way to the hospital. I want you to set up a protection detail for him. And I want our people to handle it, *no* military. Got it? And double the detail on each of the scientists. The secretaries too."

"Yes sir, right away."

"Good. I'll see you after I stop at the hospital," Demir said. He hung up and gave the phone back to Wallingford.

"The secretaries?" Abraham asked. "You think they might be targets?"

"I doubt it, but why chance it?"

They drove the rest of the way in silence, each lost in their own thoughts. Demir could understand the guilt Abraham felt. Had he taken the time to listen to Sandrovsky, the search would have been started that much sooner. But by the time the dumb ape was ready to say anything, the men had been missing for over two days.

At the hospital, Demir and Abraham trailed behind Doctor Owen as he supervised Matt's arrival in emergency. They stopped at the door of the treatment room.

"Doctor Owen," Demir held his arm, "he's to have a guard on him at all times."

"Of course, my boy," Owen said, giving him a fatherly pat on the shoulder. "But don't let them get underfoot."

"No problem," Demir said. Seeing Wallingford arrive after parking the car, he said, "I want round the clock watch on him. Someone will be here to relieve you, but for now, you're it."

"Got it," she said, and took a position outside the examining room.

Demir turned to find Abraham returning with two cups of vending machine coffee. He handed Demir a cup.

"It'll be okay," Abraham said. "We'll find them."

"They went missing last Friday, now it's Tuesday. Trail's too cold."

"We're not giving up, no matter how cold it is."

"I wasn't planning to." Demir took a sip of his coffee. Black, strong, and hot. Yet the caffeine didn't help his mood.

"Mr. Demir?" Dr. Owen called from the door to the exam room.

Demir and Abraham turned to the doctor.

"He's awake, but very groggy," Owen said.

"I need to talk to him," Demir said.

"I know you do," Owen said, "but only for a minute." He turned and they followed him inside.

Matt lay on the examination table, dressed in a hospital gown, hooked up to an EKG, an oxygen monitor clipped to his index finger, and an IV line. And he did look a hell of a lot healthier. Demir handed his cup to Abe.

"Dr. Stoddard?" he leaned over the bed and whispered. "It's me, Demir."

Matt's eyes flickered open for a moment and he seemed to focus. But all too soon, they closed again. Demir put his hand on the other man's shoulder, wanting to shake him, but settled for a firm grip instead. "Dr. Stoddard? Matt! Do you remember anything that happened?" Eyes flickered open. "Did you overhear anything to tell you who they were?"

The eyes blinked, he opened his mouth as though to talk. But again, the eyes closed.

"Doctor?" Demir shook his shoulder this time. "Did you overhear anything to tell us who they were? Matt!"

"That's enough for now," Owen said.

"What's wrong with him?" Demir asked. He reluctantly moved away from the patient. "Shouldn't the drugs have worn off by now?"

"I've ordered a battery of blood tests. Also scheduled an MRI." Owen broke off. Lowering his voice, he added, "I just worry that there may have been some brain damage. There are some bruises on his chest, consistent with CPR compressions. But without knowing what medication they gave him, or how long his heart was stopped…"

"Do what you can for him," Demir said, his voice tight, his chest heavy with anger. "Call me if there's any change."

"Of course," Owen said.

Taking his coffee back, Demir left the room with Abraham close behind. He stopped to talk to Wallingford.

"We'll be heading out now. You don't leave this door for anything. You gotta pee, hold it. No one gets in to see him unless they have hospital ID and then, you watch them like a hawk."

"What about visitors?" Wallingford said.

"What part of no one gets in did you miss?" Demir snapped.

"Uh, sir, what about him?" she pointed at the entrance to Emergency.

Demir turned to see the doors closing with Aidan peering in through the glass.

"He just arrived," Wallingford said.

"I see. He can visit." Demir knew that he shouldn't have snapped. In a lame attempt to apologize, he added, "Good job."

"Yes, sir," Wallingford said. "I'll make sure it's clear that he's the only visitor." After Demir left, she turned to Abraham, adding, "I didn't mean to make him mad."

"He's running on adrenaline. He's not really mad."

Demir heard the tail end of their conversation, realizing that no amount of apologizing was going to help. He *was* tired. He was frustrated. And now he'd have to deal with an overly emotional boyfriend. The doors swung open and Demir found Aidan near the door, shifting from one foot to the other. He hurried forward extending a hand.

"Thank you for bringing him home," Aidan said, giving a firm handshake. "Please, can I see him?"

"How did you find out so fast?" Demir asked, surprised to find Aidan calm, not the emotional wreck he was dreading.

"Laura called me. She called everyone. So, can I go in?"

"Yes, it's all right," Demir said.

"Thank you," Aidan said, hurrying past Abraham, who was on his way out. Before the doors closed, Demir saw Aidan standing by the exam bed reaching to touch the unconscious man's hand. But more importantly, he saw Wallingford discreetly enter the room.

"Everything's under control here," Abraham said. "No one's getting in to see him that doesn't belong. And you, old son," Abraham wrinkled his nose, "need a shower."

"You're no bouquet yourself, you know." Demir gave a dramatic sniff while wrinkling his nose, only to have a yawn take over. Covering his mouth, till it was over, he looked at his friend and said, "Home sounds like a plan."

CHAPTER NINETEEN

Demir let the pulsing shower jets pound out the stiffness and the frustrations. Eventually, he shut off the water, put on a bathrobe, and looked in the mirror, trying to remember the last time he'd shaved. A lifetime ago.

He reached for the auto-dispenser on the wall by the sink and started to methodically spread the gel on his face. This routine task helped clear his mind and centre him. Abraham had driven him home in Wallingford's car, with the suggestion that he rest and re-energize himself. Well, he'd slept enough on the flight home.

He had a lot to do. Find out where his men were. Find out where the leak was. Make sure the other scientists stayed safe.

Find out what the hell Kirby was really up to.

Dressed in jeans and a t-shirt, he sat on the edge of the bed to put on his runners. He forced himself to make time to eat a quick breakfast of buttered toast and instant coffee and was backing his car out of the garage long before the sun had even thought about rising.

He pulled into Cyber's parking lot twenty minutes later and, with a sense of déjà vu, parked next to Abraham's Volvo. Though the wind wasn't bitterly cold now, it was still pretty brisk and so he zipped up the windbreaker, trying to duck his neck deeper into the collar, lamenting the fact that he hadn't grabbed the weather-sensitive jacket instead.

"Glad to see you're feeling better," the elderly commissionaire said. "A tough flu going around."

"Sure was, Frank." Demir continued past to the next checkpoint.

"Good morning, sir," The security woman said. "Congratulations on bringing the doctor back."

"I see Abe's here already," Demir said. He ignored her comment and punched the elevator button.

"Yes, sir. Came in about an hour ago."

He probably came directly here after taking him home. Demir gave the security guard a faint smile as the elevator doors closed. On Sub 1, he passed Operations and headed directly for Abraham's office. Opening the door quietly, he peeked in to see Abraham asleep on the floor by the wall, covered with his ski jacket, using his arm for a pillow. That was something Demir could never get used to. He always needed to have something under his head. A rock had done the job in the past.

He quietly closed the door and returned to Operations.

"Welcome home, sir," the Ops man said. "It's great that you found Dr. Stoddard alive."

"Any developments?" Demir's jaw tensed slightly. Alive. But how much brain damage did he suffer because Demir waited too long to go after him?

"Nothing new. Kirby still insists that Mr. Henderson is on some hush hush mission. But we can't get confirmation on that. Mr. Abraham made a few calls when we came in."

"And I would have called you if there was anything new." A voice spoke from behind Demir. He turned to see Abraham standing in the doorway. "Ty, you're supposed to be sleeping."

"Plenty of time to sleep later," Demir said. He nodded thanks to the Ops man and signalled Abraham to follow him to his office. He asked, "Did you talk to Kirby about this mission?"

"He's not forthcoming with any info. Like, what a surprise."

They sat down, Demir behind his desk, Abraham in the opposite chair.

"Where's Sandrovsky?" Demir asked. "What does he have to say about all this?"

"According to others, they say he's been frantic. I left a message on his sat. I sent someone to his place, but he wasn't home. He sometimes spends the night at his girlfriend's. I was going to send someone there, but it's almost time for his shift."

"I want to see him the second he gets in," Demir said. He shrugged off his jacket and leaned back in his chair. "You know, I wonder if the car was left somewhere and it got towed?"

"We've checked that. Remember? Maybe you should get some shut-eye?"

"But what if it got towed across the river?"

"To Quebec?"

"Why not? A different province is the perfect place to hide a car. I know someone in the SQ that might be able to help out." Demir called his friend in the Sureté du Quebec—the Quebec provincial police. After a few minutes on the phone, he hung up saying to Abraham, "He'll check into it and get back to me."

The phone rang and Demir answered. It was Operations.

"Mr. Demir, Dr. Jessup just arrived in the complex. She called asking to see you when you've got time."

"Thanks, I'll be right there." Demir hung up, checked his watch. "It's barely six and Dr. Jessup's in."

"I guess she couldn't wait once the word spread," Abraham said.

Absentmindedly, Demir smoothed down his hair and was bewildered by the wide smile Abraham gave him. Both left: Abraham to Operations, Demir to see Laura Jessup.

Demir knocked on her office door and entered. Before he could say a word, she ran to him throwing her arms around his neck in a tight embrace. He automatically returned the embrace, breathing in the hypnotic fragrance of her perfume, before he realized what he was doing and loosened his hold. She kept her hands on his shoulders as she smiled up at him with tears streaming down her cheeks.

"Thank you for finding him," she finally said. "Let's sit down."

He was openly surprised at the clean sofa. In fact, the entire office was neat, with not a single file folder to be seen. He sat down as she settled next to him.

"I stopped by the hospital, but they wouldn't let me in to see Matt," she said.

"Mr. Monette said you called everyone. I'm curious how you found out."

"Edna called. She said Major Kirby from DND phoned to tell her once you had landed safely in Ottawa. Now," she said, curling her legs under her, "tell me everything."

Demir was taken aback by her comment. Apparently, Kirby wasn't beyond undermining his authority with Internal Security. It was Demir's job to contact Laura, and he would have done so once Matt had been safely delivered to the hospital. One more thing to add to the list of questions to look into. Returning his attention to the conversation at hand, he said, "I'm sorry I didn't tell you. Orders. We suspected a leak and thought it better to limit who knew. As it was, things didn't work out as expected." He summarized his mission, leaving out the lives he'd sacrificed and Anton's name.

The storytelling over, he suddenly became aware of her warm hand on his arm, attentively taking in every word.

"By the way, good acting," she said, removing her hand. "We all thought you were really sick."

"I wish," he said with a laugh. "Someone slipped me something. And if I ever get my hands on them..."

"Well, after a good meal and some sleep, I'm sure you'll figure it out." She smiled brightly and with such conviction that he almost believed her.

"Thanks," Demir said. He realized that she didn't know that Henderson and Mitchell were missing. Best to keep that information quiet, for now. In any investigation, it was always a good idea to hold back information. Damn, he was treating her like a suspect. But with the source of the leak still unknown, it would be easier to gauge everyone's reaction to the news. Shit, was this how Kirby justified his secrecy and lies?

He recognized the telltale signs that she wanted to ask something else by avoiding eye contact, the twirling of a strand of hair.

"Doctor," he began, "I may look tired, but believe me, I'm fine. If there's something else you need, please ask."

"Well," she gave a small, embarrassed laugh. She looked down at her hands, folded neatly on her lap before continuing. "There is something I'd like your help with. I want to look at the access logs, but Security won't release the information without your approval."

"Is there a problem with someone?"

"No." Her neatly folded hands twitched once, but he noticed. She gave a nonchalant shrug and added, "It's just for some budget information I need. That's all." She looked up at him with those green eyes that always reached into his soul, melting him from the inside out, making it hard to say no.

He also recognized that she was lying.

"I can't really give you full access to the records," Demir said. "But if you have specific dates in mind, I can have Ops send those records to you."

"I'll get it for you." She went around her desk. He didn't miss the fact that she unlocked the drawer. She paused, looking at the paper, then returned it to the drawer and locked it.

"Actually, it's a range. The last several weeks. Here, I'll write it down for you." She pulled a sheet of paper off the notepad on her desk and wrote quickly.

He stood and took the sheet of paper and tried to decipher the scrawl. All the scientists had a similar scrawl, except for Drake with his neat block script.

"I'll make sure you get the information as soon as possible."

"Thank you." She came around the desk as though to hug him again. She stopped short, perhaps sensing his discomfort.

"Please don't hesitate to ask me if there's anything else," Demir said, and left.

In the reception area, Edna was just coming in. Her back to him, she removed her long, burgundy coat, unzipped her boots, and slipped into black low heeled pumps. All with the air of someone very much at home.

"I see it's snowing again," he said.

She spun around. At first, her look was one of surprise but within a second, she recovered and extended a hand.

"Welcome back and congratulations," she said, with a trembling smile.

"Thanks." He waved Laura's list adding, "I guess you couldn't bully my men into giving you the info for Dr. Jessup."

"What?" She looked confused for a moment, then added stiffly, "Not for lack of trying."

"You're in pretty early, even for you." The momentary look of confusion on her face surprised him. Had he just given Laura away? Obviously she hadn't gone through her secretary for the info.

"Oh, I thought Dr. Jessup might need me," she said, her voice tight. Her smile looked forced.

"At some point today, I'd like to discuss your talent for clairvoyance," he added.

"Excuse me?"

"How you know things before they're announced. My promotion. Knowing the director would be in early. What is it, an underground secretaries' network?"

The pretend smile froze for an instant, then quickly returned to life. She seemed to be searching for something to say. Taking pity on her discomfort, he added, "I'll see you later."

But pity only went so far. He wanted to take another look at her background check. He stopped in at Operations. As soon as he entered, the Ops woman reported.

"We got a lead on the car," she said. "A man phoned Colonial Towing, in Quebec, claiming they'd broken down. He said he lived in the area and would come by later to pick it up."

"Where'd they pick it up from?"

"Ottawa River Parkway. Deschênes Rapids Lookout, just before Carling Avenue."

"At least we know where the car is," Demir said.

"Not really, sir. The company that towed it has several lots and well, their records aren't the best. They're not sure which impound lot it went to. And with the heavy wet snow Gatineau just had, the land lines are down."

"Don't they have a sat number?"

"Unfortunately, no."

"Okay," Demir sighed. "Have someone check each one till they find the car." At least they had a lead. He turned at the door and added, "Also, I want a deep dive into Edna Esteban's background."

In the meantime, he wanted to inspect the Lookout. Deciding that was something he'd rather do alone, Demir sent Abraham a message telling him where he was going and to hold down the fort till he returned.

He got his windbreaker from the coat rack, double checking to make sure he had his phone with him. It was the disposable sat he'd bought in England. Useless here. He tossed it into the wastebasket, then, with an afterthought about recycling, he took it out and left it on his desk.

He opened his top left drawer to get his own sat phone and found a folded sheet of paper on it. Probably a message from Abraham reminding him to eat. He read the message.

How about that Queen?

It was unsigned, but he recognized Henderson's handwriting immediately. Obviously, he was supposed to know what that meant. But he had no idea. Folding it up again, he put it back in the drawer, farther to the back this time and picked up his sat phone.

He turned it on and was relieved to see it was still fully charged. Leaving his office, he noticed Yasmin had come in. As soon as she saw him, she threw her arms around his neck, hugging him. This time only slightly better prepared, he returned a paternal hug.

"Welcome back," she said, with a bright smile.

He managed to get out of her embrace and move to a more comfortable distance when a new voice spoke behind him.

"You're back, eh."

He turned to see Jeanette standing behind him. Yasmin stepped aside as Jeanette gave him a strangling hug. Jeanette was a small woman, but deceptively strong. He looked up in time to see Elton hobbling at a pace too fast for his crutches to keep up. Eventually, he let them fall to the floor and dove for Demir, who managed to catch him and actually keep both of them standing. Demir held onto Elton while the women retrieved his crutches. Apparently, everyone had come in to work as soon as they got the good news, knowing that Demir himself would be in soon. All this attention unnerved him a little.

"It's wonderful to have you home," Jeannette said.

"They won't let us see Matt," Elton said.

"I know," Demir said. "It's just for a while."

"You look tired," Yasmin said.

"Tell us everything," Jeannette said.

They looked at him in anticipation of his tale. Unaware that, until his missing men were found, the story had no ending.

"I'll tell you what, we'll get together later today and I'll fill you in. The important thing is that Dr. Stoddard is safely back."

"Aidan stayed at the hospital, until the nurses threw him out,"

Yasmin added. "He called to say he's coming in to see you."

"Can you get a hold of him before he does, please?" Demir said. "I'll be going out for a while, so he might as well go home. I'll call him when I get back."

"Sounds like a plan," Jeanette said. "Hope you're going home to rest yourself."

"Soon," he said, and headed out.

He arrived fifteen minutes later at the Ottawa River Parkway Deschênes Rapids Lookout. He parked across the parking lot entrance to block any other cars from pulling in. Unlikely in the unplowed lot. A vain attempt at protecting a scene that had been open to traffic and the elements for four days.

He walked along the edge of the parking lot, where most would tend to park. He stood at the end of the lot to watch the river. Ice still covered it near the shore, but further to the middle of the river, he watched as the white-capped river rushed by. Any bodies would resurface in the spring somewhere down stream. His skin prickled at the thought.

He ground his teeth, thinking about Kirby's insistence that Henderson was still on some mission. Mitchell would never have left his pregnant wife without telling her something. Knowing from his own undercover days, families might not know details of where you were, but they *always* knew that you were working and had a general idea when you'd return.

What were they doing here? Mitchell was supposed to be driving the boss home, so what the hell were they doing in the opposite end of the city? A sight-seeing detour? Or a meeting gone wrong?

He continued along the outskirts of the parking area, studying the fresh snow. The lot hadn't been plowed, but he could see undulations where vehicles had been here between snow falls. If this was the VidCast of a forensics reality show, nice, neat flashback shots would appear, allowing the audience to follow as the investigator solved the case.

He walked along the side closest to the river, trying to ignore the growing wet around his ankles and the snow that slipped into his runners. This wasn't a damn TV show. He wasn't a goddamn forensics investigator. He was just a failed RCMP agent. And now, everyone was hugging him, congratulating him because of what? Blind luck had brought him to Matt? He'd paid with two lives to bring him home. And now two more men missing. Not bad odds. One alive. Two dead, two more missing.

He was no hero.

Fuck this. Fuck the snow that destroyed his evidence. He cut across the grass area, heading towards his car, as he glared at the parking lot and any evidence destroyed by the snow. Frustrated, he took longer, less careful strides, but with little traction from his runners, he slipped on a rock and tripped over another, then stomped on one more.

He stopped. That last one wasn't a rock. It didn't snap under his foot like a twig. He deliberately retraced his footsteps, then knelt down and carefully brushed back the snow with his bare hands. Layer by layer. To uncover what had tripped him. He left it in place.

He pulled out his sat and phoned his friend at the RCMP forensics team.

"Hi, Bob."

"Hey, Ty."

"You heard about my missing people?"

"Yeah, Abraham told me. Sorry to hear about it. Any word yet?"

"We found the spot that the car was towed from. I'm here now and I could use your expertise." He brushed back some more snow.

"I may have found Mitchell's gun."

Hands clenched in his pockets, Demir stamped his feet to warm them, impatiently watching the forensics team remove the gun from the frozen mud.

When he and Abraham were in the RCMP, they had worked with Bob on several occasions. Demir knew him and wanted him to process the scene rather than the local police, feeling he could better control the investigation. Jurisdiction might be a bit blurry, but since Cyber was on federal land and the crime started there, RCMP could be called in.

"It won't be long now," Bob told him. "After four days, I'm amazed that it's still here. But with the snowfall on Saturday, then again now, it's like the gun was waiting for you. You sure it's your man's?"

"Yes. I just got confirmation on the serial number. If he drew it—doesn't look good." Demir looked beyond the forensics team to the river.

"I've ordered the river searched. But with the spring runoff and the high flow rate, a body could have travelled quite a distance."

"Bodies," Demir corrected. Voice monotone, he added, "Our chief's still missing."

"I know."

One of the other investigators came over to report, "The gun's unfired. We'll have to process it for prints at the lab."

"So, he only had time to draw it," Demir said, his voice low.

"Okay, bag it," Bob told the forensics people.

Demir's sat pinged. "Demir here."

"Ty, they found the car," Abraham said. "A couple of our guys are there keeping an eye on it. I'll text you the address. And I'll meet you there."

"Good," Demir said, "make sure no one touches it till I get there with the forensics team." He checked the text message and to his friend he said, "My people found the car. Can you..."

"A team will meet us there," Bob said. "You drive."

"Your people staying here?" Demir asked, as they got into his car. "After so much time has passed..."

"Hey, my people can work miracles. If there's anything left here, they'll find it."

They drove across the river, making their way up the winding road into the Gatineau Hills. Though the snow had been cleared, the roads were still slick, especially on the sharp inclines. He loved driving through here in the fall when the leaves were brilliant with colour. Soon, if the snow ever gave up its stranglehold, the trees would start to grow buds and before you knew it, the bare branches would form a canopy against the sky. Let nature sort out her seasons in her own time. For now, Demir just wanted to get there. Check out the car. Search through the evidence and find his missing men.

After forty minutes, they reached the impound and parked near Henderson's car. The area was tied off with police tape. Two SQ policemen from Quebec stood guard with two I.S. men. Another man and woman stood by waiting. As Demir and Bob approached, the man turned to Bob.

"They won't let us near the car!" he snapped.

"They're on orders," Bob told him, "can't fault them for their loyalty, can we?"

Demir noticed a slight edge in Bob's voice. Either the man was a rookie or a hardcore bastard. It didn't matter because the boss' tone shut him up.

Demir asked his men, "Do you have the spare key?" One man handed Demir the key, who in turn handed it to Bob.

"First thing, let's open her up," Bob said, putting on disposable gloves to protect the scene. He tried the door handle, reporting, "Door's unlocked."

"Can you pop the trunk, please?" Demir said. The trunk sprang open. Before Demir could move around to look in, he heard a gasp from one of his men, then the other man covered his eyes with a groan.

In the heavy slow motion of a nightmare, Demir's eyes fixed on his men. One looked up at him, his eyes red, mouth gaping silently.

Finally, he came around to look inside the trunk.

Laying on his side in a partial fetal position. Hands near his face.

Mitchell.

CHAPTER TWENTY

Demir knew people were talking to him but the rhythmic thump in his ears blocked their voices. He didn't want to hear them. Vaguely aware of Abraham's hand on his shoulder, he looked at him and through a haze, saw his friend's furrowed brow, mouth moving slowly, facial expression softened in gentle understanding. Concern? For him? Everyone looked at him with a similar expression, even the rookie guy. Why? Didn't they know he was trying to work? He had to concentrate on the body in the car. Had to gather in all the information he could.

There was a stain on Mitchell's light brown suede jacket. Over his heart. His jacket had been partially unzipped. The young man hated the cold and wouldn't have done that. Had he suspected trouble and reached for his shoulder holster?

"Bob," Demir said, not looking away from the body in the trunk. "After you process the scene, let me know when you tow the car back to Ottawa. I want to be there when you go over it." His voice echoed calmly in his head. He forced his eyes away from Mitchell, then started to back towards his own car, calling over his shoulder, "Let me know as soon as you have the autopsy report."

He pulled the car keys out of his pocket, but Abraham took them from his hand and guided him towards the passenger door. In the distance, he thought he heard him say, "I better drive." Good idea. That would leave him free to sort things out in his mind.

Free to think about how he was going to rip Kirby's throat out.

But all he could think about, all he could see was Mitchell. The young Black man's face was calm, restful as though asleep. His hands close to his face.

Despite Mitchell's doubts in his ability to guard Elton Chan, the young security man had died trying to protect Henderson. Was Henderson still alive? What were they doing on the Parkway? So many questions. There was only one question Demir knew had an easy to find answer. Why did it take so long to know something was wrong?

If they'd known right away, they might have been able to save Mitchell and Henderson, or at least the trail wouldn't be so cold.

Demir's hands tightened into fists as he imagined Kirby's throat being crushed in his hands, only to have the scene dissolve when Abraham patted his arm.

"We're here."

Demir looked up from his fists and stared dream-like at the sign on the building. Cyber Inc.

He entered the building like some sort of automaton. He was oblivious to the world around him. Only saw his feet walking, taking him farther into the building. Into the elevator. Into his office. He sat behind his desk.

He needed answers. He needed facts.

There was a loud knock on his door and Sandrovsky burst in.

"Is it true? You found Mitchell?" Sandrovsky's voice was near hysterical, his eyes wild.

"He's dead," Demir said, vaguely aware of Abraham standing behind him with a hand on his shoulder. To calm him? Or was it to keep him from lunging at Sandrovsky's throat? To Sandrovsky he said, "Sit down. Tell me what happened."

"I don't know." Sandrovsky shook his head with such conviction that Demir wasn't sure which of them he was trying to convince.

"I said, sit!"

With dog-like obedience, the larger man slumped into the chair, looking up at his boss with miserable, confused eyes. Harshly, Demir continued.

"When I last saw you—you were packing up Henderson's things from his office."

"Yes, sir," Sandrovsky began. Gulping hard, he continued. "Kirby called and told me that the chief had resigned and to pack up his personal stuff. Not much, after all these years, you know. It fitted into two boxes. Then the chief himself called and asked me to make sure I packed a few extra things, like that poster behind his desk. It's his favourite you know, just like the picture of..." At the impatient huff from Demir, he got back on track. "Kirby called me in the afternoon to say the chief was ready to be picked up. I asked Mitchell to take the boxes and get him."

"He took the boxes?" Demir interrupted, "Where'd he put them?"

"I helped put them in the trunk. Then he went to pick up the chief. That's the last I saw him."

Abraham removed the restraining hand from his shoulder, but maybe he should have kept it there. Demir rocked back in his chair, studying the pathetic mess before him. He wondered if Sandrovsky was letting his hair grow back or if he just hadn't shaved his head for days. His suit jacket looked like it had been slept in, his shirt mis-buttoned. With the size of his neck, he never tolerated a tie, claiming it felt like a noose. But today he wore one, loosely knotted and nowhere near the centre of his collar. Was this noose his way of showing remorse?

Then he remembered something that he'd dismissed at the time as an emotional mistake.

"As I think about it, you knew about Henderson's resignation before I did."

"Major Kirby called me in the morning. Told me not to say nothing to anyone," Sandrovsky said, more than willing to answer every question without hesitation.

"If I find out that you did suspect something..." Demir began.

"You think I'd let my own man get killed? If I'd known there was any chance of trouble, I'd have gone myself."

"If I get even a hint, I won't call the police, I'll take care of you myself." Demir leaned forward, white knuckled fists on his desk. "Get out of my sight!"

"Don't think of leaving the complex," Abraham added.

Before the larger man retreated to the door, Demir called to him. "Are you the son of a bitch that drugged me before the mission?"

"Major Kirby said to," Sandrovsky answered, turning to face him. "He told me to sneak chloral hy-something out of the infirmary. Just to make you pass out. I never thought you'd get so sick." He waited to see if there was more but when Demir remained silent, he turned and left the office, closing the door slowly behind him.

Demir became vaguely aware of Abraham's hand on his shoulder again. "Now we know how Kirby gets his information." Demir said.

"Ty…"

"I'm okay." Demir rubbed his eyes, then picked up the phone, dialling his RCMP friend's number. "Bob, are there a couple of boxes in the trunk?" He paused. "I need them ASAP. I know, but I need to go through them." After a short pause. "Thanks, I'll meet you there." He hung up.

"Ty…" Abraham started.

Demir looked up at him, seeing the pain of losing a man mirrored in his friend's face. "Bob's forensics team is about to tow the car back to their labs so they can go over it more carefully. I'm going to check out the boxes."

"I'll come with you."

"No, Abe. I want you to stay here. Let me know when they identify the bullet?"

With a reluctant nod, Abraham left.

Demir went to Henderson's office in case Sandrovsky might have left something behind.

The desk surface had been cleared of everything except the desk lamp. He searched through the desk drawers, checking for secret panels. Nothing. The file cabinet contained work files, memos, reports, personnel files. Nothing out of the ordinary at first glance. He activated the desk to see the computer screen. Still silent and asleep. But Demir already had full access to it. Besides, the chief had never really taken to computers, preferring things old school, as he said on countless occasions.

He looked around the room. The missing poster and pictures left a lighter coloured shadow on the wall behind the desk. He'd already searched the office and another quick search didn't result in any hidden messages. He left to check out the boxes in the car.

Demir slipped on the ident gloves that Bob handed him and stepped around the car to the trunk. He took a deep breath, waiting an eternity for the forensics woman to open the trunk.

When he'd first looked in here, he'd only seen Mitchell. Now, with the young man's body removed, Demir saw the boxes. It seemed like they were already rummaged through and some things were strewn around in the trunk. There was blood on top of some of the items; which meant that Mitchell's body had been put in after the search. Had they found what they were looking for? He methodically searched through them, careful about preserving evidence. He found blank memo pads, paper clips, pens. Sandrovsky had really got carried away with packing.

He found a bottle of Tylenol. A quick inspection of the pills verified it. He found an unopened pack of gum. The gum seemed odd though. Ever since Henderson got dental implants two years ago, he'd refused to chew gum, saying he didn't want people to see his teeth stop chewing before he did. The gum could be old but Demir found a drugstore receipt for it and the Tylenol, dated last month. He picked up the gum package and he felt something hard inside. Closer examination revealed a neat slit at one end. He looked around. The forensics team had courteously moved away to give him some privacy. He unceremoniously ripped the package open. A metal key fell out landing in the trunk. He picked up the key and studied it.

An old fashioned, three-centimetre-long key that seemed oddly familiar. Not for anything at Cyber. Most of the offices and labs had keypad or palm print access. With a silent apology to Bob, he pocketed the key and continued his search.

Saying Sandrovsky had been a little slap-happy packing was an understatement. The photo of Mrs. Henderson made sense, but the fool had also packed the black and white photo of the queen and the team spirit poster of the relay race with the caption, IT TAKES TEAM WORK TO REACH YOUR GOAL.

No, Sandrovsky had said that Henderson had called and had specifically told him what to pack. His wife's picture made sense, maybe even the poster, but the other picture...

How about that Queen?

The note that Henderson had put in his desk made sense now.

He picked up the old black and white photo of a very young monarch in an eight by ten wooden frame. Examining the back, he took it apart to see if anything was hidden behind the photo. Nothing. Tilting the frame in the light, he found something engraved into the frame. A single word. Basement.

He looked through the boxes to make sure there was nothing else there. He double checked the poster. Nothing but the message for teamwork.

He smiled. Henderson preferred to do things old school. A teamwork poster. An antique key. An old photo with the clue 'basement'.

Like the antique cabinet Henderson had given him to take care of because Mrs. Henderson insisted it would clash with their new furniture, but he didn't have the heart to get rid of it. He was sure that the key in his pocket would fit into the chief's cabinet.

With the key feeling heavy in his pocket, he thanked Bob and his team and sped home.

In his basement, Demir found the cabinet with several boxes in front of it... He cleared everything out of the way and tried the key. It fit.

He opened the cabinet door to reveal two shelves. On the top, he found Henderson's marriage certificate. His will. On the bottom, he pulled out a large manila envelope, thick with papers. And a letter, addressed to him.

Carefully he opened the letter. When he read the first line, he got a sick feeling in the pit of his stomach.

Tyler,

Not to sound overly melodramatic, but if you are reading this it means that I am missing or dead.

I am sorry that I've left the operation of I.S. more and more to you the past year. There are reasons that will come clear as you read on. It was hard not to confide in you, but I wanted to keep you safe.

As a joint project with military interests, DND has kept close tabs on all aspects of security. This is how Kirby has justified his involvement. Dr. Jessup managed to keep interferences in the research area to a minimum, but couldn't fully eliminate it.

I merely had to provide security for secrets that many would pay handsomely for.

I was approached by an outside group for information about the research. They wanted information, progress reports, all the things that I have access to. Money, of course, was NEVER something I would consider, but threats were. My wife and daughter are the only family that I care about. When they threatened them, I had no choice but to co-operate but only enough to keep them happy and cause minimal damage.

To further keep the damage low, I had to distance myself from the operation of Internal Security. It was incredibly hard to act the disinterested, doddering old fool. But it did work. For a while.

Sandrovsky helped me a lot. He also took photos of my meetings to keep a record. He's completely loyal to me; even though he took his orders from Kirby, he always let me know. Don't judge him too harshly. At heart, he's a good boy.

I have included several documents, a detailed list of the times I've been contacted, a detailed record of everything I gave them. I trust you to do the right thing.

Henderson

Demir's face burned with the heat of shame. All the horrible things he'd thought of Henderson. Incompetent. Lazy. Old.

His sat rang, interrupting the self-pity. It was Abraham.

"Looks like we may have a break in figuring out who sold out Stoddard."

"That's great, I'll be there in fifteen minutes." Demir said, hanging up quickly, in no mood to talk at the moment. That's when he noticed the date on the letter.

The letter was dated last Monday, the day Matt was kidnapped. Years ago, Demir had given Henderson a key to his place to be used for emergencies. That had to be why he insisted on going home after returning from Toronto: to prepare the papers and hide them in this cabinet. He must have known that his days were numbered.

He opened up the manila envelope and slipped out the thick stack of papers, plus a slip drive. Quickly flipping through them, he realized it was a combination of transcripts of conversations and notes. At the bottom were several photos of Henderson meeting with the same man at various public locations. He returned everything to the envelope, put it back in the cabinet and locked it. He hid the key in the overhead air vent, an old hiding place that Abraham knew about. He also had a secret hiding spot at his home.

And if anything unexpected did happen to him before he could tell his friend about it, Abraham would know to check the vent. He would also find the key which would lead to the papers in the cabinet. Abe would know what to do with them

Time for *him* to take charge.

Wasn't that the last thing he'd thought as he'd hailed a cab in New York? An outsider looking in wouldn't think that he was in charge of anything. But he was. They'd tried everything in their arsenal of interrogation that would make the wardens at Guantanamo Bay envious. They'd been disappointed but he could also see that they were somewhat impressed that they couldn't get any information out of him. He wouldn't tell them the security access codes. He wouldn't tell them what new progress the scientists had made. He wouldn't tell them about their security schedule. He wouldn't tell them anything.

He had decided over a year ago that it was time to start preparing for a day like today. A day he would say, enough. The day he would stop co-operating with an agreement that he'd never agreed to.

But those dark, compact minds hadn't anticipated that their tin soldier in charge of the information flow would lock the gate in the best way he knew how. An important principle of Aikido stated that true victory was victory over one's self. And that had led to his victory over his captors, who tried every tool from their arsenal of interrogation.

How could they get information that he didn't have?

For over a year now, Henderson had made sure that he didn't read any of the reports. The security access codes were automatically changed right after Stoddard's kidnapping, and he made sure he never looked at any of the changes. A tough task at times, but he'd asked Yasmin to have his computer turned on and ready for him when he arrived at work until it soon became habit for her to log him in, even without his asking. He made sure he didn't look at any of Dr. Jessup's monthly reports before they were filed on the secure network, though honestly that was easy because he'd always found them boring. He wasn't a scientist. He was a security man with a military background. If he'd wanted to go into science, then maybe he would have paid attention in high school physics class, instead of writing love notes to future wife Brenda.

He never regretted that bad mark.

He did regret hurting Demir by callously bringing up that doomed undercover operation. From the day he'd met Demir, Henderson had recognized the shadow of pain that existed behind his eyes. The same look Henderson saw reflected in his mirror after his tour of duty in the Far East. He would have given anything not to be the catalyst for that expression, but Demir's concern about Henderson's recent behaviour meant he kept coming into his office, calling him, trying to find him, making it difficult for Henderson to finish what he needed to. It was a last resort that worked. And as he knew it would, the revived memory made Demir turn his back on Henderson.

He wondered now, as he frequently did, if he should have told Demir what was really going on. But now as before, he dismissed the thought. If the young man had known, there was no force on earth that would stop him from taking care of things immediately instead of waiting until the time was right. And that time was now.

Demir would take care of everything, as long as he found the hidden note about the queen's photo. And understood the clue. He felt confident that Demir wouldn't let Kirby run all over him with orders and national security excuses. Kirby was used to giving orders and having them followed. He'd taken advantage of Henderson being ex-military and of his loyalty to the so-called chain of command. When Kirby had asked what was going on with Henderson at DND headquarters that last

Friday, Henderson had originally told him that it was simple burnout caused by the scientist's kidnapping. Not a total idiot, Kirby hadn't believed him, and had demanded to know the truth.

But he couldn't exactly tell him that he was distancing himself from daily operations so that even under the most expert of interrogations, he wouldn't reveal anything. He'd told him instead that he was sick. A fatal disease. One that no one knew about. Not even his wife. He remembered proudly how he'd even managed to throw in watery eyes. He watched the old military man soften right before his eyes. His obsessive need to verify everything meant that it wouldn't be long before Kirby discovered he was lying. But by then it would be too late for him to do anything about it.

Of all the regrets in his life, the largest and most painful was the fact that his vocal surprise at the arrival of Smitty's men had distracted Mitchell and delayed him from reacting in time. The young man had so much to live for, and still he'd protectively stepped between Henderson and Smitty's men, shouting, "Run sir!"

As the men bundled Henderson into their car, he heard Darius Mitchell take a last breath, speaking a single name—Meesha. Mitchell's last thoughts were of his wife. Probably wondering how she would manage alone. How their child would be born and grow up without a dad. Painful last thoughts, but at least his death had been quick and relatively painless.

Henderson heard the metallic clunk of the lock turning. A flutter of air cooled his face as the door opened.

Amidst all his regrets surfaced one source of relief. That he'd kissed his wife Brenda goodbye and told her that he loved her that last morning. He smiled even more as he remembered the feel of her lips. The smell of strawberries in her hair. The taste of her breath. The warmth of her embrace. Each goodbye was as though it was the last time he'd see her. He knew that she suspected something was wrong, but he knew she'd never question him. She'd wait for him to feel ready to talk, if he could. It was a habit from military days. And when the missions would haunt him, she was always there. Ready to be supportive with words or with a silent embrace.

The door opened wider. A loud explosion seemed to fill the room.

A warmth flowed through him. Surrounded him. The pain was gone. He thought of Brenda going on alone. He knew that she was strong and independent and would eventually find comfort. He was so very tired. He wanted to rest. To close his eyes. He started to take his final breath.

"Brenda..."

At Cyber, Demir sat at his desk and took the memory slip from Abraham. He inserted it into his computer and quickly scanned the highlighted phone records for the complex, complete with dates, times, and duration.

"There are all kinds of overseas calls," Abraham began, as he pointed to the screen, "but one number was called an inordinate number of times. Especially just before Stoddard left for the conference. And every single call was made from Drake's phone."

"Not what I expected," Demir said.

"I've always known he's guilty."

"I know. Just feels too easy."

"Easy? You got any idea how many calls the handful of people here make in a month? The computer sorted every call made. There's no doubt." Abraham continued, his voice rising in pitch. "It all makes sense. He never wants people around him. Probably the only reason he let Stoddard work with him was because he was planning to sell him off all along."

"Look, Abe, I hate the bastard too. But let's get more evidence before we execute him."

"Why can't we shoot him, then get the evidence?"

Muttering curses, Abraham retreated to his office with the phone records, slamming his door shut. He slumped into his desk chair. What the hell more proof did Demir want?

Was he angry because Demir refused to believe Drake was behind everything?

Or was it knowing that he'd brushed Sandrovsky off when he tried to tell him about the missing men? If he'd listened, the search would have started Sunday night, not waiting until Sandrovsky couldn't keep quiet anymore. Abraham was more furious that the son of a bitch hadn't spoken up on Friday – when they were first overdue.

Abraham also kept wondering if he should have run off to England to offer back up when it wasn't really needed. Demir got to Newcastle safely. But he knew Demir and that he'd have tried to save both the old man and the scientist, getting himself killed in the process. The old man would be dead and the scientist would be gone.

It hurt too much to try to make sense of everything that had happened. He couldn't change it. He couldn't bring Mitchell back. But he could try to find Henderson and track down who was behind the turmoil that had attacked their lives.

He opened a copy of the records he'd given Demir. Rather than let the computer do it, he painstakingly compared the phone calls to who was in the complex at the time.

After a while, he discovered some of the calls were made when Drake wasn't in the complex. Damn! He'd been so sure that the bastard was guilty. Next, he checked the scientists and again several calls were made when none of them were in. How about the secretaries? No, they were clear. With a sinking feeling, he accessed the logs for I.S. and was relieved to find that Sandrovsky was also clear. It had to be a computer glitch.

It sure as fuck better be a computer glitch. Otherwise it meant someone had tampered with the computer records. And if that was true, then the security breach was definitely internal.

The only way to be really sure would be to check the handwritten logs made by the guard on surface duty. Abraham went to Operations to get the logs, anticipating the headache he was going to get trying to decipher some of the prescription-like handwriting. But looking forward to giving more than a headache to the person that was the source of the leak.

Fully dressed in pants and a sweater, Edna sat on the edge of her bed staring at the clock. 4:37 a.m. How did the events of the past week come to this? Life at Cyber Inc had started out so innocently. A group of scientists working on research that they enjoyed, in a dilapidated building where people were grateful to have running water and never complained about its temperature.

Then the military took over and life changed. Dietrich, the first research director, had changed from an interesting, aging man, to a senile, old fool with a touch of paranoia. She chuckled at the memory of when she told him about a movie she'd just seen where the crime was solved by taking a shredded letter and putting it back together. She couldn't order the new shredders fast enough, but in the meantime he'd ordered I.S. to actually re-shred the paper. She laughed aloud, remembering the frustration of the security people trying to re-feed the small squares through the shredders. She had been amazed that no fingertips were lost, although the use of skin glue had significantly increased. That is until Doc Owen had put a stop to the insanity. Edna had to admit that she'd been sad to see the old director and his endless antics retire.

He'd been so easy to control.

But she'd enjoyed her new boss's arrival. Laura Jessup was much nicer, not to mention saner. Even in the midst of the loss of her mother, Dr. Jessup surpassed that other fool in efficiency.

And they became more than boss and secretary. They became friends, their relationship cemented by the tragic death of Laura's mother. That bond made following Kirby's orders to keep track of the research director much easier.

Or so she thought. After Matt went missing, Kirby had ordered her to keep an even closer watch on Dr. Jessup and submit daily reports. Edna exploited the crush Demir had on the director, obvious to everyone but the target of his feelings. Edna hoped that he'd confide in Dr. Jessup secrets that he shouldn't. Unfortunately, in an attempt to further endear herself to the director, Edna's clingy methods had the opposite effect. So no further information was forthcoming from that route.

Kirby had told Edna that Demir would be absent for a short time and that she was ordered to keep an even closer watch on Dr. Jessup. To know where she was at every moment. He'd assured her that "this situation would be over soon." It didn't take a rocket scientist to figure out that Demir had been sent to retrieve Matt.

She couldn't allow that. She'd had no choice but to slip Demir a mild poison, not lethal but it would have made him too sick to move. She never anticipated the strength the man had.

Damn that stupid, overbearing Kirby. Just because she was ex-military, he thought that he could order her about like she was one of his underlings. She'd put up with it for a long time.

But if he'd only agreed to give her more money, as she'd wanted, then she wouldn't have gone looking for a better paying boss.

Edna peeked through the blinds out the front window. The Internal Security car was still there. Damn! Matt was back, so why didn't they call off the protection? Did they suspect someone?

She turned from her window. Picked up her suitcase carrying the essentials and a few mementos. She patted the front pocket of her pants to ensure the access code to the off-shore bank was in there. The account contained more than enough to live comfortably. However, had the sale of the scientist gone as planned, she would be living in luxury now.

She took out a set of car keys belonging to a friend who lived a few blocks away. The car would be in his driveway. She'd arranged with him to pick it up tomorrow evening from the airport.

She slipped out the back door, unseen by her security shadow. Just one stop to make and then she'd leave her familiar life behind and catch any flight headed out of the country.

CHAPTER TWENTY ONE

By 6:00 p.m., the nurses once again ordered Aidan Monette to leave Matt Stoddard's side, claiming his presence was agitating their patient. Just because his BP, heart rate, and even brain waves went off the chart whenever Aidan spoke to him didn't mean he was agitated. They just didn't understand. It was obvious to anyone that knew him that Matt recognized his voice and was fighting to stay conscious.

Yesterday, when he'd first seen Matt lying in the bed, looking so pale and vulnerable, he wasn't sure he could bear it. But after staying by his side, talking about nothing really, Aidan started to believe that everything would be okay. Matt's vital signs were getting stronger. He'd accidentally dozed off in the chair several times during the day, until the nurses insisted he leave. Go home and get some rest. Knowing that he'd be more use to Matt if he was better rested, he did go home to shower, change into fresh clothes, eat a peanut butter and jam sandwich, and was back at the hospital in less than and hour and a half. Rest was overrated anyway.

So, he'd stayed overnight again, coffee keeping him awake, as he spoke to Matt. Hoping his voice would bring him out of the coma.

Matt was scheduled for an MRI overnight to check for brain damage, but the test had been delayed due to some technical problems. He'd offered to take a look at the machine but the ungrateful staff had brushed his expertise aside with claims of voiding a warranty or some shit like that. What the hell did a warranty matter when lives stood in the balance?

The horse-faced nurse finally lost patience with his constant suggestions for repairs and had hospital security escort him out.

In the hospital parking lot, Aidan leaned his head on the steering wheel, feeling exhausted and emotionally drained.

Where had the time gone? Two years ago, Aidan was ready to leave his career, his home, everything, to try to find what was missing in his life. He handed in his resignation but promised to wait until a replacement was hired. The longest few months of his life.

Then, Matt Stoddard arrived.

He never did ask Laura to tear up his letter of resignation, though he knew that she had.

Their lives blended well together. That was why a few months ago, Aidan had thought it was time for another change and suggested that they move in together. But Matt hadn't quite felt ready for that kind of commitment.

When he'd arrived at the hospital, Doc Owen had broken the news to him, as gently as it was possible for that kind of news. It was very likely that Matt had suffered brain damage. He might never fully recover. Aidan vowed to take care of him for as long as he needed. Ironic that it looked like they would be moving in together after all.

Aidan sat up with a jolt. No! If they did live together, it would be from choice, not necessity.

He'd planned to talk to Demir and get him to force the nurses to let him stay at the hospital. But just as he was heading to Cyber to see him, Jeanette called to tell him that Demir wouldn't be around for a while. That meant that he could go home, eat an actual meal. Maybe even sleep.

But by the time he got home, laid on the bed for maybe a minute, he was ready to keep going. So he'd grabbed a bagel from the freezer and driven to work.

At Cyber, Aidan brought a large mug of black coffee to his desk and settled into the chair to prepare for a long evening. He'd discovered an interesting mystery the other day in Drake's computer, which he'd copied to look at later. Eight mysterious files. He picked one at random and clicked to open it. Strange. Only gibberish?

No, it was encrypted. He tried a few tricks that he knew, but the level was far more complex than he'd anticipated. That made him even more determined. Deep down he knew that once he broke the code, he'd uncover one of Drake's many secrets.

Several hours later, Aidan leaned back in his chair, stretching his back as each muscle protested. He was exhausted but definitely didn't want to go back home. Maybe a coffee break would be enough.

He slid his chair back and pushed himself to his feet. Exhaling, he grabbed his coffee stained mug and left for the lunchroom. This late, no one else was around. The corridors were quiet. Too quiet. He put on a pot of coffee and concentrated on the drip drip.

All he could think of was Matt lying in emergency, semi-conscious, barely reactive. There was no telling what drugs the kidnappers had given him. Doc Owen had said that the kidnappers had to do CPR. What if it had taken too long to restart his heart? What if the brain had been starved of oxygen too long? He'd have to wait for the results of the MRI scan. If that damned machine was ever repaired.

The neural chip they were developing would hunt down and repair damaged brain tissue, and they were close to the testing phase. Those notes would have brought his phase of the work even closer to making the theory a reality.

Filling his mug and taking a sip, the caffeine energized him. He marched back to his office for one more attempt at the files.

A few more minutes and yes! He succeeded. Damn, he was good.

Scanning the file, and it's several sub-folders, he saw that it was mostly raw data: electrical and action potential results in tables and several charts. There were several preliminary calculations, as well as experimental procedures. Moving on to the next file, he opened it with ease. In total, seven cracked open under his expert manipulation. It took him a moment before he recognized the file names. These were projects that were going nowhere and were abandoned.

When Laura had first started work here, there had been a lot more scientists at Cyber, with each of them busy doing their own thing. She'd sorted through the numerous independent projects. As a first step, she moved several scientists to work in a lower security clearance outside of Cyber. That left him, Elton, Jeanette and—unfortunately—Drake. With their input, she'd streamlined everything towards a common goal—to improve the nanites' ability. Any projects that didn't directly impact it, were cancelled.

And he remembered that there were a handful that looked like they might have some future use, so with the military's almost paranoid insistence, everything related to them was moved to a secure server that only she had access to.

These were definitely the shelved projects. He had no idea that they been encrypted. Guess that way, if someone wanted to look at them, and she'd made it clear that they could, she'd have to decrypt the files for them. Or he could do it himself, he chuckled quietly.

Yes, he was beyond good. His arrogance ended when he reached the last file. Though much smaller, it was encrypted differently.

As he concentrated on trying to open it, everything outside of his computer screen ceased to exist. Time passed at a different speed than the rest of reality. He only became aware of its passage when his lower back cramped and time resumed its normal flow and he was thrown back into the real world. Past midnight, Monette stretched his arms over his head. A little exercise while he got more coffee and he'd be good a few more hours. About to stand, he had a new thought. A few more keystrokes. One more permutation.

Got it!

He should have realized from the size of the file that the encryption might be different. It was plain text that the encryption program painstakingly translated one word at a time. Soon it became clear that the last file was a letter with the salutation, *Only serious offers*. It was a sales pitch.

The text unravelled at a frustratingly leisurely rate. As he read, his expression transformed from satisfaction at his success to one of confusion. Then, his face hardened. His eyes narrowed. His mouth became a slit. No more guesses. No more suspicions. He knew now who had betrayed everyone. Caused so much pain. All those questions, every inconsistency, made sense now.

He took hold of both sides of the screen, trying to strangle some sense out of the words. He stood up, still holding the screen. His hands gripped the screen edge harder. He ignored the crackling protest of straining plastic and glass. With a growl, he pitched it against the wall, his anger barely quenched.

Tired of watching the shadows that flittered on her ceiling, Laura tried staring at her clock. The time changed from 11:44 to 11:45. A heavy sigh and she threw off the blankets. There was no point in pretending to sleep, so she padded to the bathroom to wash her face. Patting it dry, she was taken aback by how pale she looked. How gaunt her face had become. Common sense told her she should sleep. Stoddard was home safe. But the emotional side wouldn't let her rest until she figured out who was responsible for nearly killing him.

Figuring out who had hacked her computer could answer that question. When she'd left work today, Mr. Demir still hadn't given her access to the security records. He'd seemed distracted and had probably forgotten about her request.

She could spend the night wide awake, her mind caught in endless what-if loops, or she could go to Cyber and try to sweet talk Internal Security out of those records herself.

Aidan Monette raced out of the parking lot, tires squealing, catching his security shadow off guard. As Aidan's car screeched around the corner and down the street, his shadow was left far behind. He sped along the deserted streets, only then remembering his sat, tore it off his wrist and threw it out the window so that it wouldn't broadcast his location.

After spending all day searching for information, Demir finally acknowledged that he was exhausted, both physically and mentally. He lay down on his sofa, aimlessly channel surfing, not stopping long enough for the audio to kick in before he swiped for the next screen.

He'd visited Mrs. Mitchell to deliver the news that her husband was dead. Fortunately, her sister had been there and was able to help when she collapsed in an agony of tears. He'd waited for her to calm down, if the comatose-like state could be called calm, and he managed to answer a string of questions from her sister. Not an easy task, since he had the same questions and the same lack of answers.

He'd left a half hour later, promising he'd keep them informed.

Next stop, Mrs. Henderson, to let her know her husband was missing. As soon as she'd answered the door, he realized that she was expecting bad news. Though she kept her voice even, he could tell by the tightly clenched hands on her lap, the exaggerated straight back, and the overly calm expression, that inside she was crying. He left her to her privacy and the opportunity to let the veil of bravery fall.

He called Bob several times during the course of the afternoon and early evening to check on the forensic team's progress. The bullet, from a Glock, hadn't been traced. There were no useful prints on the car. Bob's team found a few fibres that hadn't led anywhere.

Frustrated, he now stared at the VidCast of some movie he'd lost interest in the moment it started. A knock at his front door saved him from the boredom.

He opened the door, not surprised to see Abraham carrying a bag from the nearby BBQ Chicken n' Chips restaurant.

"What's this?" Demir asked, indicating the bag as he ushered his friend in, locking the door behind him.

"It's called dinner." Abraham slipped off his boots and followed to the sofa.

"I'll get us a couple of beers." Demir shut off the vid-unit and went to the kitchen. By the time he returned with the beer, his friend had set out the paper plates and bamboo cutlery on the coffee table.

Abraham took the offered beer and said, "Got you a half chicken and ribs combo with avocado fries."

"Avocado?" He frowned.

"Thought you might like a little excitement in your life."

"Thanks, I guess." Demir gave him a half smile, then took a long drink of his beer.

"I went through the records," Abraham said, opening his own beer. "Okay, so you were right about not shooting Drake before all the evidence was in."

"Who *was* in?" Demir sat up from his slouch and felt a rush of excitement. They would finally have their leak.

"Well, that's just it, I don't know. A couple of times, none of the scientists were in."

"Sandrovsky?" Afraid of the answer.

"I checked him first. No, he's clear." Abraham took a drink. "I went through all the records and duty-rosters but there wasn't a single person that was here at each of the times. I've got Ops checking other ways to track who might have come in. Sorry, but we're no closer to narrowing the list of suspects."

Not eating, both men nursed their beers. Finally, Abraham reached for the remote.

"How about we check out the sports network? There must be some game playing somewhere."

They tuned to the half-time commentary of a football game.

"Montana and Dakota, eh?" Demir said, as he settled further into the sofa, twirling the beer bottle in his hands. "Guess naming a team after a city is old fashioned."

"Are you kidding?" Abraham said. "What city can afford to pay those salaries? Trust me, it won't be long before it'll take two or three states to buy a team."

"At least in Canada, our team salaries are less obnoxious," Demir said. He gave a grunt of a laugh, as he moved food around on his plate.

Occasionally taking a drink.

He watched the announcers having an animated discussion about the first half of the game without really listening to them. That's what he needed. Someone to elaborately dissect each play. Starting with the convoluted rescue and return to Canada of Matt Stoddard. Followed by the discovery that two I.S. men were missing. Finding Mitchell's body. And of course, ending with the endless parade of suspects. His mind raced in ever widening circles trying to come up with a theory. Any theory, good or bad.

"Ugh!" Demir rubbed his eyes, muttering, "It must be a ghost."

"What did you?"

He looked at Abraham, shaking his head. "Nothing, just that it has to be a ghost. The invisible man. Or a simple puff of smoke."

Demir bolted upright with a sudden thought. He looked at Abraham, who straightened up as well.

"You okay?" Abraham asked.

"We have a complex full of mental giants. It can't be that hard for one of them to circumvent our security system," Demir said

"But there's only one way in or out of the installation and there's always a man at that entrance."

"We need to think outside the box, Abe. Literally." Demir said. He called I.S. to put the underground complex on alert.

Laura took off her coat and paused to look at the picture of the sunset in her office. She would give anything to be there, rather than be here and do what she was planning. What she had to do. Her eyes glanced at the photo of her mother on the corner of her desk.

She'd died almost the same day that Laura had taken over the research director position. Nine years ago. A part of her always missed her mother's absence, but it had become a distant ache. Until this past week. She felt so alone. There was no one that she could talk to. Bounce ideas off of. Drake was back to his old, paranoid, isolationist self. Aidan was with Matt at the hospital. Demir was distracted and hard to track down. That left Jeanette and Elton, both of whom she'd never been that close to and didn't feel comfortable trying to start up a closer friendship.

And Edna. She was once had been a cherished surrogate mother figure but had recently transformed into a stalker. Her mere presence made Laura uncomfortable and she wasn't really sure why. She sucked in a breath as she prepared to violate everyone's trust. As director, she had access to everything, including everyone's computer. Whoever the hacker was, they would have left a trail. Though she could access each computer from here, it was easier to go to each station in person. Especially since at this time of night, no one would be in.

And though it was unlikely that she'd find anything on Matt's computer, she checked it first. As she thought—all clear. Next, she cleared Jeanette's computer, then Elton Chan's. Both good. She headed next to Aidan's office.

She thought she heard a footstep behind her. She stopped dead in her tracks to listen.

"Hello?" She called out and waited. Silence. It could be I.S. doing their rounds. But they would have answered her. No one was there except her guilt at violating her people's trust.

There was privacy that she should respect. There was also secrecy that they all had to respect. And everyone knew that security trumped privacy every time.

She continued.

The car parked in the lot as far from Cyber Inc. as possible. At 2:15 in the morning, no one was around as the silent figure trudged through deep snow in the woods, making a direct line to the ventilation shaft behind the building that led into the underground complex.

Few had the knowledge, or intelligence, to reprogram the security computer and isolate the ventilation shaft, which doubled as an emergency exit from the rest of the complex. And no one would have the knowledge of how to set up a false feedback loop to deceive the morons in Operations.

But could they have tightened security and changed all the codes? Would alarms sound when the ventilation cover was removed?

No alarms sounded. The lights on the panel just inside the airshaft remained green.

Perfect. This had been a useful route to bypass the ridiculous security policies for months. Unfortunately, after Demir's successful rescue, everything would be coming to light. Time to take the information and leave. The loss of the first sale meant the auction could start anew. With a well deserved higher minimum bid.

Climbing down the ladder to Sub 2, there was a brief moment of apprehension as the access hatch opened. Still no alarms. Feeling invigorated and emboldened made walking silently in the corridor an arduous task. But again, the long, endlessly convoluted corridors and dead ends were an asset in reaching the office unseen.

Laura plodded with measured steps to the only computer left to examine. Drake's. How could she have been so blind? So deluded into giving her heart to the man who had betrayed her trust. Betrayed everyone. Almost killed Matt Stoddard.

All too soon, she stood at the door of the last place she wanted to be. She used her palm print to access the office. But it was unlocked. At 3 AM, it wasn't unusual for Drake to be here. She prepared to face him. And ask why he hacked her files.

She entered.

It took a moment for what she saw to register. To push through the confusion.

But it took a moment for her brain to realize who it actually was.

"Matt!" she exclaimed. He looked up from the computer and smiled. She continued happily, "My God, you're all right. When I saw you at the hospital... I thought... I'm so glad you're okay. After all you've been through, you shouldn't have come to work."

"Well, my pretty Laura, I'm just so dedicated."

"It—it mu—must have been horrible," Laura stuttered. Uncomfortable with the uncharacteristic compliment.

"Nah," he waved a hand. "Those idiot goons that grabbed me, gave me a knockout drug. It was touch and go until they figured out who I was."

"At least Mr. Demir brought you home where you could recover."

"I actually recovered before we got home."

"Matt, no, it was after you got home," she explained. He'd been unconscious, close to death for so long that... "You're confused. You should go back to the hospital? I'm surprised the doctor released you too soon."

"Well, to be honest," he paused to type for a moment, then looked at her again. "He didn't. And I was recovered *before* Demir got me to Newcastle. I came to on the way, and it was so hard to pretend I was still unconscious. I wasn't sure if I could fool the doctors here, so I just pretended to be half awake. Ha! They were so worried, thanks to Doc Owen, that they never stopped to think."

Only now did she notice that he was wearing a suit that was far too big for him and his smile was more of a sneer. But the worst—his eyes were hard and cruel. Her own wavering smile vanished as an echo of nausea hit her. What hospital would discharge a patient with possible brain damage? And Stoddard had no business being in Drake's office at this, or any, hour.

"Matt, what have you done?" Her words came out slow and tentatively.

"I think you've already guessed."

"You let yourself get kidnapped?"

"No, that wasn't my plan," Stoddard said. "Imagine my dilemma, here I was, having already sold Drake and then he refuses to go."

"What?" She kept hoping she'd misunderstood.

"Come on, you know how misguided and altruistic he is. That he actually believes he's doing research for the good of mankind." He laughed. "I was doing him a favour. He wasn't happy here with all the secrecy. I know that it wouldn't be long before he started working openly with them.

"I kept trying to phone about the change in plans, but," he shook his head, then added, "they didn't have voicemail. In this day and age." He shook his head again.

"How could you do this?" Her voice trembled with anger. Her greatest fear had been that Drake had betrayed her. Somehow this seemed much worse.

"Oh, it was okay. They finally answered when I called using Demir's phone. While we were waiting to get on the boat. With all their fuck ups, I didn't think they'd get there in time. But of course, goddamn Abraham shows up and saves everyone."

"I meant, how could you betray us?"

"Quite easy, actually," he said. "I put out feelers for potential buyers, then a US Black Ops group approached me. But they were way too cheap. When the conference came up, that's when I decided to add Drake to the deal. It more than tripled my payment."

"And you turned on us for money?" Laura snapped. She fought to get her anger under control.

"Come on, you can't be that naive? But," he sighed, "looks like I can start the bidding again. And this time for a little extra fee, I can offer my own services to help interpret the info." He pulled out the memory slip, showed it to her like a child teasing another for a toy he'd taken. He laughed and put it in his jacket pocket.

Slowly, she backed out the door, sure she could outrun him, but not sure for how long.

"Hold it!" Stoddard yelled. She froze at the sight of gun in his hand. "You know I can't let you go." He came around the desk, closing the distance between them quickly.

Damned if she was going to let him see how terrified she was. "You know you can't get away." She jutted out her chin in defiance. "You'll never get past security."

"How do you think I've been coming in and out of here all these months?" He said, smiling proudly. "Those toy cops are no match for me. Now," he grabbed her arm and pulled her towards him. "I don't want to kill you unless you give me a hard time. We're both leaving."

Laura resisted as much as she dared, trying to delay him. Trying to give herself time to think. Once she got to the surface, she could try to signal the security guard for help. But Stoddard would expect that and get a shot off before the guard could draw his own weapon. And then the poor, unarmed commissionaire would be next.

No, she had to do something before he got into the elevator. She started to struggle, expecting him to loosen the grip on her arm to get better control of her and that would be her chance to break free. A shove, or a stamp of heel onto his foot, or a well placed knee where it counted and she'd get away. Then she could lock herself in the nearest office and call for help.

Instead of releasing her arm, he jammed the gun hard against her cheek.

"I don't really need you to get out. Your choice," he whispered.

She calmed her struggles. Her last hope was for security to be making their rounds. No matter what, she couldn't let him reach the surface.

Feeling a knot grow in her stomach, she continued around the many twists and turns of the corridors, getting ever closer to the elevator.

As they rounded the next corner, she saw Demir and Abe come into view.

Eyes wide, Demir and Abraham both exclaimed, "Stoddard!?" Abraham drew his weapon from a shoulder holster and aimed at Stoddard.

The knot relaxed for a moment. But Laura's relief vanished as Stoddard wrapped a strangling arm around her neck and pulled her in front of him as a shield.

"I suggest you don't try to stop me." To punctuate his intentions, he shoved the gun against her temple, as though trying to push the numbing cold steel barrel into her brain.

"Dr. Stoddard," Demir began. He slowly took a single step forward and held both palms up. Abraham stood behind him, pointing his gun towards the floor. "Please let Dr. Jessup go."

"I'm walking out of here."

"We can talk about it," Demir said, keeping his voice level.

"I'm walking out of here. There's nothing to talk about."

"Doctor, I know how hard it is to deal with everything that's happened to you, being kidnapped and drugged. Almost dying." When Demir said that last part, Stoddard relaxed his strangle hold on her. Laura believed that Demir was getting through.

"No one easily gets over trauma like that," Demir continued. He took another step forward. "And waking up back in Canada, in a hospital, that had to be very difficult to cope with. To understand."

Unexpectedly, Matt started to laugh. A hearty laugh that turned Laura's blood cold.

"I hate to destroy your philanthropic ideals, but I regained consciousness soon after you pulled me out of the hospital. Those bastards kept me sedated and it took forever for me to wake up. The hardest thing was to keep quiet while you prattled on and on. Though I did like that sheep story at Hadrian's wall."

"Doctor," he continued, the only sign that he was annoyed was a tightening of his jaw line.

"And that damn doctor in Newcastle!" Stoddard said, tightening his arm around her neck, releasing it slightly when she gagged. "He had the audacity to tell me that his people would be arriving soon to take me away. I started to fight him, and I would have won, but he'd already put a sedative in my IV. After all my hard work, can you believe that they were going to get everything for free."

"Doctor," Demir continued. Laura was amazed that he could still sound so calm. "So far, you haven't done anything really wrong. Why don't you give me the gun? And it'll all be over."

"Yeah, nice idea," Matt said, as he pushed the gun harder against her temple. She knew it would leave a bruise – if she lived long enough for a bruise to form. "Enough talk! We're both leaving." He started pushing her forward. Both Demir and Abraham backed up, but slowly.

"Doctor," Demir said. Softening his voice further, he continued, "Matt. What about Aidan?"

"You're joking, right? No, I guess you're not. I knew once I got close to him the rest of you fools would accept me more quickly. I have to admit, it was fun at first, until he started getting serious. He kept talking about moving in together." He tightened his hold on her throat. "Enough chatting. We're leaving." He stared pointedly at Abraham's gun.

Demir signalled for his friend to put the gun away. In the tight corridors, there was little chance to rush him without getting Laura hurt. They had to wait for the right moment. Stoddard backed up faster, now dragging Laura by the hair. Demir rushed around the corner, but saw that he'd anticipated the move. His gun was levelled at Demir's chest.

"You guys are just too eager. Back off, for the director's health." Demir watched as though in slow motion as he started to raise the gun to Laura's head.

A shot echoed in the corridor. Matt Stoddard screamed in pain, collapsed to the floor, clutching his leg. Demir grabbed Laura's arm and shoved her towards Abraham, then kicked the gun out of the fallen man's hand. He picked the weapon up, handed it to Abraham and looked behind Stoddard expecting to see one of his I.S. men. Instead, he found Aidan pointing a steady weapon at the man writhing in pain on the floor.

"Sir, please drop your weapon," Demir said, pulling out his gun though he kept it pointed at the floor.

"What?" Aidan shook his head like he was trying to wake himself. He looked at Demir, adding in a trembling voice, "He would have killed her once he didn't need her anymore. I couldn't let him do that."

"You bastard!" Stoddard screamed, as he clutched at his thigh. "You shot me!"

"Mr. Monette, please. Drop your weapon," Demir repeated, keeping his voice level.

Aidan looked at the gun in his hand as though surprised to see it there. He let it fall. Then he leaned heavily against the wall. Demir picked up the weapon, slipped it into his belt as he returned his own gun to his holster.

"Where did you get the gun?" Demir asked.

"Armoury," Aidan answered, as he impassively watched the man writhing on the floor. "Picked the lock."

Demir cursed silently. First the airshaft, now the armoury. He'd have to revisit security – everywhere.

"How did you know?" Laura asked.

"I found some files. Decrypted them. The last was the message Matt sent out, selling our research and Drake. I didn't want to believe it. But when I went to the hospital to check," he paused to look at the man writhing on the floor. "He was scheduled for an MRI but never arrived. I found his guard unconscious on a stretcher. That's when I knew it was true. Guess that's why he kept getting agitated when I was at the hospital. He couldn't make his move with me there."

His voice was calm, even. But Demir understood too well that the pain and guilt...

Would come later.

Edna buckled her seatbelt and looked out the airplane window, relieved to have got on the first flight out of the country. Once she landed in Lisbon, she could afford the time to stop and think about where she'd like to go next. Preferably a country without an extradition treaty with Canada.

As the plane started to taxi for takeoff, she wondered what Matt had told them? With minutes to go before boarding, she decided to check her home answering machine for messages. It was quite a shock to hear Dr. Jessup's voice filling her in on his stupidity. Honestly, the fool actually thought breaking into the complex and taking Dr. Jessup hostage was a good idea.

Yes, he was an idiot. But she was the bigger idiot for thinking that working for him would be better than Kirby. Kirby had her keep an eye on all the scientists, especially Dr. Jessup. But in turn, she'd made friends with Kirby's secretary, Corporal something-or-other, who was dumb enough to easily fall for a motherly smile. He kept her informed about everything that had to do with Cyber, no matter how top secret it was. But Kirby was really beginning to annoy her with his bullying tactics. His recent order to search Laura's home for anything that looked 'interesting' pissed her off even more. Kirby's own people could have done it. She was no fool. He just wanted to have something to hold over her head in case she didn't want to work for him.

Matt, who was by nature more diplomatic, had a knack for reading people. A few months ago, with a few strategic questions, he'd discovered her dissatisfaction with Kirby—or as Matt had called him, a megalomaniac puppeteer. Matt had persuaded her that working with him was a great idea, a lot more fun, and definitely more profitable.

All she had to do was let him know about any developments in the research that wasn't made available to him and to give him access to sealed documents. She'd also supplied him with Dr. Jessup's security computer codes.

So, when he went missing, she wasn't surprised or worried. It meant the deal was in progress. She'd be rich soon.

When she'd suspected that Demir was being sent to rescue him, and she confirmed it through Corporal what's-his-name, she had to act fast. She had no choice but to try to stop Demir from going. But who could have guessed that even though he was physically incapacitated, he still managed to find Matt and bring him home.

Now, thanks to Matt's incompetence, her comfortable life was torn to shreds. Though to be honest, with no family or serious lovers, there really wasn't much to keep her here. She wouldn't miss this place at all.

Well, that wasn't really true, was it? Laura Jessup would always have a special place in her heart.

CHAPTER TWENTY TWO

Later, much later, Demir sat with Laura in her office. She settled in next to him, curling her legs under her. Missing were the warmth and comfort that he'd felt from her the last time they'd sat here like this.

"I suspected Drake," she said, her voice tinged with guilt and pain. "And all along, he was the one who couldn't trust me or anyone. He'd thought of a new approach to his original work idea that I'd shelved when I reorganized Cyber. He was so afraid that I'd take the work away from him again that he kept it secret, even from me. He admitted that the papers he took from Matt's apartment were copies of his new secret work on the old research. That's why he shredded them – to keep them from Aidan."

"But why refuse to go to the conference?"

"It's stupid really. He eventually admitted that he's afraid to fly. Now that I think of it, he's never been on a plane. Any conference he's attended, he's driven or gone by train. Coming over from England, he took the boat." She laughed, but it sounded hollow. Her voice lowered, and Demir wasn't sure she meant for him to hear her add, "He couldn't even tell me that. "

"Have you spoken to Mr. Monette?"

"He finally returned my call to say he'd be in next week. He sounded okay, but I think it's going to take more time. Coming back to work will help him heal. It's better than sitting alone at home with only his thoughts. And it'll be good to see him." She paused, then asked, "Any word on Edna yet?"

"She seems to have vanished. I found out that she worked for Kirby, from the start, keeping on eye on you, just like she did your predecessor."

"I'm just so angry. I didn't even get the satisfaction of firing her."

"There's something else. When we did another sweep of the complex and also everyone's houses, we found several bugs in yours."

"What? My home?"

"Checking them, we found Edna's DNA. Any idea when she could have planted them."

"That bitch," Laura said, under her breath, shaking her head.

Demir's mouth opened like he was going to say something, but couldn't think of anything. He'd never heard her swear. Ever. She looked at him as though his presence was enough to calm her.

"She came over on Sunday with the pretense of bringing lasagna and helping with the cleaning. That's why she was lingering upstairs for so long."

"No, those bugs have been there for a long time." Demir paused, thinking for a moment. "I wonder why Kirby didn't just hack in through your electronics. Why bother making her do it?" As soon as he asked the question, he realized the answer. To blackmail Edna into continuing to help him.

"First Matt, now Edna. How could I be so gullible?"

"I wouldn't say gullible. She preyed on your relationship and she was damn good at it."

"Any bugs here?"

"None. I doubt she wanted to risk having them be discovered during routine sweeps," he said. Then asked, "How did your meeting with the government go?"

"Like beating your head against the wall. It felt good once the meeting was over." She sighed and settled deeper into the sofa. "I tried to persuade them to reduce security around our project. Not remove it completely, but at least relax it. Thanks to recent events," she paused, swallowing hard, "we know that our work isn't so top secret. I recommended that if we at least release some minor details to the general scientific community, it would take some of the pressure off."

"Should I guess their answer?"

"They assured me they would take all my suggestions under advisement and do a risk assessment. Translation—don't hold your breath. But they can't keep our work hidden forever." She gave him a brief smile, which faded as she turned to gaze at her sunset poster.

Demir watched as the sadness in her eyes, tempered with anger, threatened to overwhelm her. He resisted the urge to hold her in his arms and to tell her that everything would be all right. A knock on the door and those thoughts of comforting her faded.

The door opened and Drake entered, pausing when he saw Demir. He nodded a greeting. Demir thought he saw something he'd never seen before in those black eyes. Emotion. Perhaps gratitude? Perhaps sadness. It was hard to tell.

"I should get back to work," Demir said. Just as he closed the door, he saw Laura step forward into Drake's waiting embrace.

It took effort not to slam the door. He inhaled deeply, realizing how out of reach she'd always been. Finally letting go of the door handle, he turned and looked at Edna's empty desk.

He hesitated outside Henderson's office, trying to convince himself that it was his office now. He should move in. And Abraham should move into Demir's. He went to Abraham's office and knocked. Hearing the muffled "come in," he opened the door to find Yasmin talking to Abraham.

"I'll find the files for you, Mr. Abraham," she said. On her way out, she gave Demir a warm smile and closed the door behind her.

"Sorry, didn't mean to interrupt," Demir said.

"I was going to see you but I heard you were with Dr. Jessup." Abraham beckoned for him to sit. "You okay?"

Demir wanted to say no. That the man he'd rescued at the cost of two lives was not worth saving. That their boss was still missing but presumed dead. That he'd had a major fight with the military powers that be, highlighting how their interference had precipitated the loss of two men. One dead. One presumed dead. That they grudgingly agreed to let I.S. do their job.

That Drake and Laura...

"Sure, I'm just tired."

"Ty," Abraham hesitated, then said, "I don't know how to say this, except to just say it. They found Henderson."

"Dead?"

Abraham nodded. "Henry, my FBI friend, just called. Port Authority in New York were doing a routine inspection – they found his body in a cargo container. Looks like they really worked him over." Abraham paused, then added, "I guess I'd always hoped there might be a chance."

"Yeah," Demir said. "And I doubt he ever told those bastards anything before they killed him."

"You think it's the same Black Ops unit Stoddard mentioned?"

"Probably. I gave DND a copy of the papers Henderson left me. I didn't want the originals to get..." he made quotation marks with his fingers, "*lost*. By the way, after work we need to stop by the bank so you can sign the access papers to the safety deposit box."

"A little safer than keeping them in your basement."

"And I feel better keeping them somewhere other than here," Demir said. "I've got to make sure that Henderson's sacrifice wasn't in vain. Or Mitchell's."

Demir took a deep breath before continuing, "I managed to find out that Kirby knew all about the pressures that Smitty's bunch were putting on Henderson. He insisted that Henderson keep with the status quo. That bastard Kirby figured he was some great badass, in control of everything."

"It's funny though. He's been sketchy as hell lately, that I figured he was behind everything." Abraham added, "Found out how tough it was to play in the big league."

"Right. And that, plus Henderson's notes, was the extra ace I needed to get rid of anyone like Kirby once and for all. *We* are in charge of security now."

"So, where's that son of a bitch now?" Abraham asked.

"Well, you know the military and their secrets," Demir said, then laughed as he added, "but they did give me the impression he needed to pack long underwear." Sobering, he asked, "What about Sandrovsky?"

"He packed up and left this morning," Abraham said.

"Good," Demir said. "I know Henderson asked me not to judge him, but I can't keep a man around if I can't be sure who he's loyal to." Unable to trust Sandrovsky was an understatement. The son of a bitch was so busy trying to keep too many bosses happy that he'd let down the people he worked with. People like Mitchell. Demir had purposely avoided seeing him since he'd fired him, not willing to trust himself not to beat the shit out of him.

"I think you made the right decision."

"Yeah, I guess so," Demir stood to leave.

"You know, it's lunch time. You should eat."

Demir stopped in his tracks and started to laugh. The look of surprise, mixed with confusion and concern on his friend's face, made everything even funnier. How would he explain the feelings of a heavy heart trying to handle one crisis, one complication after another, feeling suddenly lighter? That while he was in England, imagining Abraham's voice scolding him for taking too many risks, constantly reminding him to eat, had kept him going.

"It's nothing," Demir said, the laughter gone, but the feeling of relief now in the background of his emotions. And at a bearable distance, was the pain of all that had happened. "Sure. The cafeteria?"

Abraham started to say something, then obviously changed his mind with a shrug and said, "Don't ask me. Ask Yasmin." Abraham gave him a smile adding, "I invited her to join us. Hope that's okay with you."

"No problem," Demir said. Next thing he knew, Abraham was guiding him out of his office into the reception area.

Abraham looked at the secretary, saying, as he rubbed his stomach, "I'm afraid breakfast didn't agree with me. Yasmin, you and Ty go ahead without me. I heard there's a new Italian restaurant nearby that you might want to try."

"Mr. Abraham, I'm sorry. Should we bring something back for you? Some soup?" Yasmin asked.

"No, I'll just take a couple of antacids." He patted Demir on the shoulder and returned to his office, adding before closing the door, "Have fun you two."

Demir turned to look at Yasmin, who smiled expectantly at him. A pretty smile. He smiled back and said, "I'll get my jacket."

In his office, he slipped on his windbreaker, glad the warm weather had finally arrived and he wouldn't need to buy a replacement ski jacket just yet. About to leave, he noticed the message light on his desk. He checked in case it was important. Only one from his friend from North Bay.

Ty, old buddy. Did you drop off the face of the earth? We heard you made Chief of Security. Congrats. You still coming back up for a visit? Gotta make it a bit longer this time. At least 24 hours maybe? Give me a call, if you're not too busy, boss.

Demir tried to remember that trip. It seemed like a lifetime ago. So much had happened. So much had changed. He surprised himself when he realized that he'd accepted those changes. Accepted that he was in charge, but wasn't sure when that had happened.

A knock on the door interrupted his thoughts. Yasmin came in.

"You know we can postpone lunch until Mr. Abraham feels better."

And something else had changed. He'd made contact with an old friend and would take the time to go back to visit for more that twenty-four hours this time.

"I was checking messages. Nothing that can't keep," he said. First, he'd take Yasmin out to lunch.

Then, he'd start having a life.

THE END

ACKNOWLEDGEMENTS

Getting a book ready to be published is much more than writing the story. I'd like to thank Renaissance Press, especially Nathan Caro Fréchette who was always there, answering questions and addressing concerns at all hours of the day or night. A special thank you to Myryam Ladouceur, a wonderful developmental editor who fixed all my time travel issues (this is not a time travel story!) and despite my best efforts to hide them, she found the smallest inconsistencies. I'm grateful as well to editors Victoria Martin, Evan McKinley, and Phillip Tran, as well as Marjolaine Lafrenière.

Nathan also worked to create Shifting Trust's wonderful cover design using the perfect artwork that my daughter Louise Koren managed to interpret from a lot of hand gesturing and half sentences on my part.

However, before all of that, Shifting Trust has had a long and convoluted path to publication. In its early days several people did look at it. Among those is Alex Brett, whose critique and advice was extremely helpful. A special thank you goes to long time friend and fellow author Barbara Fradkin, who was there from at the beginning of this book. And when I was ready to give up, she was instrumental in encouraging me to keep going.

A special thank you as well to John Park, a good friend of many years and member of my critique group. He reviewed this book in its initial stages as the plot was still developing. More recently, he answered my desperate cry for help in the 11th hour without hesitation.

No book is complete without mentioning the rest of my critique group, whose honest comments over the years helped me improve my writing. Hildegarde Henderson, Andrea Schlecht, Lynne MacLean, Leslie Brown, Valerie Kirkwood and Jim Davies; all great writers and wonderful friends.

When the idea for Shifting Trust first came to me, I'd only ever written science fiction. I found myself constantly fighting to keep my characters in the present. Seeing the struggle, my very close friend Marjorie McKenna suggested that I stop fighting the novel's desire to be Science Fiction. But for some reason I was determined to write a thriller. It took several more years before I finally decided to listen to that early advice. And to believe my characters when they tell me what kind of world they want to live in. I am after all just the scribe that records their lives.

No book or story would ever see the words "The End", without the constant support of my husband, David and daughter. They keep me going during the difficult moments of self-doubt, with their simple actions that remind me that they are my biggest fans.

Renaissance
Diverse Canadian Voices

Renaissance was founded in May 2013 by a group of authors and designers who wanted to publish and market those stories which don't always fit neatly in a genre, or a niche, or a demographic. Like the happy panbibliophiles we are, we opened our submissions, with no other guideline than finding a Canadian book we would fall in love with.

Today, this is still very true; however, we've also noticed an interesting trend in what we like to publish. It turns out that we are naturally drawn to the voices of those who are members of a marginalized group, and these are the voices we want to continue to uplift.

At Renaissance, we do things differently. We are passionate about books, and we care as much about our authors enjoying the publishing process as we do about our readers enjoying a great Canadian read on the platform they prefer.

pressesrenaissancepress.ca
pressesrenaissancepress@gmail.com

FROM THE SAME AUTHOR

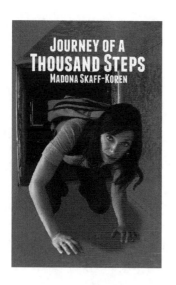

NAYA INVESTIGATES
VOL 1: JOURNEY OF A THOUSAND STEPS
VOL 2: DEATH BY ASSOCIATION

Naya had the perfect life. Co-owner of a fast growing security software company, she ran marathons in her spare time. Suddenly everything changed when she developed multiple sclerosis, and now she can barely climb a flight of stairs. Hiding at home, her computer the only contact with the outside world, she reconnects with her childhood best friend.

But when her friend disappears and the police dismiss her concerns, Naya leaves the safety of her home to find her. She ignores her physical limitations to follow a convoluted trail from high tech suspects to drug dealers, all while becoming an irritant to the police.

If you enjoyed this story, you
will also enjoy these other
Renaissance titles